CW01559098

CAPTIVE HEARTS

DEVIANT HEARTS BOOK ONE

ALI RYECART

Hello, Booklover!
I'm a local indie author —
if you enjoy Captive Hearts,
maybe check out my other
books.

Ali
X

March 2026

READER CAUTION, DISCLAIMER & COPYRIGHT

To find out more about the author visit:
www.ryecart.com

Reader Caution
This book contains strong language, scenes of a sexual nature and references to domestic abuse. It is not intended for readers under the age of 18 years.

Disclaimer
This book is a work of fiction. No part may be reproduced, by any means, without the written permission of the author. Names and characters, businesses, organisations, products or services and places and events are either the product of the author's imagination or are used fictitiously. Any resemblance to actual persons, living or dead, is entirely coincidental.

All trademarks are the property of their respective owners.

All rights reserved

© Ali Ryecart
2018

DEDICATION

For Mark

1

DASHIELL

"Dig deep, lads, the kitty's running low."

I caught Andy's eye and answered with a tiny shake of my head as I chucked twenty quid into the middle of the table. Andy would've been happy to pay for me all night, but I wasn't having any of that. I'd always paid my own way, and that wasn't going to change even if my circumstances had. With five of us, there was a fair bit of cash in the kitty, but in an over-priced place like Blue, it wouldn't last more than a round or two.

I knew agreeing to go had been a bad idea, and that was confirmed when I had to hand over a tenner just to get in. It was just a bar, for fuck's sake. I'd suggested meeting at Push. Okay, you had to pay to get in there, too, but I knew the main security guy on the door, so I, and whoever I was with, could always get in on the nod. And the drinks were cheaper at Push, a lot cheaper.

Birthday drinks, then a club. I'd been doing the mental arithmetic as soon as Andy had called me up as to how much it was all going to cost and trying to think up a good excuse on the fly to say no, but he turned the screws. The arsehole boyfriend of my oldest friend had not long walked out, and Andy needed a good night out with his mates. He was determined to draw a line under the past and go into his future with all guns blazing, he'd said. And I'd fallen for it. I was hooked, reeled in, and landed like a fish. Andy had already reserved a table at Blue.

Everybody was already there when I turned up and was knocking back the Happy Hour cocktails, but I just got myself a beer. I almost had a heart attack when the sulky looking young guy behind the bar told me how much it was. I was going be nursing that pint for a good long while, which would give me time to work up an excuse to get out of the rest of the evening.

Blue was the latest must-go-to place, from what I'd heard, but it was my first visit and likely would be my last. It was busy, but there was a large cordoned off section just behind where we were sitting, preventing the crowd from spilling into it. It was a couple of steps up and had sole access to the end of the bar, so I guessed it was some kind of VIP area. Whoever had hired it for the evening was yet to arrive, and I wondered how much it had cost them. Money always seemed to be at the forefront of my mind, but I soon lost interest as I was pulled back into my friends' lively conversation, otherwise known as the latest filthy piece of gossip.

"I think you've got the wrong table," I said when a guy who looked like a replica of the one behind the bar turned up with two bottles of champagne and five glasses.

"No, he hasn't, and this is on me." Andy gave the waiter a dopey smile, and I suppressed a groan. The guy had the same androgynous look as every one of Andy's arsehole ex-boyfriends.

"None for me, thanks, I'll stick with the beer."

"One glass, that's all I'm asking you to have. To celebrate my new life. You can have beer any day of the week."

Andy poured the champagne and pushed a glass towards me. I pushed it back.

"I don't like the stuff. It's like sour cat's piss."

"You really are uncouth, unrefined and uneducated, despite all my attempts over the years to smooth your rough edges. This *sour cat's piss* is high end. It's the stuff of gods. Now, take a sip and don't look so sulky. Cheers." Andy glared at me, but it didn't disguise the smile he was trying to suppress.

I couldn't help laughing. We'd had variations of the conversation for years, from when we'd shared a house way back. Somehow, through a friend of a friend, I'd ended up living with three posh-boy students. As they'd pondered life's big issues, I'd dragged myself up from bed each morning at some godawful hour to bust my guts on various building sites before I'd taken my filth and dust covered self to night school a couple of times a week . Oh, I could be uncouth and unrefined in all sorts of ways, and the men I'd known over the years, and that had included Andy, had never complained. But uneducated? Perhaps in Andy's world and in that of the other men around the table, but their world wasn't mine.

Andy's face broke into a full-blown grin as I downed the champagne in a few gulps, and grimaced, before I took a swig of my beer to wipe the taste away.

The music had grown louder, and our voices and

3

everybody else's raised in order to match it, but it didn't stop me from becoming aware of the commotion breaking out behind my back. I turned around to take a look, and a party of a dozen or so was filling up the raised, roped-off area. I started to turn away. I didn't know or care who they were, and besides, I'd made the decision it was time to leave, but just as I did so, my attention was caught and held. The men milling around parted like the Red Sea as a short, stocky guy in a dark suit walked through and took up his place at the table. But it wasn't him who held every piece of my attention; it was the kid who was hanging off his arm, as pretty and shiny as a diamond bracelet. He may have been just another teenage twink, but there was no doubt the kid was in a class of his own. Messy, bright blond hair that probably came out of a bottle, low slung black jeans and T-shirt that were too tight even for his skinny frame. He looked like one of those arty black and white fashion photos from a funky, cool, style magazine. For all that he was as far from my usual type as you could get, his beauty was undeniable and arresting.

"Oh wow, I think I'm in love," Andy said, gawping.

"I thought you'd taken a vow to broaden your horizons." I shook my head. Andy's declaration after the arsehole left *not* to run after the next guy in a pair of skinny jeans who happened to walk by had fallen by the wayside, just as I knew it would.

"I'd make an exception for him. And anyway, I saw you looking. You wouldn't normally glance twice at somebody like that, so something's grabbed your attention." He nodded to the blond, and his lips lifted in a sly smile. "Maybe time you had a change in direction, too?"

I shrugged and took refuge behind my pint glass. Andy was right, the kid was everything I'd never been interested in. The skinny teenager look was not my type, not at all. I liked a bit of meat on my men, some muscle, somebody I wasn't worried about snapping in two when I pounded them into the mattress. Or against the wall. Anyhow, you get my drift.

The conversation around the table moved on, but I was only half-listening because most of my attention was still on the group who'd arrived.

The blond and the older guy he was with sat down first, followed by others. One of the group looked like a bit part player in a Mafia film, all dark suit and dark glasses even though the lighting in the bar was low, which to my mind made him look like a bit of a jerk. The sulky barman who'd charged me and arm and a leg for my pint rushed over to the group with a lot more enthusiasm than he'd had for me. More people joined them, and the kid disappeared behind a wall of men. With nothing else to see, I lost interest and turned my full attention back to my friends.

When the discussion turned to which over-priced, über cool bar to go to next, I took that as my cue to leave.

"I'm heading off now." I squeezed Andy's shoulder as I got up.

Andy, along with the others, tried to get me to stay, but I just shook my head. I knew how the evening would likely pan out. It would turn into a bar crawl before crash landing in a club, with the option of some fun and games out the back somewhere. Nothing wrong in that, I'd spent many a night doing just the same thing, but it had lost its lustre and appeal in recent months. Maybe recently hitting the midpoint of my thirties had something to do with it, or maybe I'd been there, done that one too many times and was just bored. The men gathered around the table were friends, and decent to a man. They all earned big money in the City, and any one of them would have stood me drinks for the evening or lent me money accompanied by a vague 'pay me back when you can'. I appreciated that they'd have done that without a second thought, but I wasn't a charity case.

"Come over in the week, and we'll have supper. I'll text you."

I smiled down at Andy. He was the only person I knew who used the term 'supper.' A few drinks always brought out the neatly concealed, well brought up posh boy from the Shires. I leaned down and gave him a quick peck on the cheek and waved to the others as I snaked my way through the crush, my thoughts already shifting to the beers and the remains of a pork pie in the fridge at home, and sitting in my boxers as I watched some late evening telly. That pulled me up short.

There I was, walking out of a bar filled with plenty of men I could have some no-strings fun with, and I was thinking about supermarket own-brand lager, some dried up pie and the fucking *telly*. On a Saturday night. It was almost enough to make me turn around, go back to the others and let Andy stand me drinks all evening. But not quite. Maybe I'd drop into The Crown on the way home; the drinks were a fraction of the price, and there was always some fun to be had. My hand went to the back pocket of my jeans, feeling the flat little packets. Yep, everything was there for the night ahead. But there was one thing I needed first, and that was to take a leak.

Instead of pushing my way out onto the street, I followed the sign to the toilets, pointing the way up a narrow set of stairs. At the top and down a long corridor, and through another set of doors, they were cut off from the busy bar at ground level, and very little of the noise from downstairs filtered its way upwards. Which was why I could hear the muffled cries and grunts and gasps, and the laughter. I hesitated. I didn't want to walk in on a couple of guys getting down and dirty, but I was straining to relieve myself, and I wasn't going to make it more than a hundred yards, let alone home, if I didn't. If anybody was getting their end away, they could do the decent thing and lock themselves in one of the cubicles.

I pushed the door, and it didn't move. I pushed again, harder this time, and it opened an inch or two before it was slammed back. Somebody was deliberately blocking it. Another cry came through the door, and a sharp gasp. My stomach knotted, and my chest squeezed hard. Whoever was in inside wasn't there because they wanted to be, and they weren't having fun. I put my shoulder to the door and shoved hard. It flew open, and I staggered in, just keeping my footing. And stopped dead.

The blond kid from downstairs was pushed front first up against the wall. There was a smear of red on the wall tiles, from the blood that stained his nose and upper lip. His jeans and briefs were halfway down his legs, but they were tight enough that they didn't allow him to splay his legs, and all I could think was *thank Christ for that.*

A guy was pressed up against him, one hand clamped to the back of the kid's neck. With the other, he was rummaging around his flies, his dick already out.

"Fuck off, this is none of your business," he hissed.

7

"Yeah. Do yourself a favour and go, or wait and take your turn." The words were accompanied by a filthy laugh from the guy I'd shoved away from the door. He was sharp featured and vicious looking.

Outrage surged through me as the memory I'd tucked away and all but forgotten exploded into full-blown neon colour behind my eyes. A teenager, excited and hyped-up, and out on the scene for the first time, his exit from the filthy toilet in the dive of a club barred by an older, heavier man with a leer on his face and one thing on his mind. Then, it'd been the fear of what I knew was to come that had prevented me from being shoved against a wall, and I'd fought my way free. As every detail of that night raced through my head on fast forward, I didn't stop to think as I pulled my arm back and slammed my fist forward, knowing in some dark part of my brain that once again I was smashing my fist into that bastard's face, just as I'd done years before.

With a sickening crunch, blood sprayed from his face as he crumpled to his knees with a high-pitched wail, one hand clamped to his face as he dragged himself away with the other. The guy who had the kid against the wall fumbled his dick, now as limp as spaghetti, back into his jeans. Maybe he thought getting into a punch-up with his cock flapping around wasn't the best of ideas, but what-ever, it delayed his reaction and he jack-knifed into two when I yanked him away and landed a punch in the centre of his stomach before I kicked his legs out from under him, leaving him groaning and gasping on the tiled floor.

"Let me give you a hand." All my attention was on the kid. His eyes were wide, the blood dark against the stark pallor of his face. I knew I was hovering, and I only meant to guide him to the sink, but he shook his head and stepped away.

I understood, I really did. After what had happened, the last thing he'd have wanted was to have another man, a stranger, touch him.

My hands were clenching in and out of fists as I tried to control the tremble that took them over. The realisation of what I'd stopped happening, not just moments, but years before, too, hit me hard in the chest. I didn't know what to say, but I knew what I needed to do.

I pulled out my phone, ready to call the police.

"No. No, don't do that," the kid barked at me as he fumbled with the belt on his jeans, buckling away everything that had just happened.

"What? But—"

"I said no. The police can't be involved."

His voice was shaking, but I heard the determination in his words. And the fear. *Why—?* And then I recalled the scene down in the bar, the older guy whose arm the kid had been draped over, and the men milling around looking like extras in a gangster film. Men who wouldn't appreciate the involvement of the law, even if it were to investigate the attempted rape of one of their own.

"They didn't get what they were after, so there's no evidence. Nothing happened, and there's nobody to take in for questioning. Look around you, they've gone."

I turned around. He was right. I'd been so focused on him that I hadn't heard the vermin who'd attacked him make their escape.

"Thanks for your help, but I'm okay and I don't want any fuss. I'm just going to clean up before I go back down."

He stared at me, and I had the feeling I was being dismissed. I'd served my purpose, and now I was being given my marching orders. That pissed me off no end, but I also knew his sharp tone and snotty attitude were in part a defence, a barrier against what had – or almost – happened. He was in shock, whether he knew it or not.

"No." I crossed my arms over my chest and met his stare.

He scowled and turned to the sink and grabbed a handful of paper towels, which he soaked and dabbed away the blood with. Whether he liked it or not, I was going downstairs with him and was going to explain what'd happened to his boyfriend, or whoever the stocky guy was. At least I'd have done what I could.

Drying his hands, he turned back to me. You wouldn't have thought anything had happened. He looked composed and calm, and somehow bland, which was one hell of a trick to pull off for somebody as gorgeous as he was. He narrowed his eyes as we studied each other. He was certainly a lot younger than me, by a good fifteen or so years was my guess, but as I looked into a pair of jade green eyes, 'kid' no longer seemed right. There was a deep-seated wariness about him, and I suppressed a shiver as he stared at me through eyes that were far too old for somebody so young.

"So you're not going to go and forget this happened?"

He said the words slowly, as if he were considering the consequences, and my resolve wavered. Maybe he had his reasons for not wanting anything to be said and I was just going in heavy with my size tens.

"*O-kay*. But can you just say you saved me from a mugging? Please?"

That didn't seem right. What had almost happened was too serious, but I already knew I'd lie for—

"What's your name?"

"Billy. Billy Grace."

Billy Grace. The name tap-danced down my spine.

I let out a frustrated sigh. "Yes, all right. I don't like it, but—"

"Good. Right, we'd better get back down there, and quick. And remember, it was an attempted mugging. Keep it simple." He threw the last words over his shoulder at me as he strode past and pushed the door open and walked out, leaving me to follow.

The crowds in the bar had thinned a little, and I was relieved to see my friends had gone because it would have been difficult explaining why I was still hanging around. But all thoughts of them evaporated as I followed Billy to the roped-off area. Everybody fell away as Billy approached, and I saw the older guy full on for the first time.

Early to mid-fifties, I reckoned, which easily made him old enough to be Billy's father. His carefully cut hair was thinning, and under the expensive tailoring I imagined a body already gone to seed. Maybe they had some Daddy thing going on, who knew, but the thought of the two of them together made me queasy. It was more than that, though. He looked mean and hard, and I recalled the ripple of fear I'd detected in Billy just minutes ago, and I knew I'd say whatever Billy wanted, make up any story he demanded.

"Where the hell do you think you've been, eh? And who's this you're dragging behind you?"

The guy jerked his head towards me, but he kept his

eyes fixed on Billy. My hands fisted, and I clamped my teeth tight together. I didn't like being treated as though I wasn't worth an ounce of his attention, and I wanted, I *really* wanted, to tell him to fuck off, but surrounded by his gang, or whoever they were, that probably wasn't a good idea. So I just stood there, played dumb, and hoped I was doing the right thing in putting my trust in Billy.

"I'm sorry, Frankie. I was followed into the toilet by a couple of guys. They jumped me and tried to steal my phone, but he came in." Billy nodded towards me. "He saw what was happening and beat them off."

He. It sounded dismissive, and irritation briefly spiked in my chest. But of course, I knew Billy's name, but he didn't know mine.

The guy he'd called Frankie didn't say anything for a moment, but his eyes shifted between Billy and me, and back again. I got the impression he was trying to decide whether he believed the story, and I took that as my cue to pitch in.

"What he says is true. Your friend was being mugged, and they'd obviously got a bit rough before I walked in because he had blood running down his nose."

Billy nodded and produced a scrap of blood-stained tissue.

"Sit down," Frankie snapped, not at me but at Billy, who slipped into the chair next to him without a word as though he'd been waiting for permission.

"So you were a knight in shining armour, eh? What happened to these would-be muggers?" Frankie turned his attention back to me.

"I waded in and gave them both a smack, and they soon scarpered."

"And not a scratch on you?"

"No, not a scratch."

"And all for the sake of a mobile phone. You're either brave or stupid."

I didn't like the sneer on his face, but I had to tuck away the urge to make it a hat trick of men I'd caused physical harm to that night. Instead, I kept my stare level before I added the casual afterthought that CCTV would bear out what I was saying.

"Two guys, both white with short, light brown hair rushed out of here about ten or so minutes ago. One would have had blood on his face because I reckon I broke his nose. The other one I punched in the guts, so he might have been walking a bit funny. Contact the police and get the management to show them the footage." I added the last bit because I wanted to see the guy's reaction. Maybe I'd gone too far, but he was seriously pissing me off by then.

All the time, Billy was sitting with his hands in his lap and looking down. He didn't say a word, and I'd had enough of the whole charade. I didn't know who these people were, and I didn't want to know. As far as I was concerned, my part in what had happened had come to an end.

Without another word, I turned to go, but my way was barred by some of the suits. At least these ones weren't wearing sunglasses, but it was all starting to feel like I was in a bad film. I more than matched them in height and build, but there were four of them and only one of me, so I turned back to the guy.

"I've told you what happened, and if there's CCTV, it'll confirm what I've said. I'm only glad I walked in when I did, but what you do now is your business. And I'd like to go, so I'd appreciate it if you'd call off your guard dogs because I'm getting more than a little bit pissed off by being given the third degree."

Billy gasped and looked up, but the shock I saw in his face fell away almost immediately as the bland, expressionless mask fell back into place. There was some shuffling and shifting around on seats. Frankie cocked his brow. It was clear he wasn't used to being spoken to in the way I'd just done, but I was beyond caring. The last thing I expected was the smile that broke out on his face. Yes, it may have been the smile of a man who the next moment would slice your throat open, but hey, at least it was a smile.

"I'll have CCTV checked. That'll be easy enough because I own this place."

Now, that did surprise me, but I was well-versed in keeping a poker face. But his next words surprised me even more.

"I should thank you for intervening. Billy here is very precious to me. Very precious."

He clasped his hand to the back of Billy's neck. It was an act of possession, a public statement that the kid was his property. It was as predatory as the attempted rapist's hand, and like then, I wanted to smash it away. I ground my teeth so hard, I was surprised I had any left. Whatever I'd stumbled into, I wanted to stumble right the way out of.

"Stay and have a drink. It's the least I can do."

Frankie turned to one of the suits, snapping his fingers for him to pour me a drink I didn't want. I opened my mouth to refuse, but the words died on my tongue as I caught the tiny, barely there nod and very slight widening of Billy's eyes. I knew a warning when I saw one. Frankie obviously didn't like taking no for an answer. One drink, and then I'd be gone, but after everything that had happened, walking away, and leaving Billy with Frankie left a sour taste in my mouth. But what choice did I have? I didn't know the deal between them, but whatever it was, it was their business and not mine.

I accepted the whisky that was poured for me. It was as smooth as liquid silk, and I sighed at the quality of it. Frankie turned to speak into the ear of one of the suited guys, and I stole another quick glance at Billy. He was like a statue, and I didn't understand how anybody could be so still and passive. It was as though he wouldn't, or couldn't, move or talk unless he was given express permission. That wasn't far off the truth, but I wouldn't discover that for some time to come.

"What's your name?"

Frankie made the question sound like an accusation. I took my time in answering.

"Dashiell Slater. And you're Frankie who?" I looked him full in the face. The whole set up of the cordoned-off area, the suits in sunglasses and the boy toy screamed that he was a man not to be messed with, but by this time I was fed up with his attitude. I didn't care if I hacked Frankie off, so I was surprised when he laughed.

"Haynes. Frankie Haynes. Dash—*what?* What sort of name is that?"

I got this all the time, and I smothered a groan.

"Dashiell. *DASH*-uhhll. Emphasis on the first syllable. My mum had a thing for hard-boiled crime novels. Dashiell Hammett? The author?" I added, but Frankie just looked blank.

"I'll call you Dash."

"I'd rather you didn't." My shoulders stiffened. I hated being called Dash. I wouldn't even let my closest friends call me that, and Frankie Haynes didn't, and wouldn't, come into that category.

"So tell me, Dash," he said, ignoring what I'd said. "What do you need most right now?"

What sort of question was that? What the hell was he talking about? Another drink? A lift home? Or a reward for rescuing his best boy? The one who was snotty and dismissive, who'd persuaded me to lie, but was also the one who'd shot me a warning glance to play along with Frankie, even though it was clear as day that he was scared out of his wits by the guy. So I did something stupid. I opened my mouth and told Frankie the truth.

"A job."

"A job? Really?" Frankie's brows shot up in surprise, just for a moment, before he grinned.

The truth was, money was tight. I was working two or three shifts a week in a pub, strictly cash in hand, plus I was claiming unemployment benefit, which meant I was okay as long as I stuck to a carefully worked out budget, a budget that didn't include nights out in overpriced, pretentious bars like Blue. I had a tidy sum in the bank, severance pay from my last job, which had come to an end earlier in the year, but I didn't want to touch it unless I was desperate. I wasn't at that point, but if I didn't start earning, it wouldn't be long before I was.

"So what did you do before you went into the white knight business?"

Keep it simple, that's what Billy had said earlier. It was good advice, and I intended to take it.

"I was a building manager, I made sure it was maintained and kept in good order."

"So you were a caretaker? A handyman? A fixer of squeaky doors, jammed locks and blocked sinks?"

No, that was *not* what I did. Or used to do. It was a gross oversimplification, but I couldn't be bothered to put Frankie right.

"Well, in that case, maybe I can be your fairy godfather, because one good turn deserves another, Dash. And I suddenly have a very important vacancy I need to recruit to. You need a job, I need somebody to look out for Billy, make sure he doesn't get into any more trouble—"

"Frankie, I don't need—"

"Shut up."

Billy's quiet murmur, the first words he'd said in several minutes, were cut off by the vicious command. I looked at the kid, not caring that Frankie was looking at me, and saw utter, abject misery in those big, green eyes before his gaze once more dropped to his lap. My stomach twisted. Billy Grace, whoever he was and whatever arrangement he had with the hard-faced man who sat across the table from me, was too damn young to be as defeated and beaten down as he was.

"I don't want a repeat of tonight's adventures. I want somebody to run him around and keep an eye on him when I'm tied up with business. There'll be other general duties, too, because even he can't spend all his time shopping and wasting my money."

Frankie's hand slipped to the back of Billy's neck once again, and he squeezed, hard enough to hurt if the look on Billy's face was anything to go by.

A minder. *That* was the proposition Frankie was

offering me. I may have wanted a job, but babysitting hadn't been my first thought.

"Why can't one of the suits do it?"

"Because I'm asking you."

It wasn't an adequate answer, but I had one for him. I swigged back the last of my drink and stood. It really was time to go.

"I was in the right place at the right time, and I'm glad I could help, but my involvement stops here. Thanks for the drink, and the offer, but no. And now, I really am going. Goodnight." If I expected any of the suits to stop me from walking out, I was wrong. It was Frankie's next words that did that.

"A grand a week in cash. Some driving, and a few other ad hoc duties. The hours might be a bit unsociable, but we can't have everything in life. A grand in your pocket at the end of every week, Dash. No tax, no NI, no pension fund contribution. I could say think about it, but what's there to think about?"

Frankie Haynes had me. There was nothing to think about. Even if I stuck it for just a few weeks, the money would bump up my savings and give me more time to find a job I really wanted. And I could ditch the shifts in the pub. That the guy was a crook was like asking if the Pope was Catholic. The offer was tempting, too tempting, and to be honest, the fact that he was a crook was the least of it for me. Frankie made my skin crawl. I didn't want to think about what he might be into, but maybe that's exactly what I should have been doing . . . but a grand a week. It wasn't just the money that stopped me from walking away, though, it was the look I saw in Billy's eyes when Frankie had slapped him down for daring to talk. And that hand, tight on Billy's neck, like it was on the collar of a dog.

"Yes."

It was madness. Absolute fucking madness. As I sat back down, as Frankie smiled and poured me another drink, I wondered if I'd made a deal with the devil.

2

BILLY

I knew I was in trouble as soon as I heard the door slam behind me. I hadn't even wanted to go to the toilet; I just wanted to get away for a few minutes. Blue was Frankie's latest venture. He owned bars and stuff, like restaurants and clubs, all over London, all of them high-end. They were the legitimate places, the ones his other business interests hid behind. I wasn't totally sure what they were, because business was never discussed with me, but I could take a guess because I wasn't stupid despite what Frankie thought.

Frankie had 'business associates' with him, and my job was to sit there looking pretty, just like always, but the constant yakking, half in English and half in Romanian, had been giving me a headache. The Romanian guy sitting next to me, on the other side from Frankie, had been freaking me out because he kept pressing his leg into mine and squeezing my thigh under the table. If Frankie caught him, there'd be trouble. For me, later, and back at the house. So, I'd muttered about needing the loo and slipped off just to get away. If Frankie heard me, he didn't give a sign. He was deep in conversation and hitting the whisky hard. With any luck, he'd drink too much and wouldn't be able to get it up later. So that's what I'd been thinking about, how to avoid Frankie's whisky-breathed slobbering, when the door slammed behind me and I swung round.

They were on me in an instant, and it wasn't my phone they were after, top of the range or not. And I fought back. I kicked and spat and threw punches, or tried to, but there were two of them and one of me, and one half of my brain was screaming *no*, but the other half? That was telling me to let them have what they wanted. Get it over and out of the way. It'd be quick and nasty, but it'd be over. I mean, it wouldn't be much different from what Frankie liked to dole out to me. But in a dark little corner of my brain, it made me ashamed to think that way, because I still had the capacity to feel shame and degradation. So I fought because somewhere I still had a shred of pride.

When Dashiell burst in – not that I knew that was his name then, of course – I was, like, *thank God for that*, but when he got his phone out and started talking about getting the law involved, I freaked. Not that he'd have noticed because I'm well used to not letting anybody know what I'm thinking or feeling; that's what living with Frankie for nearly two years had done to me. So I was off hand in the hope he'd turn and walk away, but instead he'd wanted to make sure I got back safe. Safe? That was a laugh. Going back to Frankie was as far from safe as it was possible to get.

I didn't know for sure how Frankie would react. He may not have acknowledged my slipping out, but he'd have noticed, and he wouldn't have liked me being away for too long. I hadn't wanted Dashiell to come back with me; what I wanted him to do was walk away and forget what had happened, just like I intended to, but in a way it helped that he didn't take no for an answer. He gave Frankie somebody to focus on rather than me. I did what I always did, which was to sit there and not say anything because it was the safest course of action. I'd learned that in the early days, if I was to escape bruised ribs, or worse.

I was more shaken up by what had occurred than I was making out. I hadn't taken too much notice of my rescuer because I'd been too concerned about getting back down-stairs and soothing any ruffled feathers Frankie may have had, but as I sat there next to Frankie, it gave me time to study Dashiell properly.

I might have made out I was gazing down into my lap, but it wasn't what I was really doing. I was looking at Dashiell through my lashes, but I had to be careful not to be seen staring when staring was exactly what I wanted to do. He was the kind of man who made my spine tingle. Tall and broad, with short, dark hair. And tatts. Yeah, there was something about ink, and there was plenty of it spiralling down his arms, out from under the sleeves of his shirt, which were carefully folded back to his elbows. Did muscles and tattoos make him into a bit of a stereotype? Yeah, maybe. Who was I to judge, because hadn't I got the whole twink look down to a T? Yet that whole masc thing just did it for me. But that wasn't all; in fact, how he looked was the least of it. After he'd dealt with the two attackers, Dashiell had been kind of thoughtful, I suppose, because he wanted to make sure I was okay, and to get the police involved, which was the proper thing to do. That had really touched me, not that I showed any of what I was feeling. Dashiell had been a decent man, and I hadn't come across too many of them recently.

I almost jumped out of my seat, though, when he was offered a job. It didn't make much sense. Frankie employed any number of aides, as he called them, and any one of them could, and did, drive me around. So why did he offer a complete stranger, who hadn't been afraid to answer him back, a job? As I sat there and drunk everything in, my brain was on overdrive. Maybe Frankie was being the big man in front of his business associates, doling out well-paid jobs like they were sweets. Who knows? But I was praying Dashiell would say yes, because he'd been concerned and thoughtful and I couldn't remember the last time somebody had been like that with me.

Of course, it'd been the cash that had made the difference. I didn't fool myself it was anything to do with me, because why should it have been? I'd been snotty and not that appreciative of his help, and then got him to lie for me. A grand a week, cash that'd go straight in his pocket. He'd said he'd needed a job, and on the face of it being some kind of gofer and just doing as he was told, even if it did mean he had to drive me around, was pretty cushy. So I didn't blame him when he said yes. It was easy money, and after all, wasn't that why I'd said yes to Frankie when he'd offered me my 'job'?

Frankie's words had made me cringe when Dashiell had sat back down and taken another drink to seal the deal.

"I like nice things in my life, Dash, and Billy's one of them. I don't like it when others try and take what's mine. If I choose to give, that's one thing, but somebody taking the piss and trying to help themselves to what belongs to me? That's something I don't look kindly upon. And that includes this lovely creature."

He squeezed my neck hard, and it was all I could do not to cry out and pull away. A lovely creature, nothing more than a dumb pet to play with. He was laying his claim, making it clear who I belonged to. I was just another one of his possessions that was to be kept out of the hands of others. I was as bought and paid for as one of his houses, or cars, or a tin of bloody baked beans. *He's off limits.* That was Frankie's message. I understood it, and I had no doubt Dashiell did, too. It was a message for both of us, not that I ever needed reminding. Despite the money on offer, I half-expected Dashiell to tell Frankie to stuff it, because he'd made it plain he was capable of it.

"A grand a week in cash? All right, you're on, but I want the money in my hand by 5.00pm each Friday. If it's not, I walk."

I almost wet myself that Dashiell said that, and I half-expected Frankie to have him bundled outside just for his nerve for talking like that, but instead Frankie laughed, stuck out his hand and said they had a deal. Everything was done and dusted, without a word from me. I didn't know whether to be pleased, scared, or pissed off, but none of it mattered. My life had changed, had been decided by others, and there wasn't a thing I could do about it.

3

DASHIELL

I spent all weekend flip-flopping between trying to forget everything that happened on Friday night and thinking about the cash. Because the money was a bloody big hook, there was no two ways about it, but it was more than the offer of easy money. I couldn't get Billy out of my head. With me, he'd been off hand and snotty, which given the circumstances I'd found him in, ticked me off, but there had least been a bit of spark about him. When he was back with Frankie, well, that was another story. It was as though he faded away. He was gorgeous, no doubt, but it was his eyes I'd dreamed of. They were the saddest, bleakest eyes I'd ever seen.

As soon as I'd walked out of the bar, I'd googled Frankie Haynes. Restaurateur, bar and club owner. A man who gave to charity, according to the many photos I found of him, shaking the hand of one civic dignitary or another. There was even a photo of him outside a church with a vicar, a group of kids and a lamb. Yes, a lamb. He was holding a *fucking lamb*. No doubt once the cameras had stopped clicking, he'd had it slaughtered and served up with roast spuds and mint sauce. The smiling public face hid something darker, but what that was I had no idea. Or not then.

At the house, I was buzzed through the heavy solid gates and told exactly where to park. It was one of those ultra-modern houses you might see on a building design programme on the TV, a huge square block of stark white walls and glass and designed for style rather than comfort. I crunched my way along the pea gravelled path to the front door and knew every step I was taking was being recorded. It hadn't taken me more than a glance to know there were security cameras in place. They weren't obvious except to the trained eye, but if you knew what to look for. . .

The door was opened by a chunky guy with a buzz cut, small piggy eyes and a tight, mean looking mouth, and I recognised him as the sunglasses wearing jerk from Friday night. I was told, in not overly friendly terms, to wait in the large, bright hallway. Apart from a couple of very tall vases which held what looked like a bunch of twigs, there was a very uncomfortable looking chair, but it was the only one, so I sat down and waited.

After fifteen minutes or so, the same guy returned and escorted me along a corridor coming off the hallway. If he was typical of my new workmates, I was in for a whale of a time. I was shown into a large room that functioned as an office where Frankie sat at a desk by the window where a laptop, tablet and a couple of smartphones lay on top.

"I was debating with myself whether or not you'd show up. I really didn't know what you'd do, once you'd thought my offer over properly. On the one hand, you seem to be a man who knows his own mind and speaks it. Which can be refreshing, when you're surrounded by flunkies and yes men the way I am. But the lure of easy money is a hard one to resist, and it will be easy money as long as you stick to my rules."

No greeting, no preliminaries, no small talk. Not that I expected any, but still, I felt myself bristling. The lure of easy money had brought me to the house, and for a moment I felt cheap and sullied. But it wasn't the whole truth. The desolation I'd seen in Billy's eyes had haunted my dreams for the last two nights, and I couldn't rid myself of the image. But I had to push that aside. I was there to do a job, to drive the kid around, take him shopping while he loaded up his sugar daddy's credit card, and to keep the dogs at bay. Easy enough, but I didn't know why Frankie was willing to let a stranger be his much younger boyfriend's babysitter. There must have been somebody he could have given the job to, and returning my so-called good deed with a job seemed a bit excessive.

"Of course the money was an enticement. I'm not going to lie or insult your intelligence by saying otherwise. But a thousand a week to drive a kid around? That seems a bit excessive, especially when you don't know me. Why not have one of your existing employees do what you're paying me a lot of money for? I don't get it."

There, I was displaying some of that refreshing speaking my mind, although I doubted he'd put up with too much of it. Frankie didn't say anything for a few seconds, but if felt a whole lot longer as he stared at me across the table and tapped the end of the pen he was holding on the desk, as steady and regular as a metronome. I held his gaze, determined not to drop mine first.

"The men I employ have specialised skills, and driving around a kid, as you put it, is not the best way to utilise those. Doing what you did, you put me in your debt, and that's not something I like. Offering you a job when you blurted out your situation seemed the best way to disgorge that debt. I'm good at reading others; I wouldn't be the successful man I am today if that were not the case. And do you know what I read in you? Pride. You'd have spat in my face if I'd offered you a cash reward for your assistance, although spitting at me isn't something I'd recommend. But a reward you had to work for, to earn? Your pride would let you accept that."

He never shifted his eyes from mine, and he kept tapping the end of that pen on the desk. It was as if he were underlining each and every word. Because he'd read me right. I was proud. If he'd held out a bundle of cash for what I'd done, while I might not have spat in his face, I'd have told him where he could have shoved it; but to work for it, well, that was a different thing entirely. As he continued to stare, I admit I wanted to flinch, and not many men provoked that in me, and that's when I knew at a primitive, deep level in some dark place in my lizard brain that this man was very, very dangerous. What I said before, about him smiling as he slit your throat? I had no doubt he'd do it and then walk away without a second thought. It took all my power to keep my expression impassive and my eyes steady. I shrugged and hoped I pulled off the nonchalance I definitely wasn't feeling.

"So, what are my duties?" There had to be more than driving Billy around the shops. Nobody could spend all their time shopping.

"Show me your hands."

"What?" The sudden change of direction caught me off guard.

"Dash, don't make me ask twice."

I ground my teeth together as I laid my hands, palms upwards, on the desk.

"Hardened skin, rough and calloused. A man who's done more than push a pen or tap a keyboard," Frankie said as he studied my hands.

"I told you on Friday, I fixed gates and mended jammed locks." No, *he'd* said that, not me. Frankie's comments had got up my nose, where they were still well and truly lodged. I pulled my hands back and straightened my cuffs.

"General maintenance," he said, sitting back in his chair and ignoring my terse comment. "Fixing stuff. The type of handyman work you're used to. Keeping the cars clean, maintained and ready to go at a moment's notice." Frankie gave me his cold smile again, the cat playing with the mouse. "Taking Billy where he needs to go. Getting him what he wants, carrying the bags containing his many, many regular purchases. I don't suppose any of that will impinge too much on your pride. I'm sure the money will mollify any qualms, eh?" His grin fell away. "Stop anybody sniffing around him."

Ah, was that what it was really all about? Had somebody shown some ill-advised interest in Daddy's favourite boy? So, driving and a bit of muscle when required, in between carting Billy's shopping around. I seldom needed the muscle; I could look pretty menacing when I wanted, and that was usually enough.

"And to inform me directly of any unusual activity."

This wasn't about driving the kid around, this was

about being Frankie's eyes and ears. The obvious thing would have been for him to have had one of his existing employees do what he was asking of me, despite what he'd said. Did that mean one of his trusted employees hadn't been so trustworthy after all? Had somebody stepped out of line, or crossed a line? Had their employment been terminated? Had *they* been terminated? Maybe that last thought was a bit over the top, but with Frankie's cold eyes boring into mine, I wasn't sure it was. I suppressed a shiver.

Frankie tossed aside the pen and got up, and just like before, I suspected the beautifully tailored suit he wore hid a growing paunch. The sunlight streaming through the windows revealed what had been hidden in the muted light of the bar on Friday. He'd been handsome once but was showing signs of wear and tear, his jowls were heavy and his thinning hair was more grey than light brown. An image of him nailing Billy to the mattress, sweating and panting, exploded in my brain. There was something obscene and deeply wrong about it, and my stomach turned. Frankie had intimated Billy needed protecting, but I already knew that the one Billy really needed protecting from was Frankie.

I nodded, I didn't speak. It was as though by not speaking, I wasn't actually agreeing to what he wanted of me. Childish and silly, I know, but it made me feel better.

"I've business to attend to. There's a black Range Rover parked in the garage. I assume you can drive?" He quirked his brow at me as he held a key aloft that he'd fished from the desk drawer.

"Clean license. Never even been done for speeding." I

didn't need to tell him I'd passed every advanced motorist test there was and was trained in car hijack prevention.

"Good. I had no wish to rescind my offer."

He threw the key at me, which I caught with ease. I stood up, too, as it seemed our discussion was at an end. I didn't know where to go, and I felt awkward, and too late, I realised that was Frankie's intention, and I mentally gave myself a kick for allowing myself to be put on the back foot so easily.

"Before you go, I want to make sure you understand something. I've employed you to do a job, the duties of which I think I've made clear. I like clarity and clean lines. You're not Billy's friend. Friendship blurs those lines. Keep to the strict remit of the job."

No fraternisation. No sniffing around. Frankie had made himself very clear indeed. That smile crept over his face again, and I itched to smack it off. Instead, I told him I was happy to adhere to the job description.

He walked me out of his office, across and further down the hallway and opened the door to a lounge. Billy was perched on the edge of a sofa, a jacket lying over his lap. He jumped up and shrugged it on.

My new job as driver, gofer and hired muscle was about to start.

4

BILLY

I climbed into the back of the car and told Dashiell where he was to take me before I turned my attention to scrolling through my phone. I didn't know what I was looking at; it was just a handy way to avoid conversation and eye contact. I felt really awkward, being alone with Dashiell for the first time since he'd come to my rescue like he was some super hero or something. I'm not saying I'm not grateful, because believe me being attacked in the toilets wasn't my idea of fun, but I could've handled it. Living with Frankie had done that to me. I've become, what's the word? Desensitised. Yeah, that's it. Desensitised. I'd let Frankie Haynes desensitise me to degradation, but it was the price I had to pay to fulfil my obligations.

When I moved in with Frankie and he insisted I had somebody drive me wherever I wanted to go, I thought, *shit, this is great*. It was way better than trying to push onto the Tube or queue up in the rain for the bus, but it wasn't long before the novelty wore off. The driver, always one of Frankie's aides, never spoke to me, and once we'd arrived where we were going more often than not would follow me around like a stray dog. I spoke to Frankie about it once, in the early days, and asked if I could have an Oyster season ticket instead so I could get around on my own (reckoning it was cheaper than Pay-As-You-Go). He'd explained, in words of one syllable like I was stupid or something, that he didn't let his pets roam free, before he hit me. That was my first real taste of what being with Frankie would be like. I never asked again.

I had my own secret name for Frankie's aides: zombies. Most of them had about as much brains as the walking dead, and the personalities to match. I'd play up, telling them to take me here or there, ordering them to queue up in a café somewhere and bring me my coffee like they were my own personal servant or something. But when we were out and about, they didn't have any choice but to do as they were told, and they hated it, running after Frankie's spoilt little whore. I'd overheard a couple of the zombies talking about me one time, and the things they said, and called me, weren't pretty, but the way I saw it, they were just as much Frankie's whores as I was. So, yeah, I acted up. It was a petty form of revenge, but it was all I had.

"Are you okay? After Friday, I mean?"

Dashiell's words caught me off guard. My eyes snapped away from my phone, and I frowned as I caught his glance in the rear-view mirror. His job was to drive me around, not make conversation.

"Yeah. Fine."

"I still think the police should have been called, but I suppose you had your reasons for not wanting the law involved. And Frankie, too."

His words made me jump. I looked into the rear-view mirror again, but Dashiell had his eyes fixed on the road ahead. How did he expect me to answer that? What had he and Frankie talked about when they were locked away in the office earlier? What, exactly, were Dashiell's orders? Was he more than my driver, and a general dog's body? Was I being tested in some way, to see what I said about Frankie? Depending on the score, I could expect a present or a punch. Paranoia. Yeah, that's something else I'd learned in the last couple of years.

"How long until we get there?" I asked, ignoring his comment.

I was going for a fitting for a new suit at a place just off Saville Row, and it was taking ages to get through the traffic as we got nearer to the West End.

"About ten minutes."

"You obviously don't drive in London that much."

I think I may have eye rolled. There was no way we were ten minutes away. I slouched back into the seat and began flicking through my phone again, but almost immediately I was thrown to the side as Dashiell made a sharp turn down a narrow road between a couple of shops.

"What're you doing? This isn't the way."

Where the fuck was he taking me? Nerves gnawed at my guts, but Dashiell threw me a quick glance over his shoulder.

"I know a shortcut."

He was grinning, the cocky bastard. But he was right. He swung down one little side street after the next, and then suddenly there we were, pulling into the tiny private carpark of the tailor's shop. I looked at my watch. Dashiell had made it in nine minutes, not ten.

"Wait here in the car." I used my best spoiled whore's voice, rude and snotty in other words. To be honest, I was interested to see how he'd react. It was how I spoke to the zombies, and I wanted to see if he'd seethe the way they did.

"Shouldn't I be coming in with you?"

So he was some sort of guard, a newly recruited zombie after all. I kind of felt more disappointed than I should have, because I suppose I'd hoped he'd be different.

"It's a final fitting, so I won't be long. But if they're your orders. . ."

He didn't say anything for a second or two, and I just expected him to trail after me, but instead he gave me a sharp nod, like he'd thought and then made up his mind.

"Like you say, you won't be long. I'll wait here in the car."

He turned the radio on and fiddled around until he found a talk show and slipped down into the seat and closed his eyes, relaxed and at ease. I was surprised, I really thought he'd insist on coming in with me, and I didn't know what to say, so I just got out of the car and made my way to the shop.

No more than a few tweaks here and there were needed, and the suit would be delivered to the house before the end of the week. I already had the shirts, as bespoke as the suit, and another pair of new shoes so shiny, I could see my face in them. It'd all cost more than most people would have spent on a luxury holiday, yet I'd probably wear the lot no more than once or twice. But then why should I have cared, because I wasn't paying?

Dashiell looked like he was asleep when I got back to

the car, and I hammered on the window. I think I wanted to make him jump, but I was disappointed because his eyes immediately snapped open and he looked wide awake. I climbed into the back, feeling kind of annoyed that my attempt to catch *him* off guard hadn't worked.

"Where to now?" Dashiell turned the ignition on and looked at me through the rear-view mirror.

"I could do with a coffee." I'd been about to add that no doubt he could, too, but I bit my tongue because that sounded too much like starting a conversation.

"Anywhere in particular?"

I thought for a moment. There was no end of high street coffee shops around, and any one of them would do, but I must have hesitated too long because Dashiell cut into my thoughts.

"I know a good place in Soho, so not too far away. Do you want to try there?"

"Er, yeah. Okay."

I could feel my face heating up. Soho, where I'd been a dancer in a club. It was where I'd met Frankie and ended up coming to an agreement that had changed my life for both the better and worse, but that was a whole different story.

Dashiell eased his way into the traffic and headed east, into Soho's narrow, twisty streets. Diversions and road blocks were everywhere; there was no way he was going to find anywhere to park, but I was proved wrong once again. In one smooth move, he manoeuvred the car into a space that looked way too small for the massive Range Rover; the warning bleeps barely sounded from the dashboard.

"It's just around the corner," he said, and I followed

him into a small side street and into a café with the name printed on the window. Barista Boys.

It was the aroma that hit me first. Coffee, chocolate, caramel, vanilla. . . it was overload, and my mouth began to water as my stomach rumbled. I'd had a small pot of plain, low fat yogurt for breakfast. I generally skipped lunch and was looking forward – if you could call it that – to a tiny, boring dinner of steamed fish and veg. I was always hungry, and although I could cope with it, I never got used to it. I drank loads of water, and coffee, because they helped fill me up.

"Black coffee." I dug into my jacket pocket for my wallet and thrust a tenner into his hand and scuttled off to one of the few free tables.

As Dashiell queued up, I looked around the place. When I danced in the club, I only really knew the area at night, and in the early hours, when the café would be closed. I was sorry I hadn't known about it. The chairs and tables were mismatched, and the walls were mainly rough, exposed brickwork. There were posters tacked to the walls and flyers for cabarets and shows lying around. It was busy, and the murmur of voices fought with the whir of the milk frother, and the hard clanging of coffee grounds being emptied into metal waste bins.

It wasn't long before I found myself looking for Dashiell. He was talking to a young, dark-haired barista, and they were laughing and joking like they knew each other well. A door to the side of the counter opened, and a tall, well-built guy came out, and it was smiles all round and a big bear hug. The three of them carried on talking as the drinks were prepared, and I felt a pang of jealousy. The barista, and the owner or manager, who the bigger, older guy must have been, seemed to be friends of Dashiell. He was pleased to see them, and they were pleased to see him. Who was pleased to see me? I didn't even think Frankie was, half the time. And who was I pleased to see? There was only one person, but every time I saw them, all I wanted to do was cry.

"Cheer up, it might never happen." Dashiell put the tray on the table before he dragged out a chair and sat down.

I didn't bother to answer because all my attention was focused on what was on the tray. A huge slab of chocolate cake. I wanted to stuff all of it in my mouth at once, and then lick every scrap of frosting off my fingers. Well, that wasn't going to be happening any time soon. I dragged my eyes away from the plateful of sugary temptation, but the smell of rich, creamy chocolate filled me up. Maybe if I breathed in the smell, I could have the cake without the calories. But that wasn't all that was on the tray. Dashiell had got himself a huge bucket of hot chocolate topped off with cream and drenched in caramel sauce. His drink and cake probably contained about three days' worth of my calorie intake.

"Compliments of Bernie – the owner," he said, nodding in the direction of the big guy who was talking to the barista. Dashiell dropped the ten-pound note in front of me. "I assumed you like chocolate, because who doesn't?"

Dashiell pushed the cake towards me. What the hell was he doing? I stared at the cake, at Dashiell, and back at the cake. I wanted it, I mean I *really, really* wanted it. My mouth was watering, my stomach was clenching down hard, and I was sure my pulse rate had picked up. But there was no way I could eat it. A tide of anger engulfed me, but

I didn't know if I was angry at Dashiell for just assuming the way he had, or at myself because I was too scared to eat the fucking cake.

"I can't eat that." I all but spat the words out as I shoved the plate away harder than I'd meant. It skidded across the table and smashed against his mug, which he just about managed to stop toppling over and into his lap. Still, hot chocolate with blobs of cream slopped over the rim and pooled on the table. Without a word, Dashiell bundled up some paper napkins and dabbed at the mess, wiping away all signs of my outburst. His face was unreadable, but I doubt he'd been impressed.

"Sorry, I didn't mean. . ." My words trailed off, and I could feel my face going red. I'd acted like a spoiled kid throwing a tantrum, and I was embarrassed. He'd done something nice and thoughtful for me, after all, and it suddenly became important that he didn't think I was nothing more than Frankie's snotty kept boy.

"Cakes, biscuits, sweets and the rest of that stuff are all off limits. Frankie, he, erm, he likes me to keep slim." I cringed inside, and it felt like the whole episode was going from bad to worse. Dashiell didn't need to know how Frankie liked me, or anything about the screwed-up relationship I had with him. But the truth was, I didn't want Dashiell to think I had some sort of weird food hang up or that I was a borderline anorexic. Being, and staying, thin was part of my unwritten job description. If I jumped head first into that cake that was making me almost hyperventilate, I didn't have any confidence that I'd be able to stick to the remit.

"Slim? Okay, if that's how you want to put it."

His eyes raked over me, and I knew what he was

seeing. Skinny, not slim. Bony, sharp angles. It was what I saw every time I looked in the mirror. I was used to it, but it didn't mean I liked it.

Dashiell tucked into the cake as he checked his phone, taking no further notice of me. I sipped on my coffee. I wasn't that keen on black coffee, it was normally too bitter, but I'd got used to it – no unnecessary milky calories for me, thanks very much – but this was good. It was smooth and rich, and I almost enjoyed it. I looked up to ask Dashiell how he knew about the café, ready to make some kind of amends, when the words stuck in my throat.

He was engrossed in something he was reading, and chewing slowly. Frosting smeared his lips, and his tongue swept its way around, wiping them clean. My backbone tingled, and warmth flared deep in my belly as the urge to lean across and lick every last bit of that frosting away, tasting not just its creamy sweetness, but Dashiell, too, took hold of me. Where the hell had *that* come from? I clutched tight to my mug to stop my hands from shaking, but I couldn't drag my eyes away. He looked up as if he knew I was staring at him and gave me that cocky smile that was too much like a smirk. It was as if he'd read my mind, and my faced heated up for the second time that day.

"Why're you having a suit made? Special occasion?"

I shrugged. "Some business event Frankie's attending. He's getting an award or something. It'll be a load of boring old men congratulating each other." I realised, too late, what I'd said. "What I mean is—" But what I meant didn't matter, because Dashiell started to laugh. He shook his head as the rich, deep rumble died and he looked at me square on, a smile pulling at the corners of his mouth.

"Not the most exciting night out for a teenager, I imagine."

Teenager? It was my turn to laugh.

"How old do you think I am?"

He tilted his head and looked across the little round table at me. Consternation flittered across his face. I'd surprised him, and I felt a tiny thrill of triumph.

"Nineteen, max."

Okay, I was whip thin and that made me look younger, but nineteen, *max*? Seriously?

"Twenty-three. Twenty-four in November." Maybe by then I'd be getting a bit too old for Frankie. The thought thrilled and terrified me in equal measure.

"Oh. Right. You look younger."

Dashiell frowned, and he seemed perplexed. He glanced away, then back. He wanted to ask me something, I just knew it, and I waited for him to speak.

"Then why do you need a, a—"

"A babysitter?"

"Your words, not mine."

I needed to pick my words carefully.

"Frankie's kind of possessive, you know? But I reckon you've already figured that one out."

Dashiell said nothing; he just stared at me. Whatever he was thinking was well hidden behind a very impressive poker face. I should have left it at that, there wasn't any need to say more, but I found myself explaining why. What had happened had been public, and he could've found out easily enough.

"A few months back, we were at the opening night of a club. Not one of his places, but a business associate's. There was free booze, and some people had more than they could handle. Inhibitions slipped, I suppose, along with boundaries. Somebody, some guy who'd had too much to drink, took a liking to me and got a bit too insistent."

I'd chosen my words with care, that was for sure. The guy had been like an octopus and had tried to kiss me at the same time he'd grabbed hold of my dick. Frankie had been furious – not with me, thank God – or not so much, but with the guy, who'd been bundled off by a couple of the zombies. Ever since, Frankie had tightened the noose he'd slipped around my neck on the day I'd moved in with him. I didn't fool myself that he was being protective of me; it was about possession and how Frankie thought it made him look, having something he owned pawed by another man.

"And he wants to make sure it doesn't happen again, which is how I come into the picture?"

"You came to my assistance and proved yourself to him. It'll be a dull job, but I'm sure the weekly grand will make it more interesting for you," I snapped.

What did I say about my mouth running away with me? Dashiell's expression didn't change, but I was sure I saw his jaw tighten and twitch.

"Yes, I'm sure it will. Unless there's anywhere else you want to go, I can take you back."

I nodded and followed his upright, rigid back out of the café and back to the car.

5

DASHIELL

When Billy had told me he was twenty-three, I was shocked because he really did look like a poster boy teenage twink – the kind of too young, too skinny type I'd never had any interest in. But there was something about Billy Grace that *did* interest me – and my dick, if I'm honest. Just about everything he'd said and done had showed him to be rude, snotty, and a brat. He was touchy and thin-skinned, everything that ordinarily pissed me off, but I didn't believe any of it. It was armour, or a mask, self-protection of some type, something to keep himself safe from whatever it was that had caused those beautiful green eyes of his to be way older than a twenty-three-year-old's had any right to be.

When we arrived at the café I saw his reaction to the display case. The kid (or not kid, because I needed to stop thinking of him in that way) was almost drooling. His eyes went wide, and when he licked his lips, my dick gave a very ill-timed twitch. I thought that maybe he'd pick at a bit of the cake and leave the rest, but his reaction had been extreme. I mean, it was a slice of cake, for Christ's sake. When he did what he did, my first thought was that he had some kind of psychological issue around food. It made sense, especially as he was so thin, and I'd called myself all sorts for not working it out, but when he said Frankie liked him slim (slim my arse, skinny as a rake more like it), it fell into place. He was starving hungry, and his tongue was all but hanging out. Billy didn't just want the damn cake, he craved it.

What would Frankie have done if Billy gained a few pounds? Given him a smack? Inflicted some sort of mental torture? That Frankie was capable of both of those, I was more than sure. I was pretty good at summing people up with little more than a glance, and I was usually right. I had no doubt that beneath Frankie's expensive, paunch-disguising suit and the chic, cool house in one of London's wealthiest areas, there lurked a vicious thug any nasty little gang would've been proud to have as a member. In short, Billy was scared, and for good reason, and that disturbed me for all that I kept telling myself that whatever the details of the arrangement the pair of them had, it was none of my business.

We got back to the house at lunch time, not that I imagined Billy was going to have any lunch, as he fled upstairs without so much as a glance my way following a silent return journey. I had no idea what I was supposed to do next, and alone in the large entrance hall I listened carefully and heard the faint sound of voices coming from deeper inside the house. I followed them because it was time to meet my new colleagues.

The voices ceased as soon as I walked into the huge kitchen. Two guys sat at a large table at the far end, near the glass doors that led to the garden. I recognised the piggy-eyed, sullen one who'd escorted me to Frankie's office earlier, and who'd looked at me like I was something he'd trodden in. The second did no more than give me a disinterested glance before he carried on tapping into his phone.

"Afternoon. I'm Dashiell, the new—"

"The boy's arse wiper," the one with the piggy eyes said. "Rather you than me, mate. I was at Blue on Friday night when you rode to his rescue."

I didn't like the sneering way he said *the boy*, but I kept my face neutral as I threw him a cursory glance.

"I'm Lee." The phone tapping guy stood up and extended his hand for me to shake.

As I shook Lee's hand, something itched in the back of my mind. I had the vaguest feeling I'd met him before, but where or when I had no idea, as I didn't make a habit of hanging around with a crook's henchmen. He looked around my age, and like a million and one other guys you could see anywhere, so I dismissed the thought as a case of mistaken identity.

"And this here's Tony. Don't worry, you'll get used to him. If you're unlucky." Lee's mouth twitched in a faint smile, before he sat down again and turned his attention back to whatever it was he was doing on his phone.

"Good to meet you both." It wasn't, but it was the done thing to say.

"So, anything I need to know?" I looked at my two new colleagues and gave what I hoped was a disarming grin.

"What d'ya mean?" Tony narrowed his eyes and screwed up his nose, making his resemblance to a pig all the more striking, although I suspected our curly tailed, four-legged friends had a sight more brains than Tony did.

"About Billy, I suppose. And Frankie. Just don't want to put my foot in it, I guess. Driving a kid around and queuing up for his coffee's a good gig at a grand a week, so I don't want to screw it up and be out on my ear."

I looked from one to the other. On the face of it, what I'd said was true, and a wise man would have just got on with the job, kept his head down and collected his very generous pay at the end of the week, but I'd never been very good at being wise. But Billy Grace had crawled under my skin. I wanted to know more about him and discover what had brought him into Frankie Haynes' orbit, a place I'd bet my last penny on he didn't want to be, so I wasn't above ferreting out scraps of information wherever I could.

"Frankie's all right. That's all you need to know."

Tony scratched at a particularly impressive patch of acne on his neck at the same time he glared at me. "Just a shame about that skinny little tart he's got hanging around him, who thinks he's a cut above everybody else." Tony sniggered, and I wanted to land my fist right in the centre of the creep's ugly face.

"You need to watch what you say." Lee's words were as cold and steady as his stare, which just made Tony scowl. So, Tony not only had a big mouth, he was stupid, too, which probably wasn't a wise thing to be if you worked for somebody like Frankie Haynes.

"Billy's been Frankie's partner for about two years," Lee said, moving his focus from the still scowling Tony to me.

His grey eyes were assessing and intelligent, and I had

that creeping feeling again that I'd met him someplace. What was clear as day was that Lee was in a whole different league to the brainless Tony.

"Just keep in mind that Frankie's very protective. Sure, Billy's spoilt, but he's kept on a short leash. *You're* that leash, when you're out and about with him. Bat away unwanted attention, fetch and carry, be friendly but keep your distance, and you'll be all right because that'll keep Frankie happy. And believe me, that's just how you want him to stay."

Succinct, wise words. Lee was a bright light to the low wattage of Tony.

"Right, understood. I'm just here to do a job." And that's exactly what I should have been there for.

"Coffee?" Lee asked.

I nodded, and a couple of minutes later I was passed something nasty and instant. I took the offer, along with the accompanying packet of biscuits that was opened up and placed on the table as some kind of acceptance, and I made idle conversation with my newfound workmates. Both were casually dressed in jeans, T-shirts and hoodies, the suits of Friday night obviously for official duties only. Both men were broad and muscular, but whereas Lee looked fit, Tony just seemed brawny, his body as muscle-bound as his brain.

"You're due to pick up Antonescu from Heathrow at 4.30pm," Lee said, looking at Tony. "You should go now."

Tony's frown deepened, if that were possible, and for a moment I thought he was going to argue, but instead he got up and lumbered out of the kitchen without saying a word. Lee hadn't been making a suggestion, but issuing a command and making the pecking order clear.

"Billy's all right, don't take any notice of what Tony says." Lee at last put his phone away, tucking it into the pocket of his jeans. I didn't ask any more questions because I didn't want to appear to be pushing for information.

"Frankie is, too."

I seriously doubted that, and Lee's next words just confirmed that for me.

"As long as you keep on the right side of him and don't piss him off. Like I say, do your job and you'll be fine. Chaperoning Billy's a sweet gig, for a thousand in your hand at the end of the week." He tipped his head to the side and looked at me. Quizzical was the first word that sprung to mind, with sharp and smart following close on its heels. "I wasn't at Blue on Friday, but I've heard what happened. You must have seriously impressed Frankie. He's very careful, and especially so when it comes to Billy. Yet he decided to take you on the payroll without any hesitation. What's your secret?"

Lee leaned back in his chair and looked at me straight on. No, that's not quite right. He didn't look; he scrutinised. He was attempting to work me out, just as I was him. It was on the tip of my tongue to ask him if we'd met, but I swallowed the words down. I'd met all sorts or men in all sorts of situations, and if one of them had been a body-guard or henchman, or what have you, for a crook, I'm wasn't sure I wanted to renew my acquaintance. Instead of asking a question, I answered one.

"No secret. I interrupted an attempted theft. I was in the right place at the right time, that's all. The stars aligned, as they say; he had a job going, and I needed one. And cash in hand, too. I'm not going to look a gift horse in the mouth." I didn't know if the stars aligning was a saying or not, but it sounded right.

"He'd have had you checked out. If he'd have found anything he was wasn't happy with you wouldn't have got one foot on the premises. So I guess you've got nothing to hide, have you?"

Lee's words brought me up short. Of course a man like Frankie Haynes would have checked me out. I kicked myself for not thinking of it. A few months of idleness had taken the edge off my thinking. He wasn't going to entrust a valuable possession to anybody who'd walked in off the street despite all his talk of repaying my good deed. I pulled up a quick mental list of what he might have looked for. I didn't do the standard social media sites, all endless selfies and photos of what people were having for dinner; I had the well-known gay hook up apps, and that was about all. I didn't show my face in my profile picture; just the usual cheesy washboard abs shot. But I'd given Frankie my name, and that would have been enough for him to search on, and no doubt he'd been thorough, but he'd wouldn't have found anything on me he wouldn't be happy to show his grannie.

"So what are you doing for the rest of the day?" Lee asked, changing the subject.

It was a good question because I had no idea. Handyman duties, Frankie had said, but from the little I'd seen of the house, it looked pristine and well-maintained. Maybe I was expected to go around and check that all the lightbulbs worked or that the doors didn't squeak.

"I haven't got a clue. Billy's disappeared, and Frankie's not around, so—" I shrugged my shoulders.

"Frankie's upstairs, but he won't want to be disturbed.

Clean the cars. The one you used today, and the other three in the garage. Frankie's very particular about a lot of things, and that includes keeping the vehicles nice and shiny. Don't go wandering around the house."

"Why? Do you think I'm going to nick the family silver?"

"I wouldn't advise it."

I waited for Lee to say more, but he didn't; he just kept his eyes on me, retaining his deadpan and disinterested expression before he got up and left, leaving me alone in the big, shiny kitchen.

Looking around me, I got a serious case of kitchen envy. It was a real fuck-off kitchen. I'd always enjoyed cooking, and if work had been a bitch, I'd put on some music, crack open a beer or a bottle of wine and sizzle up a steak, most of them eaten alone and in front of the telly. I shook my shoulders, literally shook them, to dislodge the maudlin thought that had seemed to come out of nowhere.

I craved another coffee, not the instant crap I'd just about been able to swallow, but something good, strong and mellow. I looked around, and my eyes alighted on the state of the art coffee machine on the counter. I was an addict, caffeine was my crack cocaine, and I'd just met my supplier. I had the same machine at home, and it didn't take me long before I had something worth drinking in my hand. I closed my eyes and let my thoughts wander, and they inevitably wandered to Billy.

On the face of it, it looked simple. Younger man, older man, sex in exchange for an easy lifestyle. The set up was as old as time, yet there was nothing simple about what was going on between Billy and Frankie, I just knew it. I could feel it in my bones. Whatever Billy's reasons were for being with Frankie, the price he was paying was a heavy one.

I finished the coffee, then checked my phone, but there were no messages, and then flicked through my hook up apps. Same old dick pics and Photoshopped abs. Maybe later I'd think about some mindless fun and games. Or maybe not. I shut the app down. I had to be getting old; the masc4mascs I usually found appealing had suddenly lost their savour.

A quick glance of my watch surprised me; it was 3.00pm, and I'd been back at the house for over a couple of hours. By the time I got the cars washed, it'd be time to head off home.

Lee had told me not to wander through the house, but I'd never been very good at doing what I was told, and I traced my way back to the hallway. I didn't meet anybody, and it struck me, suddenly, how quiet the house was. Tony had gone to the airport to pick up Antonescu, whoever he was, and I had no idea where Lee had disappeared to. Frankie and Billy were around somewhere, but the place was so deathly silent, it could've been empty but for me.

I'd already taken a quick look around the entrance hall, I couldn't help it, my former training still ran deep in me, but I hadn't detected any cameras. That didn't mean there weren't any, though. I was the new boy, unknown and yet to be fully trusted despite the check Frankie apparently had taken out on me. I put on my best lost and bored expression for the benefit of the cameras, if they were there, and added in a loud sigh just for extra effect. I turned back towards the kitchen, which provided a back way out across to the garage, but I hadn't taken more than a couple of steps when a cry stopped me in my tracks.

It happened again, louder and longer, and edged with pain.

The sound of something heavy, falling or being thrown followed. A wail, then a plea, shaky and full of fear.

Billy's voice.

All thoughts of making my way back to the kitchen, and of avoiding the maybe hidden cameras, or heeding Lee's instruction, of the grand a week in undeclared, ready cash, vanished. For a big man, I can be very, very quiet, and I was never quieter as I crept up the wide, sweeping staircase. I stopped on the landing of the first floor. Billy's pleas had fallen silent, and the only sound I could hear was the beat of my own heart deep in my chest. Seconds, maybe even minutes passed, and there was nothing, and eventually I turned to make my way back downstairs.

The scream was high-pitched, feral and blood-curdling, and it rooted me to the spot. It was coming from a room at the end of the hallway and was followed by Billy's begging for whatever was happening to stop. I felt sick, and the sour taste of vomit filled my mouth. The only thing I cared about was putting a halt to whatever was happening behind that door, and in just the same way I had in the toilets in Blue, on Friday night. I hadn't taken more than a couple of steps before a heavy arm locked itself around my neck and I found myself being pulled back.

I was taken by surprise as a big hand clamped over my mouth and I was dragged, like a sack of potatoes and just as fucking useless, down the hallway and through a door, which slammed shut. I was pushed forward and out of the arms of my abductor. I swung around, ready to fight if need be.

"I told you. No wandering around the house. Just do

the job you're being paid for, and don't get involved with anything that goes on here. Understand?"

Lee glared at me from across the bedroom he'd hauled me into.

"You didn't hear—"

"Didn't hear what? It doesn't matter what I heard or didn't. And the same goes for you."

He stared at me, the same scrutinising look from earlier, as if he were trying to make up his mind about something, or maybe me. He shook his head and swore under his breath.

"Billy's not a prisoner. All right? If he didn't want to be here, he wouldn't be. He's free to walk out that door and never come back. He and Frankie have an arrangement, which suits them both, but that's nobody's business but theirs. You forget about whatever it was you think you heard."

"I don't *think* I heard anything." I was pissed off. I'd been brought down with ease, and that should never, ever have happened, and now I was being dismissed. Whatever *arrangement* Billy and Frankie had, Billy's cries and pleas had sent a cold shiver across my skin.

"I should report this to Frankie. You deliberately went against my order. You're the bottom of the food chain here, and you'd be wise to remember that."

Of course he was going to let Frankie know, he was Frankie's man, for God's sake. I'd walk out the door, and I'd never see or hear from Billy again. The thought sent a chill down my backbone.

Lee huffed. "I'm not, or not this time, but you're on a warning. You're new, and you don't know the rules. Don't put me in this position again, because next time I will inform Frankie, and just like I said earlier, he's not a man you want to get on the wrong side of. Go and clean the cars like I told you, and then go. Okay? *Okay?*" he said when I didn't answer.

I nodded, unable to force myself to say yes, and earned a tight, humourless smile in response. If I were to return the following day, I had no option but to do what I was told.

Lee had said Billy wasn't a prisoner, and though Billy may not have been kept under lock and key, there was one thing I knew, and that was that imprisonment came in more than one form.

6

BILLY

"I want you to drive me to the chemist."

Dashiell was washing his hands at the kitchen sink, his shirtsleeves rolled up and revealing the tatts on his arms. It wasn't a good idea to stare, not when Lee and Tony were also in the kitchen, but they were going through some stuff together on Lee's phone and were taking no notice of me.

"Sure. Give me five minutes," he threw over his shoulder.

His tone was cool and matter of fact, and I'm not surprised after how I'd been in the café the day before. I suppose I could have apologised properly, but I just wanted to forget it.

Five minutes later, I was climbing into the back of the car. Sitting down hurt. Sitting down really, really hurt, but it was better than the pain that shot through me every time I walked more than a few paces.

"Are you okay?"

Dashiell was looking at me as I eased myself into the seat. His eyes had narrowed, and the V of a heavy frown dug down between his brows. His mouth was drawn in a tight line, and he looked angry, and I didn't understand why.

"Yeah, just twisted my back, that's all, so it's sore." I wiped away the sweat that had broken out on my forehead and bit on my tongue to stop myself from howling as the backs of my legs pressed down on the car seat.

Dashiell started up the car. I winced as he moved off, and I caught him looking at me in the rear-view mirror, that deep frown still in place.

A sore back? Yeah, right. I had bruises across my arse and the backs of my thighs. And welts. I'd covered the welts in antiseptic cream, but I needed some of those massive plasters you can get because the skin kept splitting, along with some heavy-duty painkillers.

I'd spent the whole morning in bed. Frankie was long gone when I woke up, and I'd cried, pressing my face into a pillow so nobody would hear. I cried because of the pain, because my whole body hurt so much. It had been bad, with Frankie. Sometimes he got really angry, and he'd take it out on me. I was like his human stress ball. He'd squeeze and squeeze until he broke me down, and like a stress ball I'd spring back, but it was getting harder to do that, and I knew that one day he'd squeeze me so much, there'd be nothing left to spring back.

The weather was good, it was lunchtime and the little high street was busy, so Dashiell had to park a short walk away. As I staggered out of the car, I gasped and thought I was going to be sick. Dashiell was by my side in an instant, holding me steady.

"Bad back, my arse. And what's this?"

Dashiell touched the back of one of my thighs with one

of his hands, and I flinched. When he held it up, it was wet and red. We stared at the blood that had seeped through the loose tracksuit bottoms I was wearing. I held my breath, but I could hear his, and it was heavy and ragged.

"I should take you to the hospital." His tone was hard and tight, like he was trying to keep a lid on his temper.

"No, I just need some big plasters." I probably needed bandages, but I wasn't going to say that.

"If you're bleeding, you need to see a doctor."

It was like Friday night all over again. Go to the police, go to the hospital, do the right thing. In my world, none of that happened, and the sooner Dashiell realised that, the better. I pulled my arm from the hand that was still holding me steady.

"Don't get involved with stuff that doesn't concern you. Your job is to drive me around. What it *isn't* is you telling me what I should do. All right?"

I hated talking to him like that, because all he was doing was being decent, yet I was giving him a hard time by acting like the snotty brat again. I turned and made my slow, and painful, way to the chemist. Dashiell was probably starting to hate me, and I wouldn't have blamed him.

It didn't take me long to get what I needed, and the drive back to the house was as silent and awkward as the previous day's had been.

I didn't see much of Dashiell for the rest of the week. I didn't know what he got up to, as I didn't need him to drive me. I'd spent most of my time watching films, listening to music, or reading. Escaping, in my head, which I'd been doing more and more frequently. But I'd been deliberately avoiding him, too, because despite what had seemed to be genuine concern and anger over the state I'd been in, I didn't know for sure what the deal was between him and Frankie. Like, had Frankie told him to report back anything I'd said or done? Yeah, that paranoia had reared its head again. Keeping him at arms' length seemed the smart move, so I just kept out of his way as much as I could.

By the time Thursday night came around, the welts had calmed down and the bruises had begun to fade. I was walking easier, too, just like I knew I would be because it wasn't the first time I'd been in that position, and it wouldn't be the last.

Staring at myself in the bedroom mirror, I looked good. Slate grey suit, shirt that was the palest, palest pink and a deep magenta tie. Frankie came up behind me and gripped me by the hips; my muscles stiffened with the sickening anticipation of what might happen next. A quickie before we left? A blow job to rid himself of some of the tension ahead of the evening's big award ceremony? My mind was already shutting down; more and more, I found myself retreating to some private little corner in my head every time he touched me.

"You look beautiful. I'll be the envy of every man there tonight."

I very much doubted it, but I just smiled, the way I always did. Frankie buried his face into my neck, and I thought he was going to suck down on it and leave a bruise – he really did have a thing about bruising me, even when he thought he was being gentle, which wasn't often. It was all about ownership with Frankie, it was like a bruise was a way of saying *this belongs to. . .* but instead he just kissed me and told me to be downstairs on the dot at 6.30pm, before he left.

It was never a good thing to be late for Frankie, so I made sure I was walking down the stairs at 6.25pm.

Dashiell was at the bottom of the stairs, alone in the entrance hall and leaning on the newel post. He hadn't noticed me, and I stopped dead.

Fuck, but he looked good. He was wearing a dark grey suit, such a deep shade it was almost black; it was the uniform the zombies wore when they were on duty. Frankie was a bit flash, an exhibitionist, I suppose, and he liked to make an entrance wherever he went, which meant his entourage had to look right. Thing was, the zombies always looked like what they were, thugs who'd dressed up for the night. *You can't make a silk purse out of a sow's ear.* My gran's words came back to me, and they were true when it came to the zombies. But the same couldn't be said of Dashiell.

The suit fitted him like a glove and was as dark as his thick hair that I had a sudden, blinding vision of scrunching up in my fists as he— *shit*, I couldn't think of him, of any man, like that. I took a deep breath and carried on walking down the stairs, and that's when he looked up and his eyes meet mine. He smiled, and something broke in me. I'd been rude and nasty to him, but the smile that lit up his face was so warm and friendly and was everything I didn't deserve from him, and I couldn't help smiling back. He opened his mouth, and I knew, I just knew, he was going to say something that would make me feel good, but also ashamed for the way I'd treated him, when another voice called out.

"Dashiell. You're with me in the front car, the one that's carrying Frankie and Billy." Lee strode into the hallway, and it was back to the business of the evening. A couple of minutes later I was in the car with Frankie.

Frankie was on the phone, issuing instructions or something at the same time he stroked my thigh. I tensed up again, and I breathed in deep and slow. I really, really hoped and prayed he wasn't going to make me go down on him in the back of the car. There was a glass window between the front and the back seats, and I didn't know if he thought it gave us privacy, but he wouldn't have cared either way.

I pretended I wasn't worried about what the zombies thought, just as they pretended not to see. When it first happened, I couldn't work out why Frankie did it, and I wondered whether having others watch (but making out they weren't) was a turn on, but I didn't reckon it was about that. He wanted what he wanted, where and when he wanted. I think it was that simple. But this time, on the way to that boring awards ceremony where he'd be fêted for all his wonderful charity work, I sent up prayers to anything that was listening that he wouldn't scrape his fingers through the back of my hair and shove my head down. Why? Because Dashiell was there, in the front seat next to Lee, and he'd know what was happening and would see me for what I was, and I didn't want him to see the evidence, even though he knew it.

"We're here, Frankie."

Lee's clipped tones came through speakers into the back of the car. He'd got us to the West End hotel on the dot of 7.15pm. The second car parked up behind us a minute or so later, and I walked into the hotel with

Frankie, with Dashiell, Lee, Tony and some other zombie I'd not seen before following behind.

Everybody was looking at us as we walked through. I should have been used to it, Frankie's insistence on 'security'. It was totally over the top because this was a legitimate business awards ceremony, or at least I think it was. I wondered what all the others who were gathered there would think if they knew about Frankie's less conventional business interests. I wasn't involved with the stuff that made Frankie the big money, and I didn't want to be. Maybe I was a parasite living off the suffering of others, but I refused to think about it because I couldn't afford to. The fact was, I needed Frankie, and because of that I'd do anything to keep him wanting me.

"Lee, Dash, you're inside with us. We've got a front row table, close to the stage. You two, stay out here," Frankie barked, nodding at Tony and the other guy.

Tony didn't look happy because he probably thought he was going to get a place at the big table with Frankie. The guy was such a prick. I took a very quick glance at Dashiell and wondered what he thought about spending the next three hours or so being bored to death listening to speeches about *giving back to the community*, which was probably tax deductible in any case. I remembered our conversation in the café about it all being a bit dull for a teenager, and I pressed my lips together tight to stop myself from smiling. Dashiell's eyes crinkled, just a tiny, tiny bit, and I knew he was remembering, too.

There was a drinks reception first, and Frankie was immediately whipped away by a group of men, all laughing together and slapping each other's backs in congratulations. Frankie's nod of the head was tiny, but it was enough for Lee to lead Dashiell and I out of the main crowd to stand by the wall. I wasn't to be introduced, and I was more than happy about that. Dashiell took an orange juice from a roving waitress, and I followed suit. Lee wandered off, back in the direction of where Frankie played the affable businessman with the others, leaving me alone with Dashiell.

"You know this is going to be really, really boring, don't you?" I said as I sipped my juice and stared out over the crowd.

Dashiell laughed, but quietly, like it was meant just for me, a low rumble that sent a tingle down my backbone. "Hey, don't knock it. I'm on overtime, I get to eat fancy food and hobnob with the great and the good. And if I do get bored," he said, his voice dropping, "well, let's just say there's a lot to distract me."

"It's not a good idea to be distracted when—" I turned to look at Dashiell, and the words dissolved in my mouth.

He was looking straight at me. Just as his eyes had locked onto mine when I'd been coming down the stairs earlier, the same thing happened, and I swear to God, I couldn't pull my gaze away from his. All that shit you see in films, where everything fades away until there's just the two main characters staring at each other, everything else forgotten about? Yeah, that was us. For a few moments, nothing, *nothing* mattered except the two of us and the stark, undisguised desire I saw in Dashiell's eyes as they drilled into mine.

And then he smiled, just like he'd smiled before, and all that rawness I saw in him softened, and I ached, I honestly ached, to reach up and press my lips to his to taste the warmth and sweetness of his smile.

"Billy, you need to re-join Frankie because they're going through."

From somewhere, Lee had reappeared.

"What?" I think I must have looked at him like I was stupid or something because he was peering at me through narrowed eyes. "Er, yeah. Right."

I looked over to where Frankie was, still talking to the same group of men. I glanced back at Lee, and a chill shot through me. Lee was staring hard at Dashiell. His grey eyes were like granite, and Dashiell wasn't shying away, like they were in some kind of silent stand-off.

"Come on." Lee took my elbow, pulling me rather than guiding me back towards Frankie to go through for dinner and the ceremony.

We were at a large table, with a couple of the men Frankie had been talking to. The food arrived, but I pushed it around on my plate. Normally I'd have wanted to scoff it all down, and everybody else's too, but this time I genuinely couldn't stomach it, because of the knot deep in my guts. I kept my eyes down, not daring to meet Dashiell's, who was across the large, round table from me along with Lee. By the third, uneaten, course, I was desperate to get away for a few minutes.

"Frankie? I need the bathroom. Please?" I murmured. I'd learned early on that it was always better to ask for Frankie's permission.

He answered with a curt nod of the head, and I had to stop myself from making a run for it.

As soon as I got to the Gents', I dived into one of the cubicles and slumped down onto the closed lid of the toilet. The noise and heat, having to sit still and smile and be the perfect pet for Frankie as I tried my hardest not to stare at Dashiell, had shredded my nerves. A few minutes, it was all I needed, and then I could go back and play the game again. I took a deep breath, unlocked the door, and stepped outside.

"We really must stop meeting like this."

Dashiell leaned against the wall, his legs crossed at the ankle and his hands in his trouser pockets. He looked at ease and was smiling with all the warmth of earlier.

"You okay?" He bent his head to the side and looked at me, and a small frown furrowed his brow. When I didn't answer, he pushed himself away from the wall and took a step towards me.

"Yes, I'm fine." I was anything but fine, because that smile brought back what I'd seen in his eyes as we'd stood by the wall. He had no right to look at me like that, not when there wasn't a thing he or I could do about it.

"Are you? You seem very, I don't know, muted, I suppose the word is. Yes, muted."

I wanted to scream. Yeah, I was muted all right. Muted, meek, mild, compliant, silent. All those words and more were my default mode. It was what was expected of me, and I played my part well because muted and all the rest of it got me through each day.

"I'm okay. I should get back," I mumbled, and I made to walk past him, but Dashiell caught me by the arm and stopped me in my tracks. I stared down at his hand wrapped around my forearm. A few fine, dark hairs were scattered over the pale skin. His hands were calloused, as though he was used to rough or outdoor work, but it was his fingers I noticed, long and slender, and I wondered, just for a moment, what he might do with those fingers and how they might feel as they traced their way across my skin.

"No, you're not."

No, I wasn't all right. I was as far from all right as it was possible to be, but I tugged my arm out from his grip. I needed to get back, to the noise and the heat and Frankie's insistent squeezing and rubbing of my thigh under the linen-draped table. That's what I needed to do, but instead I looked up into Dashiell's big blue eyes, eyes that were looking back at me with concern and compassion. I honestly didn't know if what I was seeing was genuine or whether Dashiell was under orders from Frankie to test me and trip me up, but at that moment none of that mattered as I stood there and unravelled.

Dashiell's arms coiled themselves around me, holding me up and holding me tight. There was no heat, nothing sexual in his touch; there was only warmth and strength, and I just couldn't hold back. I cried. Big, fat, messy sobs, and it wasn't pretty. I had snot running from my nose and drool from my mouth, and I was getting it all over his suit, the suit he looked fuck-off gorgeous in. I couldn't help any of it, and all I wanted was for Dashiell to hold me in his arms, a temporary safe haven from the mess that was my life.

"You can trust me, I'm not like the others. With whatever you need. If you want to talk—"

"There's nothing to talk about. It is what it is." I stepped back and dragged my hand across my face to wipe away the snot and tears. The wave was receding, and I was feeling a bit stupid as I battled to regain the control I'd lost that had resulted in me melting into a slushy puddle.

"He's asked me to report any unusual activity."

"So you're a spy? Your daily reports are just going to be a pile of blank pages." Perhaps I should have been angry, but I didn't have the energy.

"No, I'm not. And I never would be, for that man."

Dashiell looked down at me. His eyes were still kind, but there was something else there, too, as if he were thinking and working something out.

"You don't believe me? Would I have told you that if I intended to do it?"

"Why would you go against his orders? Frankie's not a man to make angry." If there was anyone who knew that, it was me, and I had the faded bruises and faint scars to prove it.

"Maybe I don't like being told what to do."

"I—" I didn't get any further. Dashiell pressed a forefinger to my lips, and the rest of the words melted away.

"Sometimes you just have to trust somebody, and that somebody's me."

His words were matter of fact, as if my trusting him was some kind of done deal. And you know what? In that moment, that was exactly what it felt like. I nodded, and Dashiell smiled, big, broad and this time just a touch cocky, and God, didn't I just want him to pull me back into this arms?

"Come on, let's get back out there," he said.

He was right, because being away for too long wasn't a good idea, but as I washed and dried my face and walked through the door Dashiell held open for me, I felt a calm I thought had been lost to me forever.

7

DASHIELL

I finally got away at 1.00am, after picking up my own car back at the house, and although I could have stayed over, I needed to be on my own, on my own turf, where I could think.

To be honest, I didn't know who was the most surprised by what had taken place. I was a bit rough and ready, tender was definitely not my default mode, but something about Billy brought out a side of me I'd barely known existed, let alone acknowledged. It was a protective side, I suppose you could call it, and new to me. All the men who'd come and gone in my life, and even those who'd stayed, like my friend Andy, had never needed my protection in any shape or form. Billy was different. It wasn't just physical protection he needed; it was emotional, too. When he went into meltdown mode, all I'd wanted to do was hold him close and offer him the safe haven of a strong pair of arms, a shoulder to cry on and the promise of trust and friendship, even if it were just for a few minutes.

I spent most of the night tossing and turning, in and out of fitful sleep. When I dragged myself out of bed at seven the following morning, I felt like shit and looked as bad. A shower, shave and two cups of coffee later, and I was just about ready to leave for the house.

I had no idea how Billy would react to me, and to what had happened, in the cold light of day and when he'd had time to think. He was scared to death of Frankie, and my stomach clenched when I recalled the pleas for Frankie to stop whatever it was he'd been doing behind the closed door of their bedroom. I'd heard genuine fear in Billy's voice and had touched the evidence of it the following day. It had made me feel sick, seeing the pain Billy had been in, and if Frankie had been there, I'm not sure my temper would have held. Whatever arrangement they had, I didn't believe that what that bastard put Billy through was truly consensual.

All this meant that there was a good chance he'd be regretting his breakdown. I'd seen his vulnerability, and let's face it, nobody ever wants to be that exposed. I'd known him for just a week, so I didn't know him at all, if you looked at it like that. Billy Grace, too young, too skinny, too blond, suspicious, defensive, a rude and bad-tempered brat, had got under my skin where he'd burrowed deep and got as snug as a bug in a rug. Mixed metaphors? Yes, perhaps, but then, he was mixing up my thinking.

I arrived at the house just before 9.00am, and the electric gates opened once I'd clicked the entry key I'd been given. I still suspected there were hidden cameras, but that didn't bother me too much; it was just enough that I was aware of them.

Lee was alone in the kitchen, tapping into his phone.

He was so caught up in what he was doing, he didn't notice me walk in. The phone wasn't the one he'd been using when I'd first met him, or the one I'd seen him use since. I didn't know why I should have noticed it, but I did, then promptly forgot about it. There was nothing unusual about it because lots of people had more than one phone, and I guessed it was his own, rather than for work.

"Morning."

Lee's head shot up. His face drained of all colour, and I thought he was going to be sick, all way out of proportion to being caught texting or whatever it was he'd been up to.

"Frankie wants to see you," he snapped as he stuffed the phone deep into his pocket.

"Good morning to you, too."

"Best not keep him waiting." He didn't bother to respond to my only very slightly sarcastic comment. "You'll find him in his office. Remember where that is?"

"Reckon I can find it."

I walked away without another word, and a couple of minutes later I was sitting opposite Frankie. Christ, he looked awful.

His skin had a grey pallor, and there were dark, puffy bags under his bloodshot eyes. He was dressed casually, the paunch I'd always suspected was fully on show beneath the stretched shirt. Even before I'd gone a couple of paces into the room, I could smell the booze. A brandy in his morning coffee, or gin on his cornflakes, perhaps? Maybe there was a bottle hidden in his desk drawer and he'd availed himself of a morning nip?

But it was none of that; it was the after-effects of the night before. By time we left the hotel, Frankie had had to be poured into the car, and this morning the alcohol was leeching out of his system. As Lee and I had got him into the car, the thought of him turning his drunken attentions on Billy had made me want to puke, but he'd been asleep and snoring like a pig within moments of pulling away, and he'd had to be carried into the house when we got back.

"You've been here for almost a week."

It wasn't a question, but a statement.

"And so?" he barked at me.

"And so *what*?" I asked, although I knew precisely what he was getting at: my reports on Billy I had no intention of giving him, unless they were my own carefully edited version.

"Is there anything I need to be made aware of? Think carefully and answer honestly. And remember that grand."

Ah yes, that grand, the one I wanted at that moment to stuff right up his arse. Instead, I cocked my head to the side as if I were dredging my memory.

"No, nothing."

"Nothing? Are you sure about that?"

I'd taken Billy to the tailors, and then to the chemist's on Tuesday morning, and after that I'd barely seen him until the award ceremony the night before, so I'd kept myself busy washing cars, replacing some tiles in a bathroom, fixing some leaky taps, and painting a fucking shed. He hadn't been wrong when he'd said he needed a handyman. None of it had taken me long, and other than that, I'd made friends with the coffee machine in the kitchen again; in all honesty, I wasn't really earning my pay. I needed to feed Frankie something, something to keep me employed, something to gain his trust. It was time to tempt him with an edited titbit.

"There was one thing, but it was minor. Not even worth mentioning, really."

"Anything and everything's worth mentioning."

He leaned forward. I'd got his interest, and it was time to throw him the bait. I screwed up my eyes, like I was thinking back over the week.

"He wanted a coffee after the tailor's on Monday, so we stopped off on the way back." So far, so true. "To one of the chain places," I added. My first edit. I wasn't going to tell him about Barista Boys, and I knew we weren't followed, so he couldn't check out my story. "It was busy, but I snagged us a table, and by the time I'd got back with the drinks, a guy, another customer, had taken one of the spare places and was getting a bit too chatty. Borderline flirty. Billy was ignoring him, but the guy wasn't taking the hint, so I made sure he took it from me. I told him to fuck off," I added, for good measure. Well, at least going for a coffee had been true.

I was pretty damn pleased with that. Just enough to make keeping me on worthwhile.

Frankie narrowed his eyes at me, but with the hangover he must have had, it was clearly too much effort, and he sagged back into his chair.

"Okay. Good. I don't like anybody taking an interest when it's not theirs to take. You won't get any trouble from Billy, he knows the rules."

Frankie grinned, smug and self-satisfied, and vicious, and my stomach shrivelled.

I kept my face neutral, but it took everything I had not to reach out and yank the bastard over the desk and slam his face down so hard, it turned into a bloody pulp, dripped over the edge and pooled on the carpet. So Billy knew the rules, every one of them no doubt hammered home with a punch, a slap or worse. I think it was then, when I looked at that smile that made me feel sick, that I understood how much I hated Frankie Haynes. *He* was the one Billy needed protection from. The only place Billy had any chance of getting that from was me. Walking away after a few weeks, when my bank balance was nice and fat, would have been like throwing Billy to the sharks. I wouldn't do it, I couldn't. And that meant I had to box clever.

Frankie pulled open the drawer to his desk and threw two wads of notes towards me. I'd chucked him some scraps, and he was doing the same to me. It made me hate him even more.

"I won't be around later. We're going away for the weekend, so I won't be able to put the cash in your hand on the dot of five. We're going to celebrate my award with a special group of friends, for all the good things I do for the community."

He laughed, and my stomach turned some more because there was something dirty and sick in the sound that came out of his mouth. I glanced at the bundled notes on the desk. My first grand. It felt like blood money.

"You can count it if you like, but it's all there. You've made a good start, just make sure you keep it up. You can leave at lunchtime, and as we're not going to be here over the weekend, you can report back in at 8.00am on Monday morning." He waved his hand, indicating the door behind me. I was dismissed.

I wanted to pummel him into the ground, I wanted to hit him until he screamed and begged for me to stop, I wanted to stick his head in a meat grinder because he was a nasty, vicious fucker the world could do without. I wasn't a violent man, I honestly wasn't, but Frankie Haynes dragged something dark from deep inside of me. I clawed the money towards me, stuffed it into my pockets and got out before I gave in to what I itched to do. I had to because if I touched as much as one hair on his scummy head, it wouldn't be me who'd suffer.

8

BILLY

"Where's Dashiell?"

If it had been Lee sitting at the table and flicking through the newspaper, I'd have at least said good morning first, but it was Tony, so I didn't bother.

Tony barely threw me a glance before he shrugged. "How should I know? I'm not his keeper."

I didn't say anything to that; instead, I just looked at him. His mouth was pressed closed, but his jaw worked up and down as if he were chewing something he didn't like the taste of.

"I think he's in the garage," he finally added.

Tony was stupid, he really did have shit for brains, but he had just enough going on between his ears to know I could make things awkward for him with Frankie. Frankie could treat me pretty much how he wanted because I was bought and paid for, but that privilege didn't extend to the zombies. They were expected to treat me with a certain amount of respect, not for my own sake, but because Frankie felt that in disrespecting me, they were disrespecting *him*. It was kind of like it was a slur on his choice of, let's say, companion.

I headed off towards the garage without a word because Tony wasn't worth wasting any more breath on. I needed to go shopping, and there was a ton of stuff I wanted to buy, so I was going to load up the credit card and be laden down with bags. Well, I wasn't; it was Dashiell who'd be doing the carrying, not me. It wouldn't take me long to get through a few hundred quid, or even a grand or more. I mean, I wouldn't technically be paying for any of it, although ultimately I *was* paying, but not in cash. It was all part of the deal, you see. No, that's not strictly true; it was the *heart* of the deal, the very essence of it. The reason I was going to be spending all that money was the reason I was with Frankie.

I wouldn't be spending a penny on myself.

Sure enough, I found Dashiell in the garage. He hadn't seen me, and he was bent over the open bonnet and fiddling around with the engine or whatever. Other than the suit he'd been wearing the previous Thursday, the one he'd looked so good in, I'd only ever seen him in smart jeans and a shirt, but he wasn't wearing any of that stuff then.

"Just a tick. . . let me just. . . there, all done." The bonnet closed with a hard click, and he turned to me and smiled. "Do you need me to take you somewhere, Billy?"

It was the first time I'd seen him since Thursday night, and I didn't really know how to act now that I was alone with him. The whole episode in the toilets at the hotel had been intimate, but also kind of embarrassing. I'd always been able to hold it together and keep calm in public, but with a kind word or two I'd come apart. Dashiell had offered me not just a real shoulder to cry on, but support and friendship. It was so tempting to grab what he was offering, but I couldn't. Having a friend meant getting close, and that was too dangerous. He was there to drive me about and do odd jobs around the house, that was all, and I had to remember that. What had happened needed to be forgotten, by the both of us.

"Billy?"

Dashiell quirked his head to the side when I didn't answer, but the smile stayed on his lips. He wandered over to me, wiping his hands on an old bit of rag, and I swallowed hard.

The old jeans he wore were covered in greasy stains and hung loose and low on his hips. Instead of a smart shirt, he was wearing a T-shirt, just as worn as his jeans, but tight against his hard muscles. Jesus, he was well-built. I mean, I already knew that but seeing him in the flesh, kind of thing, well, that was different. And those tatts, snaking all the way down his arms. . . blue, red, green, pink. Loads of colour, and a complicated design I wanted to trace with my fingers, or my tongue.

"Billy? What's wrong?"

The touch of his hand to my face was an electric shock going through me, and I jerked back. I couldn't let him touch me.

"What do you think you're doing?" My snap was vicious, like a cornered dog, and Dashiell's smile faded.

"I want you to take me to Oxford Street. Twenty minutes."

Dashiell nodded and took a step back. "Okay. I'll have a quick shower, and I'll see you at the front of the house."

He threw the towel on a work bench and walked out of

the garage without as much as a glance back in my direction, leaving me standing there alone. I felt shitty, and I wanted to run after him and make him understand, but instead I wandered back into the house to collect my stuff, feeling lonelier than ever before.

We'd been driving for about fifteen minutes, but it felt like forever. Dashiell hadn't said a word to me since we'd set off, and the atmosphere in the car was as heavy as a lead weight, and it was my fault. Dashiell had stopped me from falling out of control on Thursday, but all I'd done earlier was retreat to my default position of snotty brat. He didn't deserve that, but I was also *better* than that, I knew I was, so I licked my dry lips and dived right in.

"I—I'm sorry. For acting the way I did earlier."

"It's about what happened last Thursday, isn't it?"

I nodded and glanced into the rear-view mirror, where I caught his eye. "I don't normally do that. Break down, I mean." I could feel the heat rush up my face. I'd probably gone as red as a beetroot.

"Billy, everybody needs to let off steam. If you keep the pressure valve screwed down too tight, you end up going off like a bomb."

We stopped at a red light, and Dashiell turned around. His face was serious, but at least he'd lost the hard, blank expression that had taken the place of the warm smile I'd wiped from his face back in the garage.

"If you don't want to talk about what happened, fine. I'm okay with that. But you need a friend, in that house, and I can be what you need. I don't care what Frankie's orders are, I'm not going to spy on you and report back to him. I'm not your minder, or jailer, or nanny, or—"

"Babysitter?"

Dashiell laughed as he shook his head. "No, Billy, I'm not your babysitter either. When you're with me, you can say and do whatever you want. None of it will get back to Frankie, that's a promise."

The blast of a horn behind us was a signal that the lights had changed, and Dashiell swung around and set off. Neither of us spoke for a few minutes, as Dashiell concentrated on the heavy traffic, and I thought about what he'd said. He was offering to be my safety valve and friend, to be somebody I could trust and not be wary and suspicious off. That's what he'd said, and I believed him. Yeah, I needed a friend, but I had to make sure I didn't start to think he could be more than that because if I did, it wouldn't be just me who'd suffer the consequences.

"Wanker!" Dashiell shouted at a cyclist wobbling in front of him, as he smashed down on the horn. "They're a fucking menace. Poxy bastards."

I stared laughing, I couldn't help it, and Dashiell joined in.

"Know any more shortcuts?" I asked as I leaned forward from the back seat.

I was just an inch or two from the back of his neck, and I could smell traces of the lemony shower gel he'd used. Dashiell had had his hair cut over the weekend, and the back was shaved close to his neck, and I imagined it'd feel like a paint brush if I rubbed my fingers across it, spikey but kind of soft at the same time. I sat back a bit and shoved the thought away.

"I know plenty. I could get you from one side of

London to the other without touching a main road," he said as he turned into a less congested side street.

"How come? Were you a cab driver or something? Did you do The Knowledge?" The map of London's streets every black cab driver had to commit to memory. Somehow, though, I couldn't imagine Dashiell driving a cab.

"No. I've just spent a lot of time driving through London over the years, that's all."

He didn't say any more, and I didn't push it. It wasn't long, though, before we parked in an underground carpark around the back of Oxford Street.

"The men's stuff's on the ground floor," Dashiell said when I headed to the up escalator in the large department store, just across the road from the carpark.

I shook my head because it wasn't men's clothing I was interested in.

I hadn't thought what he might think when he saw what I was buying, and it made me feel a bit funny and awkward because I'd have had to explain, and that's something I didn't want to do.

"There's a café on the top floor. I'll meet you there when I'm done." I didn't want Dashiell standing over me when I went through the cashmere jumpers, flowery dresses, and the silky, soft scarves.

"Why don't you want me to come around with you?"

Because I don't want you to see what I'm buying didn't seem enough of an answer. He'd either assume I was into cross-dressing, which I wasn't, or he'd ask me questions I wasn't willing to answer. I started to feel as awkward as I had earlier.

"When I'm shopping, I like to do it on my own." It was the only answer I could think of, and it sounded really,

really lame. Dashiell didn't believe it either, I could see it in the way he raised his brows. I felt cornered, and I lashed out without thinking.

"Look, you said you weren't my minder or babysitter, or whatever, so don't start acting like one. Just go up to the café and get a coffee. You can even get yourself a bloody piece of cake." I pulled a tenner out from my wallet and shoved it at him. I was tense and wound up, and I'd reverted to being a brat again, but what I was there to buy, and why, was private and upsetting, and I couldn't take having an audience, not even Dashiell.

He caught my hand, curled it into a fist and crushed the bank note into my palm.

"No, I'm not any of those things. I told you. If you want to go and shop on your own, that's fine, but you don't have to shout and make a scene in the middle of the sales floor like some spoilt little bitch. And don't ever shove money at me again and give me orders to run along like a good boy. Do you understand?"

Dashiell's voice was calm and measured, unlike mine apparently. I glanced around and saw nearby shoppers and staff looking at us. My burst of temper was doused as quickly as it'd flared up, and again I was left feeling stupid and embarrassed. If it had been any of the others who'd driven me, they'd have been more than happy to take the money and sit around in the café. I should have remembered, before I got stroppy, that Dashiell wasn't like the rest of them.

"I—" But I was too late. Dashiell had stepped onto the escalator and was heading for the top floor café, leaving me standing on my own for the second time that morning.

It didn't take me too long to get everything I wanted.

My purchases filled bag after bag. Pretty shoes that would never be worn, soft cashmere jumpers that would be added to the pile that was already a dozen strong, floaty silk scarves that would stay wrapped in tissue paper. I bought it all because it made me feel better. Pretty, dainty things she could never afford. If she'd known what I had to do to get them, she'd have thrown the lot on the bonfire. But she'd never know, because she'd never know anything anymore.

I flung in a few extras, and the credit card took a hit to the tune of fifteen hundred pounds. I had dark, ugly bruises on my hips from Frankie's attentions over the weekend when we'd gone away, so I had no qualms about hitting the credit card hard.

Lugging what felt like a hundred bags, I made my way to the café. Dashiell was sitting by one of the windows and was talking into his phone. For a split second, I wondered whether he was speaking to Frankie, telling him I'd had a tantrum and had ordered him not to follow me around the shop. My stomach dropped like a stone.

Dashiell looked up and saw me staring and waved me across. He was smiling and laughing, the phone still clamped to his ear. No, he wasn't talking to Frankie, I was certain. Dashiell hadn't lied to me in the car, and I shouldn't have doubted him, but I couldn't shake off two years' of fear and paranoia in one morning's shopping trip.

He was still on the phone when I dumped the bags down and pulled out the spare chair to sit down. Whoever he was talking to, he was enjoying the conversation because he gave what I reckon was the dirtiest laugh I'd ever heard.

"Andrew Pollard, you are such a *tease*. You gonna

cook my eggs for me the way I like 'em in the morning, hmm?"

The words made my stomach shrink. He was sitting there in front of me, talking to what must have been his boyfriend. Andrew. Why hadn't I thought about that? Of course somebody like Dashiell would have a boyfriend. He'd have a whole other life, one that had nothing to do with me, and the house, and Frankie. . . I pulled out my own phone to try and make it look like I wasn't drinking in everything he was saying to the man who was a tease and who he was going to having breakfast with after they'd spent the night—

"Did you get everything you wanted?"

Dashiell was staring down at the dozens of bags. His voice was cool, and so were his eyes when he looked across to me. "If you've got everything, I'll drive you back."

I nodded, and we both stood up, ready to go. But I didn't want to go, I didn't want to go back to that house that wasn't my home and never could be. But where else could I go?

"Billy?"

The frostiness in his voice had gone, and Dashiell was frowning at me, not in annoyance but with concern.

"I'm sorry," I said. "For earlier. I shouldn't have spoken to you like that. The things I needed to get, they were kind of personal, but I've got everything, so yeah, let's go."

He didn't say anything as he gathered together all my bags, and I wondered if we were in for a silent ride back as I followed him out and back to the car.

"No, don't get in," he said as I began to open the door.

"What?"

"Do you want to go yet? I know I don't. Unless Frankie needs you back at the house by a certain time?"

I thought for a moment. Frankie had meetings, and then he was going to drop in on one of his clubs, because he liked to just turn up out of the blue to keep everybody on their toes, but he hadn't said anything about wanting me to go with him. I shook my head.

"Good. Come on."

"Where to? What—?" I called out as I rushed to keep up with him. Dashiell had strode off, assuming I'd follow, and that's exactly what I was doing.

"Do you like films?"

"Yeah. Why? Do you want to go to the cinema?"

His grin was his answer. I hadn't been to the cinema in more than a year, when I'd gone one afternoon, on impulse when Frankie had been away on business. I'd sat there on my own with a big bucket of popcorn I barely touched. I didn't remember what the film was, but I remembered feeling sad and lonely. I'd lost touch with all my friends, and there'd been nobody to call up to see if they wanted to go out.

"But isn't it a bit early? Nothing'll be showing yet." I'd agreed to go without saying yes.

"There's something I'd like to see, but it won't be on for a couple of hours yet. It's a thriller but low budget and a bit art house, and it's only showing for a couple of days. I know the guy who directed it, and his wife, too, who's one of the leads. What do you think?"

"Er, yeah. Okay."

I wasn't used to anybody asking for my opinion or what I wanted to do. Anybody being Frankie, of course.

"We'll get something to eat first. I'm starving."

My stomach rumbled in agreement. I'd skipped break-fast, which wasn't anything unusual, but that meant I'd not eaten anything since yesterday afternoon and had existed on cup after cup of black coffee. I reckoned I'd be okay with a salad.

We cut down a side turning to get off Oxford Street, and as we headed into Soho, I knew where we were going. A few minutes later, we arrived at the little café where I'd had the tantrum over the cake. I seemed to be having a lot of tantrums with Dashiell.

My mouth started watering as soon as we walked through the door. It was lunchtime, and the place was packed, but a couple started to gather up their things and we were over there like a shot, almost shoving them away before they'd barely got up. We got more than a few dirty looks from people holding trays and with nowhere to sit, but they should have been a bit quicker off the mark. There were no menus on the tables, but there was a big black-board listing different drinks, sandwiches and cakes. There were no salads, except for what went with the sandwiches and rolls, which looked huge.

"What are you having?"

I glanced between the board and Dashiell. It certainly wasn't going to be the chocolate cake, the one I'd almost upended in his lap.

"I'll just have a coffee."

"You'll have something to eat."

"No, I'm not—"

"Hungry? Don't give me that crap. You're almost drool-ing. If you don't pick something, I'll pick it for you. And this time you won't try and tip it all over me."

My jaw hit the ground. I mean, he was right about me

being hungry, but telling me I had no choice about whether I ate or not made me feel like a badly-behaved kid again.

"Well?"

He was completely stony-faced, and it got my back up a bit. I didn't want to just say yes, all meek and mild, because I did enough of that with Frankie.

"I said I'll have a coffee, and that's all."

We stared at each other across the table. I was determined not to give in, when Dashiell leaned across and whispered into my ear.

"Do I have to tie you down and force some food down your throat?"

Well, that made me jump. It also sent a burst of energy to my dick. Being tied down by Dashiell flashed up some very dirty images in my head. But I was very, very hungry, no doubt about that, and if I didn't eat anything, I'd likely pass out. It'd happened before.

"A chicken sandwich," I mumbled. "No mayo." That would probably do the least amount of damage.

Dashiell gave a brief nod before he went and joined the long queue, and I let my mind wander.

When had food become the enemy? Since I'd been with Frankie, that's when. Being hungry all the time, wanting but not permitting myself to eat other than the most basic, read boring, stuff. Frankie liked me thin, and what Frankie liked, Frankie got. I couldn't afford for him to go off me, there was too much at stake. I never wanted him to touch me again, but what I wanted wasn't important. So, you see, not eating wasn't about staying fashionably skinny or vanity, and I didn't have an eating disorder, although if it went on much longer, I sometimes wondered if I'd end up with one. Everything I did, none of it was about me, it was about the one person in the whole world who'd loved me.

"Chicken salad and pesto baguette. You can share the muffin afterwards with me if you want."

The tray was piled up. As well as my own sandwich, which was the size of a suitcase, he had two huge crusty rolls so filled with sliced beef, it was poking out the sides.

"Two? You pig."

Dashiell laughed as he picked up one of the overloaded rolls. "I'm a growing boy. I didn't have time for breakfast this morning, and Barista Boys make the best sandwiches in Soho. Or London, probably. And do the best muffins, cakes, coffee. . ."

He winked at me as he bit into a roll. Mayo smeared his lips, and he let out a long groan as he slumped back into his seat. He chewed slowly, his eyes closed, and he groaned some more. I couldn't take my eyes off that creamy white that blobbed his lips, and I shifted around on my seat as my skin prickled with heat. My dick pressed against the zip of my jeans, and I looked away, just grateful the little table shielded me and that my jacket was long enough. I kept my attention fixed on my baguette as I nibbled on the chicken and wondered how much of the bread I could get away with not eating as Dashiell attacked the second of his two rolls.

Dashiell's phone rang, and he fumbled in his pocket for it.

"Hi, Babe."

Babe. Dashiell's voice was warm and familiar. Whoever was on the other end of the line was known well enough to be Dashiell's *babe*. I wondered whether it was the same man he'd been speaking to earlier, the one who was a tease and who he was going to be eating breakfast with. Andrew, the boyfriend. Whatever, it was none of my business. I put down the rest of my sandwich. I'd suddenly lost the taste for it, but I'd got through most of it, including the bread, so Dashiell couldn't have a go at me for not eating anything.

I tried to drown out the conversation as I looked at what was going on around me in the café, but the warmth of his voice as he spoke to *Babe* kind of hit me hard in the chest. I looked around for the sign for the toilets because I couldn't sit there any longer trying not to listen to a conversation that had nothing to do with me, but before I could make a move, the call ended.

Dashiell picked up his roll and carried on eating. He wasn't going to tell me who'd called, but then he had no reason to, and I wasn't going to ask. We sat in silence as Dashiell concentrated on eating and I pretended to be interested in my phone.

"You done with that?"

Dashiell nodded to the remains of my sandwich.

"Yeah. There was tons of it." I wondered whether he was going to congratulate me for managing to eat more than a mouthful or scold me for not finishing it. Or would he pick it up and shove the rest down my throat, as he'd threatened? He didn't do any of those things, but he kind of looked pleased.

His phone pinged on the table next to his plate, and he grinned as he read the message.

"Who was that?" The question was out of my mouth before I could stop it. I'd been determined not to ask, but it had just come spewing out. Dashiell took his time to answer, and I wondered whether he was thinking of a polite way to tell me to mind my own business.

"A friend. The same one I was talking to a couple of minutes ago, and earlier, in the department store. And no, Andrew – Andy – he's not my boyfriend, because that's what you're wondering, isn't it? I can see it in your face. I wouldn't take up poker, if I were you, because you'd lose."

I gawped. He'd read me like a book. It surprised but also worried me, because I thought I was good at hiding what I was thinking and feeling, keeping everything locked away, and not letting anybody know what was going on inside.

"Although he was, once. We were together for a couple of years, when we were younger and lived in a student house. It never worked out. Obviously. But he's stayed a close friend."

I didn't know what to say. It wasn't so much that the guy was Dashiell's ex-boyfriend, it was more that he was a good friend, somebody who was close and important in Dashiell's life. The friends I'd had had long gone. I didn't know where they were or what they were doing. I wouldn't be getting a call or a text, I wouldn't be laughing down the phone and making arrangements to meet up. I was alone and lonely, but that was the price I paid for my obligations, and I was willing to pay it. But it still made me feel sad and empty, if I let myself think about it.

"You were at university?" Dashiell didn't strike me as having gone to uni. It wasn't that I thought he was stupid or anything; it was more that he seemed to be the practical type I suppose.

Dashiell laughed. "University? No, you must be joking. For one reason or another, I found myself sharing a house with a bunch of students. While they were racking up their debts, I worked on building sites during the day and went to evening classes, where I took a vocational engineering course. What about you?"

What about me *what*? What did I do before I became Frankie's tart?

"Did you go to university, or college, after you left school?"

The way he asked, it was casual and conversational, but kind of gentle, too, like he'd sussed out what I'd been thinking.

I shook my head.

"Thought about applying, but the fees and that." Tuition fees and student loans. Thousands of pounds in debt and no guarantee of a good job at the end of it all. But that hadn't been the only reason. "I left school after A Levels and got a job. Accounts clerk. I've always been good with numbers. The company started putting me through accountancy training, day release once a week, but there were some changes in my personal life, so I had to leave."

That was an understatement. The gradual deterioration, then the diagnosis when everything suddenly seemed to accelerate and go downhill fast. Day after day spent in the little house and caring for somebody who couldn't care for themselves any longer.

"You don't look like an accountant to me, you're not boring enough." Dashiell grinned at me, and I couldn't help laughing.

"It was okay. I mean, it was a bit dull, but it was a good job, and they were willing to finance my studies. I even beat off the competition from a load of graduates to get it." I had, too. Gran had been really proud when I received the call telling me I'd got the job. She even made a cake to celebrate. It was a horrible cake, because she was a bit of a rubbish cook, but it was still the best cake I'd ever eaten. The memory, like the cake, was bitter sweet.

"So, you were an engineer?" I wanted the spotlight off me, but I also wanted to know more about Dashiell.

"No, the course I did was vocational, and practical. Engineering was the main but not the sole element. It helped me eventually get into facilities management. I ended up being responsible for the running of a large building: maintenance, security, health and safety. All that kind of stuff, but there were changes, and my job ended up being made redundant. It's the way of the world, or so it seems. Anyway, do you still fancy seeing that film? The cinema's just up the road."

"Er, yeah, okay."

He bundled up his paper napkin and dropped it on his empty plate as he got up. Like our time in the café, the conversation was over.

"Ready?"

I nodded and followed him out, as he waved his good-byes to the same dark-haired barista I'd seen him laughing and joking with on our last visit.

9

DASHIELL

"That was brilliant. At the end, when she found the hidden diaries, that was just so not what I was expecting. And the detective. . ."

I was grinning so much, my face ached. As Billy said, the film had been brilliant and we'd both been hooked in from the opening shot. I was glad, because if the film had been shit, it would have reflected on my friends, but I was also glad for Billy's sake. He was often so guarded and prickly. He was twenty-three and looked like a teenager, or at least he did until you looked deep into his eyes. Why he was with Frankie Haynes, I had no idea, but I really didn't think it had much to do with money. There was a whole story there, but Billy wasn't telling, and I wasn't going to push.

He was still enthusing about the film and was more alive and animated than I'd seen him before. And I wanted him to stay that way. It was late afternoon, and the rush hour was just picking up. If we attempted to head back then and there, we'd spend ages sitting in traffic. Or at least that was my excuse. The truth was, I wanted to spend more time with him, just the pair of us. The hazy sunshine was warm, and I knew a tucked away little pub with a pretty walled garden.

"I could do with a cold drink. How about you?"

"Erm—"

"Just a soft drink, that's all I'm thinking, before we head back."

I'd stopped him mid-flow about the film, and I could have kicked myself. That wariness that he always had about him was back, and that just made me so fucking angry. I wasn't angry at Billy; I was angry because he was too damn young to be so suspicious and on edge. I wanted back the Billy of just a few seconds ago, the Billy whose eyes had sparkled and who'd crackled with energy and life.

"Soda and lime, or another diet carbonated beverage of your choice? How can you refuse such temptation? I'd even offer to buy you a bag of pork scratchings if I thought you'd eat them. Go on, what do you say?" I gave him my biggest, cheesiest grin, but he just looked at me as though I were mad. And maybe I was, for wanting to make him smile at me, and wanting to hear him laugh again. Frankie had made my job description very clear. All those boundaries and clean lines he'd talked about? If making Billy smile and laugh blurred and dirtied them, then so be it. As far as Frankie was concerned, he could shove his job description.

"Pork scratchings? Fried pig skin? That's gross."

"Nah, it's only gross if you find a bit of bristle attached."

His mouth turned up in a smile, and he started to laugh. That had been my intention all along, but I'd be lying if I said I didn't get a strange fluttering deep down in my stomach.

The Stokers' Arms was about a fifteen-minute walk away, going towards Charing Cross and tucked away in a tiny back alley. It was fairly quiet, and we found a nice spot in the garden. I got us a pint of soda and lime each, but not the pork scratchings because Billy was right, they were gross and I wouldn't touch them with a barge pole.

"So, you like cinema," I said, referring back to the film. "What else do you like doing?"

There was a lot more to Billy Grace than being Frankie's *boy*, and I wanted to get under the skin of him and find out more about what he liked and what made him tick. I didn't think he was going to answer me at first because he just stared across the little wooden table, but as I looked deeper into those jade green eyes of his, I got the impression he was weighing up what to tell me and how much to open up. If he decided not to answer, I wouldn't push him, but my stomach held tight as I waited, hoping he would.

"I've always enjoyed films. Not just the big block-buster ones, but indie films like the one we saw today. I kind of like them more, really. And reading. I read a lot. Fantasy, sci-fi, romance sometimes."

He buried himself in his drink, but I didn't miss the flush that spread over his face. I don't think he meant to let that last one slip, not if the beetroot red of his cheeks was anything to go by. I mean, it's not many twenty-three-year-old guys who admit to reading love stories. I almost grinned before I realised that his life with Frankie would be as far from a love story as it was possible to get.

"I used to play the guitar. I was pretty good, I played a lot of classical stuff, and folk."

He blurted the words out, and the flush was back, lighting up his cheeks once more. He kept surprising me, and I liked it. A lot of young, and not so young, guys played guitar, but not normally the type of music he'd described. I got the feeling he'd not really meant to tell me, that he'd revealed something about himself that was private. I doubted anybody else back at the house knew this little piece of Billy, and that included Frankie. Why Billy had told me, I had no idea, but something warmed inside me and made me very glad he had. It felt like our little secret.

"Do you still play?"

I already knew the answer. Billy shook his head.

"No. It started taking up too much time, and there were other things I needed to concentrate on."

There was a finality to his voice, and he looked away. The subject of why Billy had abandoned the guitar was officially closed.

"I was a drummer in a band, a few years back. I think it's safe to say we were crap." I took a mouthful of my drink and watched Billy over the rim of my glass. He glanced at me, and his eyes narrowed. I'd piqued his interest, and I waited for his question.

"Yeah? What did you play?"

"Our own stuff. We thought we were going to be the next Oasis, and we sang everything with a faux Northern whine. The whole Manchester sound was seriously cool in the '90s. The trouble was, we weren't. We were truly, truly terrible."

That wasn't really the case; in fact, we weren't too bad,

and there were two or three pubs we played in on a fairly regular basis. The story hadn't been about whether we were a decent pub band, but about drawing Billy out and making him laugh again, which he did.

"Who knew we were both musicians, or kind of. I mean, there's no real skill in banging on a drum."

Billy grinned at me in playful challenge. No real skill? I wasn't putting up with that.

"I'll treat that comment with the contempt it deserves. I was a god when I had those sticks in my hands. I'm still friends with the lead singer, and he dug out an old photo and sent me a copy a few months ago. Back in the day, UXB were all the rage in our little corner of north London," I said with a grin as I pulled the phone from my pocket.

"UXB?" Billy quirked his head to the side.

"It's short for unexploded bomb. It's what we were, an unexploded bomb of limited talent."

I switched the phone on to pull up my photos to show Billy, but the thing almost went into meltdown as it pinged message after left message. I'd turned it off when we walked into the cinema over four hours earlier. Billy had done the same. Down deep in my gut, I knew who'd been trying to get in touch, and I was right.

"Looks like Frankie wants you back at the house." The messages weren't as polite or reasoned, but I wasn't about to read them out to Billy because I knew he'd have received similar.

"Oh shit," he muttered as he pulled his own phone out. His hands were shaking as he powered it up, and something icy gripped hard and deep in my belly.

Like mine, his sprung into life. His face blanched as he read through the texts.

"He wants me to go with him to one of the clubs tonight. He's – he's not happy I'm not home."

That poker face of mine I mentioned before? It came in very handy just then, but I was seething inside. Whatever deal Billy had made with Frankie, there was no way it was worth it, not when he was white-faced and trembling.

"I'll phone him and explain."

"No. No, don't do that."

Billy grabbed my wrist, and we both looked down at his white-knuckled hand gripping me tight.

"I know him. I know how to talk him round."

His hand slipped away, and he walked to a corner of the garden, the phone pressed tight to his ear.

Somehow I doubted Billy would be talking Frankie round, not if the tone of his messages to me was anything to go by.

"We need to go. Now."

He walked past me, shoulders hunched and eyes cast down. I nodded, at a loss for what to say, and followed him out.

I never did show Billy that photo.

———

Before we even reached the front door, it was slung open. Frankie stood on the threshold, his face hard and stony. I'm not a man to be easily intimidated, but my heart skipped a beat when he pinned his eyes to Billy. In that moment, if I had to give a name to evil, it would have been Frankie Haynes.

"Get upstairs. Your clothes are laid out. Get changed and stay there."

Billy didn't need telling twice, as he ran up the stairs without a second glance in my direction.

Frankie turned his gaze to me.

"You, in my office."

He turned, and I followed.

In the few steps to his office, I had to think fast. I needed to take the blame for Billy not being home, I was the one Frankie needed to take his anger out on, but I knew Billy wouldn't escape unscathed, and the thought churned my stomach.

"Sit down," he said as soon as the door was closed.

I did as I was told. Contrite and grovelling didn't come naturally, but I had to play it for all it was worth.

"It's my fault."

"What's your fault?"

Frankie leaned back in his seat, his eyes never leaving mine.

"Billy being late back. He had a lot of shopping to get, and time was getting on once he'd finished, and I insisted we leave driving back until the rush hour tailed off."

I looked him in the eye. It made me look truthful and full of integrity, or at least I hoped it did. And I had told him the truth, or at least some of it.

"Why were your phones switched off? I don't like my employees being out of contact during working hours. In Billy's case, that's 24/7. He needs a little reminder of that."

My hands were hidden by the edge of the desk, and they curled into fists, my nails digging deep into my palms. I felt sick, imagining what Frankie's *reminder* would involve.

On the drive back, Billy had been white-faced, and I knew he was quietly panicking. Frankie would have wanted to know why both our phones had been switched off, and I thought admitting to going to the cinema was the logical thing to explain that. Billy had almost had a seizure when I suggested it. Going to the cinema was what *friends* did, sitting together all cosy in the dark, sharing a bucket of popcorn. Just like sitting in a pub garden in the late afternoon sun, talking about films and books and music. Frankie's little talk came back to me, about clear and clean lines, when he'd warned me off befriending Billy. But we needed to tell him something that sounded plausible, and by the time we got back to the house, we'd agreed a story I prayed would fly.

"Mine had run out of power, so I turned it off because there was no point in keeping it switched on." The lie slipped off my tongue as smooth as silk.

"And Billy's, too? How convenient."

A sneer broke out on his face, and I itched to wipe it off. I clenched my hands tighter in my lap.

"He had one of those portable chargers with him, but that had run out of juice, too. After he'd finished shopping, we had a coffee while our phones charged up at one of those charging stations, but by then the rush hour had kicked in, so like I said, I wanted to wait out the worst. I didn't fancy sitting in traffic for hours."

Who knew I was such a smooth liar? Frankie wasn't stupid, and I suspected he had the cunning of a sewer rat, but I could see the doubt flickering in his eyes. The bastard had meant to catch me out, but now he wasn't so sure. I pressed home the slim advantage I had.

"I'm sorry. I'll make sure my phone's fully powered in

future. And it was my call about leaving it to come back until later. He'd said we should get back, but the traffic at that time. . ." I let my words trail off. I'd gone all out for contrite, and I just had to hope he believed me.

The silence that filled the room was heavy, and I sat in the chair across the desk from Frankie with bowed shoulders and what I hoped was a suitably worried expression on my face. Cowed, and in mortal fear of losing that weekly grand in ready cash, that was the look I was going for. But the truth of it was, I *was* worried. Not for me because I had no qualms about telling Frankie to fuck off, all for that he was a nasty bastard. I was worried for Billy because he wouldn't stand a chance.

Frankie viewed Billy as his property to be treated as he saw fit, for good or for bad, and the problem was so did Billy. I didn't hold that we're put on this Earth for a purpose, or that people come into our lives for a reason. That's all crap and mumbo jumbo. Life is random, and the best you can do with it is to try and not fuck up too much. But you know what? When I sat in the office, doing my best not to piss off Frankie too much so that he wouldn't tell me to take a hike, my doubt wavered because I knew, with a clarity that was blinding, that the only thing that stood between Frankie and Billy was me, and without me Billy would be destroyed. So, you see, I was there for a reason. The bottom line was that Billy needed protection, and the only place he could look to that was me. He didn't know it, but I was going to make sure he did.

"Get out. You've screwed up today, but you're new."

Frankie gave an exaggerated shrug of his shoulders, the big man with the power to be magnanimous. He was like a cheap, low budget version of The Godfather. Those palms of mine were really starting to hurt.

"One more cock up like this, and you're out. Understand?"

He glowered at me from across the desk. I looked down and gave a nod and mumbled another apology for good measure, but inside I was giving myself a good old pat on the back. I'd got away with it, but my self-congratulations were short lived. I may have survived another day unscathed, but I knew the same couldn't be said for Billy. The thought sickened me. I needed to be smart, to think ahead. I hadn't done that today, and it would be Billy who'd suffer the consequences. I walked out of the office, and the house, determined that would never happen again.

10

BILLY

When Frankie ordered me into the house, I didn't need telling twice. All the way back from the pub, I'd felt sick with worry about what he'd do to me. I was expecting to feel the back of his hand, at least, but when that didn't happen, I felt even worse because I reckoned he was saving up my punishment for later.

The film, talking in the pub garden about music, it'd all felt so normal. Being with Dashiell, I'd forgotten about Frankie and getting back to the house, but as soon as I turned my phone on, all that had been wiped away and the reality of my life had swept back in.

Frankie didn't speak to me in the car on the way to the club. His silence freaked me out, along with the long, cool stares, like he was thinking up new ways to punish me. When the car arrived at the club, I didn't know how I made it inside because my legs were shaking so much. It wasn't long before I asked permission to be excused to go to the toilet. *Back in five* Frankie had snarled at me. I got back in four. It's amazing how much you can throw up in the toilet in under four minutes.

The staff in the club picked up on Frankie's bad mood straight away, and that made them clumsy. God, he was vicious. I reckon a few lost their jobs that night, including the manager, but all I could think of was that, for once, it wasn't me in the firing line. All evening he'd been knocking back the scotch, and I was sure he'd have to be poured into the car and wouldn't be fit to do anything when we got back, and so I allowed myself to relax, just a little bit.

What's that saying about not counting chickens before they hatched or something? Well, I counted mine a bit too early because he was stone cold sober when we left. Frankie wasn't going to let me get off lightly, and I knew my punishment had just been put on hold.

In the early hours, I stumbled to the bathroom and cleaned up the dried blood from my backside and tried not to cry out too loud before I dosed myself up on painkillers. The bruises on my arms had already started to come out, huge black stains, and the skin on my wrists was red and puffy from the restraints he'd used. It was lucky I had a load of long sleeved T-shirts because I was going to need every single of them for the next few days. I had a tube of arnica cream, and as I rubbed it into my damaged skin, it made me think of Gran. She'd used it on my bashed knees and elbows when I'd been little. God alone knew what she'd think if she knew what I'd ended up using it for.

Despite everything Frankie had put me through when we got back, it was the thought of Gran that really hurt. She'd sacrificed everything for me, she'd always put me first. It was only as I got older that I came to understand that there had been times when she'd gone short on food and other essentials so that I didn't. As she'd provided for me then, so I provided for her now. Gran was safe and cared for, and that was all that mattered. The fact that I paid for all that in bruises, and worse, was the way it was.

I crawled back into bed, gasping with pain with every move, but I wasn't afraid of waking Frankie up. He was dead to the world, worn out by all that angry energy he'd used on me, and was snoring and grunting like the pig he was. I hated him as I stared at his heaving bulk, and I asked myself the question I always pushed to the back of my mind: Is all this worth it? But I knew the answer, and it was *yes*. It was worth it a million times over.

The following morning, I woke up to an empty bed. My whole body was stiff and achy, but I was more concerned by the blood I'd found around my arse the night before, but there wasn't any sign of any more, so I reckoned I was okay. Really, really sore, but okay. After all, it wasn't like it hadn't happened before.

As I made my very careful way downstairs, I heard Frankie's voice on the phone, even behind the closed door of his office. He was shouting and sounded angry, but then he normally did, and I wondered who was getting it in the neck from him. I was just thankful it was somebody else, and not me.

When I was about halfway down the stairs, Lee crossed the hallway. He looked up, met my eye and we both stopped.

There was something about Lee that I couldn't put my finger on. He was way smarter than Tony or any of the other zombies that turned up, but then I don't suppose that was saying much. He was watchful, like he was just clocking what was going on and noting it away in the back of his mind. I didn't know anything about him, other than he started working for Frankie a short time before I moved in. Lee had earned Frankie's trust and approval, I knew that much, and that in itself was enough for me to be extra wary of him, but his face hardened, just for a second, when he saw Frankie's handiwork on me, and it wasn't the first time I'd noticed that.

"Billy." Lee nodded at me, and I nodded back. I expected him to carry on walking across the hall, but he hesitated. He glanced in the direction of Frankie's office, then back at me. When I got to the bottom of the stairs, he asked me something he'd never asked before.

"Are you okay?"

I had to bite back the laugh. Was I okay? No, I fucking wasn't okay. I'd pretty much been assaulted just hours before, I was covered in bruises, and I'd had to bandage up my wrists, and Lee asked me if I was *okay*?

"Yeah, I'm fine."

He glanced towards the office again.

"Look—"

It was as far as he got, because Frankie slung open the office door and was yelling down the hallway for Lee to get his sorry arse to him *now*.

Whatever it was Lee was going to say was forgotten as he rushed off and seconds later Frankie's office door banged shut.

I headed for the kitchen. I needed a coffee, but more than that I needed to see Dashiell and find out what Frankie had said to him the day before. Dashiell wasn't there, only Tony, who was going through something on his phone. He looked up and smirked.

"You all right this morning, Billy?" He didn't bother to hide his sneer.

My nerves were wreaked, and I opened my mouth to snap when Lee rushed in.

"Get this list sent over, and then on the road." Lee thrust a piece of paper into Tony's chest with enough force to send Tony back a couple of steps. "There are drops offs to do, and you're late. Do you want to tell Frankie why that is?"

Tony's face fell, and he looked as if he were going to start arguing, but I think it made it through even his thick head that telling Frankie he'd screwed up because he was wasting time baiting me wasn't a good idea. He mumbled something under this breath and stomped out, and Lee was hard on his heels when Frankie's voice bellowed through the house.

I was alone in the kitchen, and there was no sign of Dashiell. For all I knew, Frankie had sacked him.

I started to shake, and I had to hang onto the edge of the table because if I didn't, I was going to go down like a ton of bricks.

"Billy?"

Dashiell stood in the doorway to the kitchen, and I sagged against the table. He was beside me like a shot, and I couldn't help wincing when he eased me into one of chairs; he didn't say anything, but his lips were pressed tight and his brows pulled together in a heavy frown.

"I thought he might have given you the sack," I said quickly and under my breath.

My relief at seeing Dashiell hit me like a punch in the guts, and I really started to shake bad. Dashiell Slater was bossy, and he didn't take any of my crap. He'd come to my rescue, he'd lied for me, and he'd caught me when I'd fallen. More than any of that, though, for a little while he'd made me forget about how screwed up my life was and had made me laugh, and that wasn't something I did much of anymore. I hadn't known him for any time, really, but already he'd become the only sane thing in my life, and I was clinging to him like he was a lifeline. And that was stupid, because Dashiell wouldn't hang around. As soon as he'd made enough cash, he'd be gone, and I wouldn't blame him. He wouldn't stay because of me. Why would he? Why would anybody? All those jumbled thoughts and questions just kept going round and round in my head, but all that counted was that he *was* still there and that he was fussing over me like I really mattered. Somebody was bothered about me, somebody cared. Real or not, it calmed the panic that had threatened to overwhelm me and made me feel a bit less lonely and alone.

"No, not the sack, but he did read me the riot act. I gave him the story we agreed on, and I think he bought, but if I screw up again, I'm out. So, I'm not going to screw up." He brushed my hair away where it had fallen across my eyes.

I swallowed. I'd been really horrible to him, more often than not. I didn't deserve the care and concern I saw in his eyes nor the warmth in his slow smile, and I didn't deserve the kiss I knew was coming as he leaned in towards me, angling his head as I closed my eyes.

"Dashiell, I want—"

My eyes flew open, and I jerked back, and my heart was beating so fast, I thought it was going to explode out of my chest because Frankie had caught us, Dashiell had been about to kiss me, and—

The door to the kitchen closed, and Lee leaned back against it. My heart calmed down, not by much, but all I could think was thank God it was Lee and not Frankie.

"You need to be very, very careful."

My mouth was so dry, I couldn't say a word, but I just about managed to swallow down the sour sickness that rose up in my throat. I glanced up at Dashiell, expecting him to be looking as sick as I felt, but he seemed cool and totally unbothered as if the near miss didn't mean a thing.

"Billy was upset, and you know why. But yes, you're right. Thanks."

I was still shaky from everything that had happened and reeling from the thought of all the shit that would have hit the fan if it'd been anybody else who'd walked into the kitchen, so I wasn't exactly sharp, but something was going on between the two of them, something that was unsaid but understood. It was like they'd forgotten I was there. Dashiell and Lee were looking at each, like they were sussing one another out. The air in the kitchen crackled with electricity, you'd have had to be dead not to feel it, but my mind was foggy and slow, and I couldn't get a proper grip on what was happening.

Lee gave a curt nod of the head, and Dashiell responded with a tight smile, like they'd sealed a deal.

"Frankie's got a couple of driving jobs for you. He's got some business associates who need to be picked up from their hotel and taken around the West End, shopping and whatever. The details are here."

Lee handed Dashiell a slip of paper before he looked at me.

"Frankie says you're to stay in the house today. No going out, anywhere, under any circumstances."

"What? No. No, not today. He can't." I jumped up and toppled over the chair, all the pain and soreness in my body forgotten. Frankie couldn't say no, he couldn't, not today of all days. It was a special day, it was more than special, it was why I'd bought all the extra stuff, all the pretty things she'd always loved but could never afford. But Frankie could, he could do anything he wanted. It was the cherry on the cake of my punishment and the thing he knew would hurt the most.

"No—"

"*Yes*. Yes, Billy. Really. He's not in a good mood. Keep out of his way unless he sends for you and don't piss him off. You can go and visit another day."

Lee was right. I wasn't going anywhere. I stared into space, thinking of all the things I'd bought that wouldn't be wrapped in shiny paper and covered in glittery bows and taken on what was supposed to be a special day.

"What—?" Dashiell asked, and I heard the confusion in his voice. Lee and I had understood each other, and this time it had been Dashiell who didn't understand. Because Lee knew, you see. He knew who the armfuls of pretty things were for.

Out of the corner of my eye, I saw him shake his head at Dashiell. The day had only just started, but I already wanted it to be over. I'd crawl under the cover of one of the beds in a spare room and pretend the day wasn't happening. Even knowing that Dashiell was still there and that he'd so nearly kissed me wasn't enough to lighten the bleakness that filled me. I was so tired, more tired than I think I'd ever been before, and all I wanted to do was sleep. But first of all, I had a phone call to make.

11

DASHIELL

I turned the engine off, slumped back in the seat and let relief flood over me. I'd just returned from dropping Frankie, along with Tony and a couple of guys I hadn't seen before, at Heathrow, and he'd be away for a week, in Bucharest and Istanbul.

The house had been filled with tension for the last couple of days, and I'd kept my head down and got on with my work, avoiding Frankie as much as possible. I hadn't seen Billy either, apart from a brief glimpse since he'd stumbled from the kitchen after being told he was effectively under house arrest.

I entered the house through the utility room which led to the kitchen. I'd expected to find Lee in there, but the room was empty, so I got the coffee on as I thought about the long list of jobs Frankie had barked out at me. They could wait. Frankie had been in a foul mood, and even Tony had the sense to keep quiet as I drove them all to the airport.

There was a spare seat on the plane, a seat that should

have been occupied by Billy, but he was upstairs in one of the spare rooms. Gastric flu, apparently. Frankie kept a tame doctor on the books, and he'd been called out at 4.00am and had promptly declared Billy far too ill to travel. Frankie, by all accounts, had gone mental, but the doctor had stood his ground and told Frankie that one look at Billy and the authorities wouldn't allow him to fly. I'd got all this from Lee when I'd pitched up for work. So Billy was on his own for the week, and my brain had been working overtime.

I decided to go and put my head around the door to make sure he was okay. Perhaps I could hold his hand, mop his brow and show him funny cat videos to cheer him up. The thought made me smile. I liked looking after Billy, and that was exactly what I was going to do.

I hadn't even gone up a couple of steps when I came to a halt. I heard a hard thump from down the hallway, coming from the direction of Frankie's office. I edged down the steps and listened. My hearing's always been sharp, but I had to strain because whoever was in there was doing their damndest to be quiet, although they'd cocked up with the massive thump. I was on high alert because nobody went in without an express invitation, and definitely not without Frankie being present. Plus, the door was always kept securely locked when he wasn't in there. I knew that because I'd tried to get in one time, just to be nosey.

Whoever was inside shouldn't have been. The door was ajar, and as I peered through the crack I saw Lee, sitting in Frankie's desk chair, tapping away at the computer before he folded down the top. I stepped back, ready to hotfoot it back down the hallway, but instead of getting up to leave, he pulled his phone from his jeans pocket and began taking photos of a paper document lying on the desk. He was using the same phone I'd seen him use before, the one he'd stuffed back into pocket when I'd walked in on him and surprised him. He folded the document in half and placed it in one of the desk drawers, which he locked. I squinted. There was something wrong with his hands, but then I realised what it was I was seeing. Latex gloves. I didn't know what Lee was up to, other than the obvious of spying on Frankie, but why he was doing it, I didn't have a clue. One half of my brain told me to turn tail and get away and forget everything I'd seen, but the other half, the half that always got me into trouble, was goading me to find out what was going on. I wasn't sure which half was going to win out, but in the end it didn't matter because I sneezed. Can you believe it? I fucking *sneezed*.

Lee was on me in the blink of an eye. And I mean on me. I was hauled through the door and shoved up against the wall, face first and arm bent up my back. He matched me for size or was maybe even a bit bigger and was heavy, too. I was trapped, and we both knew it.

"Whatever you think you saw, forget it. Okay?" he hissed in my ear.

I made some sort of snorty-grunty sound because having my face pressed into the wall wasn't exactly making it easy to talk. As quickly as he'd had me up against the wall in an arm lock, I was released. I wanted to take a swing at him for what he'd just done, but common sense prevailed as it told me that wouldn't be a good idea. Lee had taken a few steps back and was out of reach of my fist in any case.

"I heard noise coming from Frankie's private office.

You know the one? Oh, this one. The one nobody's allowed to go in. What was I supposed to do when I heard *noise*?" I was going for sarcasm in a big way. I'd been jumped and shoved up against the wall and was feeling stupid for being so easily bested, and it wasn't the first time it'd happened. I might have cocked up, but so had Lee. He hadn't made that good a job at being a spy, or whatever the hell it was he was doing.

"What are you supposed to do? Nothing, Dashiell, nothing at all. That's what."

He'd squared his shoulders and was staring right at me, and I was doing the same back. We were engaged in a weird stand-off, and my brain, now that it'd got over its shock, was in overdrive.

Lee was in a different league to Tony and the few other assistants I'd come across. He was smart and observant and didn't miss a beat. If he wanted to earn brownie points with Frankie, me and Billy had handed him the opportunity on a plate when he'd walked into the kitchen just as I'd been about to kiss Billy. But he hadn't told tales. Maybe he was a business rival to Frankie, as dirty as Frankie was himself, but there was something about Lee that made me think that wasn't the case. It was something in his bearing, and in the way he held himself. The ease with which he'd overcome me had been efficient, clean and without fuss. Lee hadn't picked up his strong arm skills on the streets, he'd been trained. And then I knew. I just fucking *knew* where it was I'd met him. It'd been a few years since I'd seen him last, but it all came flooding back.

"What are you now, Lee? Military, still, or police?"

Bingo. His eyes flashed a split second of shock I was

confident ninety-nine percent of people wouldn't notice, but I'd been trained to be the one percent who did.

He was weighing me up, assessing the situation he'd found himself in and deciding if I could be trusted. He was out on his own, and the decision was his. Lee could have denied it and told me I was mad. After all, being a rival in whatever sordid, dirty business Frankie dipped his hands into was a story that would fly. It was credible, but I wouldn't believe it, not when I'd seen that split second of shock in his eyes, and certainly not when I'd made it clear I knew who he was.

He made his decision.

"Police."

At the bottom of the garden there was a bench, and I sat there as I watched Lee, a few yards away, walk backwards and forwards as he talked into his mobile. He hadn't been prepared to say anything more when we were in the house, and once outside, he'd strode off. Whoever it was he was speaking to, it looked like it was a pretty intense conversation, which was hardly surprising seeing that his cover was blown if only to me.

It'd bugged me that I hadn't been able to work out how I knew him, or from where, but when it had come, it'd been a blinding flash. It was his eyes that had finally made me remember. Cool, grey, watchful eyes. When I'd known Lee, he'd been the sort who you just knew was quietly sussing everything and everybody out. And he'd been bright, very, very bright, and it didn't look like much had changed since we'd served together in the same unit of the British Army Reserve.

If you discounted the cock up of me finding him in Frankie's office, that is.

It must have been a good ten to twelve years since we'd been Reserve Soldiers together. To be fair, I didn't serve with him for that long because he ended up transferring to another unit. Still, he'd made an impression on me. As I watched him, I remembered him saying he'd decided to quit his day job, whatever that was at the time, and join The Met.

"So, what happens now?" I asked when he finished his call and came and sat down beside me.

"Nothing. We carry on as before."

That made no sense at all. I knew who and what Lee was, so *nothing* couldn't have been an option.

"I don't know how these things work, but my knowing who you are has got to be a risk to your operation, or investigation, or whatever it is you call it."

"Oh, you're not a risk, Dashiell. As you saw just now, I've been speaking at some length to my commander, and we've concluded you're no risk at all."

Something in the way he spoke, something I couldn't quite identify, made my stomach curl up into a tight, little ball and my mouth go dry.

"What do you mean?"

Lee turned and looked at me with grey eyes that were no longer cool, but cold and hard.

"Billy."

"I don't understand." But I did, I understood exactly what Lee was saying and why it was I wasn't considered a threat, and it made me feel sick.

"Dashiell, you're far from stupid. You know exactly what I'm talking about. If you even think about doing anything to compromise the investigation, a little word in Frankie's ear about you and Billy—"

I launched myself and dragged him off the bench and onto grass before he could even take a breath. So much for trained men, as we rolled around, scrapping and trying to land punches and kicking out. The threat he'd made fuelled my anger and gave weight to my fists. Billy had no hope of surviving a full-on onslaught from Frankie, he'd be beaten to within an inch of his life or even to death, yet that was what Lee was threatening to set in motion with his *little word*.

"Dashiell, stop it. *Stop*."

I was pinned to the ground. Lee's thighs clamped either side of my hips, my wrists were held fast in his iron grip, and his whole weight bore down on me. Once again, he'd got the upper hand, but I was gratified by the sight of blood dripping from his nose and the deep, puffy scratch that I'd torn down his cheek. I attempted to buck him off me, but it made no difference; I was only getting up if he let me go.

"If this operation goes down the pan for any reason, any reason *at all*, do you know what's at risk?"

"Yeah, your fucking overtime, that's what." I bucked again, but it was useless.

"On what I'm paid? You must be joking."

He huffed and shook his head as I glared up at him.

"I'm going to get off and let you up, but if you attempt to take another swing at me, you'll regret it. Okay? *Okay?*" he repeated as he twisted my wrists hard enough to make my eyes water.

"I don't guarantee anything," I said through gritted teeth.

"I'll take that as your agreement, then."

Lee sprung off me and stepped back, ready to defend himself if need be. The truth was, my burst of anger-fuelled energy had burnt itself out. What I wanted more than anything was answers. I collapsed down onto the bench, and after a second's hesitation Lee sat down next to me.

"When you turned up, I was surprised you didn't recognise me, because I knew exactly who you were."

"You're not that memorable, Lee."

"Good, because when you're undercover, being memorable is the last thing you want to be."

I threw him a sideways glance. The nosebleed I'd inflicted had stopped, and he'd flattened down his fair hair. For a man who'd been rolling around on the grass engaged in a brawl just a minute or two before, he was looking pretty damn composed. My ribs were sore and smarting where I'd taken some of his punches, but he hadn't marked my face.

"When I told my commander about you, I thought she'd pull me out, but the decision was taken to see how things developed, especially when you showed no sign of recognising who I was. So the decision was made to carry on as normal."

"I did recognise you, but I couldn't think from where. It would have come to me sooner or later, you just helped the process along by being caught red-handed. They don't teach you very well in spy school, do they?"

"I'm not a spy, I'm a police officer."

Lee's words may have been calm and even, but I didn't

miss the slight flinch. The fact was, I *had* caught him, and I wondered whether he'd revealed that little nugget to his boss. I didn't care either way; he was just lucky it was me who'd found him snooping in Frankie's office.

"And now they know you've been rumbled. That's got to make a difference."

"No, not really."

Lee looked me full in the face, and like earlier, I got the impression he was weighing up how much to tell me, and like then, I could see in his eyes he'd made his decision.

"Frankie's been under investigation for a long time. It was set up for me to be introduced to him and be brought into his organisation. It was tricky and dangerous for a lot of people, but it worked, and once I was on the inside, I had to bust my arse off to gain his trust. Or as much of it as he was prepared to give. This operation has cost a fortune, and I'm not just talking money. The planning, the resources. . . you can't even begin to imagine. A lot hinges upon its success."

"So what is it you're investigating?" If Lee had wanted to grab my attention, he had it by the balls.

"There are several lines of enquiry, as we in Her Majesty's Constabulary tend to say. I'm not at liberty to tell you, even if I wanted to. Which I don't. But Frankie Haynes is a vicious and dangerous criminal who has to be stopped. We're on the edge, Dashiell; we're getting to that point where we might just be able to do it. So if you do anything at all to endanger all the work that's gone into getting Frankie Haynes, for whatever reason, you might just want to consider this: I'd be out of here before he could lay a hand on me, but you wouldn't, and more to the point, nor would Billy. I'd make sure Frankie knew exactly what was going on between the pair of you—"

"Nothing's going on—"

"Maybe not. Or not yet. But it's heading that way. Frankie's a suspicious man, but you already know that, and if he thought there was even a sniff of anything between you and Billy, that kid wouldn't last two minutes. I'd throw him to the dogs, Dashiell. Don't doubt me on that or put me to the test. It's what they used to call M.A.D. back in the day. Mutually Assured Destruction. Your co-operation in return for mine. All you have to do is carry on as if nothing's happened. Do as Frankie tells you, keep your head down, your mouth shut, and collect your grand at the end of the week. Don't make waves because if you do, you'll drown, and so will Billy."

Lee got up and without another word headed back to the house, leaving me staring after him as I shivered under the warm morning sun.

12

BILLY

I thought I had things sussed out. During the two years I'd been with Frankie, I'd got to know what was expected of me. I knew how far I could push the boundaries, which wasn't much, and I'd learned a few small strategies to make my life easier and safer.

Frankie was vain, and he liked his ego stroked, so that meant lots of adoring glances and lapping up every word he said. I could do that, and make it seem like I was giving him every scrap of attention, but it was a sham because in my head I'd be someplace else. I read something once, about finding what they called your happy place, which was all about switching off from stuff that stressed you out. I had a kind of happy place. It was just a big, empty space, where I could tune out from much of what was going on around me, or being done to me, but be just with it enough that I didn't get caught out and suffer the consequences. My happy place wasn't empty anymore. It was filled with Dashiell, and thinking about him was about all that'd got me through the last couple of days since we'd rushed back to the house from the pub. He wasn't just in my new happy place, he'd become it.

I'd paid the price for not being at the house. Frankie was still angry about that, even a couple of days later, so I shouldn't have let my focus drift because I knew it wouldn't have taken much to tip him over the edge again. He was going on and on about the trip to Romania and Turkey the following day, but I stopped listening and instead found myself back in that happy place, with Dashiell. I'd let myself become distracted, and that was dangerous in my world. Frankie said something and I'd failed to jump to attention, and just that little slip up had been enough to tip him over, and I'd ended up with scratches, bite marks and more bruises, including one on my cheekbone.

In the early hours, I woke up in agony. I was screaming and crying and throwing up all over the bedding. God knows how, because there was hardly anything in my stomach. Khan, Frankie's flunky doctor, had been called and declared gastric flu. That was a load of crap. It was some kind of panic attack. Frankie had gone mad, but in the end he'd had no choice but to leave without me, probably thinking he'd rather not have me spewing up all over him on the plane. I reckon I must have been given a shot of something to put me out, because when I woke up, it was early afternoon.

Stress and always living in fear of what Frankie would do next. It was like standing on the edge of a cliff that was crumbling away under my feet, and one false move would send me plunging over the edge. I felt like a wrung out rag, but I got myself up and dressed and padded downstairs.

Dashiell was there, in the kitchen, holding a mug and

staring out over the garden and frowning hard. He hadn't noticed me come in.

"Hello."

He swung around, and my stomach, sore as it was, flipped.

The smile that lit up his whole face vanished as he spotted the growing bruise on my face. I flinched as I touched the tender skin, conscious suddenly of Frankie's handiwork on me.

"What the—?"

"It's nothing," I murmured as I looked down.

Dashiell smashed the mug down on the table and rushed over to me. His jaw was tight and stiff, his mouth pushed into a rigid, straight line. He was angry, but not at me.

It wasn't often, anymore, that I felt shame, but I felt it then. I accepted everything that was doled out to me without any thought of saying no or fighting back. That was my life, but sometimes something would come along and trip me up, and I'd see myself through the eyes of another, and I wouldn't like what I saw. So, maybe I cringed or tried to make myself seem smaller or something because Dashiell's anger fell away, just as my hand did from my face as he tipped my chin up and looked at me with those big blue eyes that were no longer hard and angry, but soft and brimming over with concern.

"This is going to need to be taken care of."

"No."

"Yes. It's puffy and swollen."

He touched the bruise, and I flinched as nervy pain shot up my face.

"Sit down, and I'll get some ice. We need to reduce the swelling."

I did as I was told. I was too sore and worn out to argue, and I gave myself up to Dashiell's care without another word.

Dashiell rummaged around in the freezer and pulled out a packet of peas that he wrapped in a tea towel. He placed it on my cheek and supported my head with his free hand, and I didn't know what felt best, the soothing iciness or the warmth of his palm.

"Better?"

"Hmm. He's away for a week."

"I know, sweetheart, I know."

Sweetheart. That one little word was silk trailing across my skin, just as his fingers were as they traced my jawline before easing through my hair at the back of my neck, where he gently kneaded and rubbed, breaking up and sweeping away the tension that held me tight. I closed my eyes and melted into his touch. I could have stayed there forever, but Dashiell's hand fell away as quick, hard footsteps approached the kitchen.

My eyes shot open, and Lee walked in.

He looked between me and Dashiell, and his eyes narrowed.

"Billy's got a nasty bruise on his face," Dashiell said. "Ice'll bring the swelling down."

"Yes, good idea."

Lee looked at Dashiell as he spoke, and I thought they held each other's gaze, but given the state I was in, I couldn't be sure of anything.

"How are you, Billy? Do you want me to call Dr. Khan?" Lee asked.

"I'm all right. And no, I don't want Khan back." Khan, the creepy doctor. His hands were always damp, and he made my flesh crawl. No way did I want to see him again.

"It's looking better already."

Dashiell took the makeshift ice pack away. My face was numb, and I doubted what he'd said was true, but he was there and looking after me, and that was the only thing I needed.

"Lee, it's fine. I've got this."

I glanced up at Dashiell. He was looking at Lee as though he was challenging him to make a comment or something. Maybe he thought Lee was going to insist on getting Khan back in, because in Frankie's absence I was effectively under Lee's control, so if he chose to do that, there wasn't a thing either me or Dashiell could do about it. I waited for him to do exactly that, but instead he backed off.

"All right. I've got some stuff to do. I'll be back this evening."

He went without another word. Lee would be staying at the house, the way he always did when Frankie was away and I was left behind. I heard the front door bang closed, leaving Dashiell and myself alone.

"It really does look better." Dashiell smiled and touched the bruise with gentle fingers, and this time I didn't flinch.

"You need to eat and then get some more sleep because you look worn out," he said as he pulled open one of the cupboards.

"No, I don't want—"

"You need to eat. Just a bit of soup, that's all I'm asking."

He wasn't pushing, and he'd done so much for me, it felt kind of wrong to say no, and it wouldn't hurt to have a little something.

A couple of minutes later, a bowl was placed in front of me at the table. I didn't have the strength to argue about not wanting it; he was trying to look after me, and all I had to do was let him.

"No arguments." He had a mock stern don't-mess-with-me look on his face.

"As if I would." I spooned up some of the soup. I had no idea how much of it I'd be able to eat, but I was determined to try, but my hand was shaking and most of it dribbled back into the bowl.

Without saying anything, Dashiell took the spoon from me, dipped it into the soup and held it to my lips. I was twenty-three and being fed like a baby, but I didn't care or put up any resistance. What should have been awkward and embarrassing wasn't. How could it have been, not when he'd already seen the shameful way Frankie treated me and had dealt with the results? After that, being fed from his hand faded into nothing.

I nibbled at the soupy bread he tempted me with, but it wasn't long before I was shaking my head. I didn't have much, but I felt better for it, though I knew the real reason for that was having Dashiell next to me. I sighed and sagged back into my seat. Dashiell scraped his chair closer and snaked an arm around my shoulders, and without even thinking I settled into him and closed my eyes as he swept his fingers through my hair. The house was quiet. There was no Frankie barking orders and no zombies jumping to them. With the rhythmic back and forth of Dashiell's fingers, there was only this moment. What should have happened next was that he kissed me, but he didn't, and I was kind of glad of that. I'd have kissed him back, no question, but that wasn't what I needed. It was his warmth, and strength, and just knowing he was there.

"Come on," he said, helping me up. "The best thing for you is sleep."

I nodded, too tired for words, as I let him lead me out of the kitchen and upstairs.

13

DASHIELL

I've always believed that if you're going to pick on somebody, you pick on somebody your own size. Billy wasn't anybody's size, and certainly not Frankie Haynes'. I wondered if Frankie would be quite so brave without his henchmen around him, and with somebody who wouldn't be afraid to hit back.

When I saw the bruise on Billy's cheek, and the shame he'd tried to hide, all I wanted was to get Frankie fucking Haynes in a dark corner and beat the living shit out of him. Did having those dark thoughts and urges make me as bad as him? No, I didn't think so. Frankie's attack on Billy had been the act of a bully and a coward, because Billy was in no place to fight back. Frankie did what he did because he could get away with it. But when I turned and saw Billy's face, well, something hardened inside me. I didn't give a damn what their arrangement was and why Billy had ended up being Frankie's toy; all I knew was that I never, ever wanted to see the hopelessness and dejection I'd seen in Billy's eyes ever again. I'd already become his friend, and that's what he needed most of all because I sure as hell knew he didn't have any in that house.

But I didn't just want to be Billy's friend, and that was throwing me way off course.

I didn't see him for the rest of the day, but I looked in on him every so often and hung around until Lee returned.

Lee and Billy, Billy and Lee. I didn't know which of the two I was thinking about the most on the drive home, and later, as I lay awake in bed. Lee's revelation had shaken me, and so had his threat. *I'd throw him to the dogs, Dashiell. Don't doubt me on that, or put me to the test.* His words had been chilling, and I didn't doubt him at all, not one little bit, that if push came to shove, he'd do it.

It hadn't just been the fall out of what would happen if Lee's cover was blown that kept me awake, it had been that he'd read me so easily. Nothing was going on between myself and Billy, but that didn't mean I didn't want it to, and I was sure Billy felt the same way. But if Lee could read the situation so easily, that meant so could others, and by others I meant Frankie. The thought wasn't just sobering, it was profoundly worrying.

Every second I wasn't busy, and even when I was, my mind kept jumping back to Billy and the screwed-up situation he was in. On the face of it, it was simple, but I knew it was anything but. Younger man, older man, sex and fake affection in exchange for a pampered, easy life. If that had been the promise Billy had gone in on, it had turned out to be a false one. But I didn't believe for one moment the good life was why Billy had got together with Frankie and why he stayed, because his life was as far from good as it was possible to get. It broke my heart seeing how scared he was. Frightened to eat, frightened to speak, frightened to push against the invisible chains Frankie had wound around him. It had been on the tip of my tongue, more than once, to just come straight out and ask him why he was there, why he didn't just leave, but I'd bitten back my questions because I knew he'd clam up or revert to the comfort zone of being a snotty brat and tell me it was none of my business. If I started questioning him, I risked pushing him away when what I wanted was to pull him closer.

If Billy didn't have options, then neither did I. If I did anything that even threatened to move an apple, let alone upset the whole apple cart, then everything Billy had suffered so far would just be a foretaste of what he could expect. Much as I hated it, and much as I was forced to sit on my hands, at that moment I had no choice but to tow Lee's line and pray that the investigation would bring down Frankie, and soon, freeing Billy from whatever it was that bound him to stay. There was one thing I could do, though, and that was be there, ready and waiting to catch Billy when he fell.

When I arrived for work, Lee was nowhere to be seen, but his jacket, slung over the back of one of the kitchen chairs, showed that he was around, maybe rifling around in Frankie's office. I was half-tempted to go through his pockets, but I kicked that thought aside. It was too dangerous to show even an interest.

Upstairs, there was no answer when I knocked on Billy's door, so I opened it, thinking he must have still been sleeping just at the moment he walked out from the en suite bathroom with a towel draped around his waist. Droplets of water were scattered across his chest and shoulders, and his hair, wet from the shower, was a dark, burnished gold plastered to his head. The bruise on his face was livid against his pale skin, but it didn't look as angry as it had the day before. We stared at each other across the floor of the room, and I tried not to let my eyes focus on the marks that animal Haynes had left on Billy's body.

"How're you feeling this morning?"

"A lot better. Thanks, for yesterday." Billy grabbed the dressing gown that was lying across the bottom of the bed and pulled it on, knotting the cord tight. In silence we looked at each other, neither of us knowing what to say; it felt awkward, and that's the last thing I wanted.

"Do you want to stay here today? It'd be a shame if you did, with the weather so good."

"I never, ever want to stay here."

Billy's response was matter of fact, but it damn near ripped my heart out. Of course he didn't want to stay in that house, where Frankie doled out violence on an almost daily basis. Well, Frankie was away, and Billy had no reason to stay.

"Fancy a day out?" What I wanted to say was *fancy packing a bag and running away with me*, but with Lee's threats still fresh in my mind, I swallowed back the words.

He answered with a smile and a tiny nod of his head, and colour crept across his face, and wouldn't you know it, I felt a little bundle of warmth expand in my chest.

"See you out the front in half an hour." I bounded down the stairs with thoughts about where to go and what to do filling my head as the whole day stretched out in front of us, with nothing and nobody to think about except us.

"Where are we going?"

"Get in the front with me, and I'll tell you."

Billy's eyes opened wide as though I'd suggested something daring, which in his world I probably had, but the day was about leaving his world behind, and he jumped in.

Out on the road, we approached a large intersection, and I took the left hand turn towards the outer suburbs of south west London and the coast road.

"Where—?"

"A day at the seaside. We can eat chips on the beach, and then gorge on ice creams."

"I don't each chips and ice creams."

"You do today." I meant it, too. Frankie wouldn't be back for a week, so there was plenty of time for Billy to purge himself of illegal calories. It was a disturbing thought, Billy crouched over a toilet bowl and throwing up, all to keep Frankie happy. I hope that wasn't what he did, but he was skinny enough for it to be a possibility.

We drove in silence for the next few miles; there were roadworks and the traffic was heavy, and I needed my wits about me, but that didn't stop me from casting glances towards Billy. He was doing his best, but I could tell he wasn't completely relaxed if the stiff line of his shoulders and his hands, clamped together in this lap, were anything to go by. All I wanted was for him to feel free and easy, like he'd been after we'd seen the film and in the pub, before it'd all gone to shit, and I needed to make that happen.

It wasn't even mid-morning, but the temperatures were already climbing.

"I can put on the air con or open up all the windows, but that might muck up your hair, and you don't want the style police on your tail."

"My hair? What—?"

Out of the corner of my eye, I could see him frowning, but that melted into a grin.

"Cheeky bastard," he said with a small laugh. "Open up those windows and just drive."

He had that messy, just got out of bed hair, which didn't look how hair really looked when you just fell out of bed, or at least mine never did. On anyone else it would have looked over styled and over gelled, but on Billy it looked perfect. I knew, too, it was soft, and my fingers tingled with the memory of me brushing my hands through it the day before. I turned to say something, but he was slouched down in the seat with his eyes closed. His hands had relaxed and lay loose and open on his thighs, so I said nothing and just drove, feeling more content than I had for a long time.

I'd been driving for about an hour when Billy stirred and spoke.

"Are we going to Hastings?" He pushed himself up in his seat, blinking away the sleep from his eyes.

"Yep," I said as I approached the outskirts of the small south coast town. "I came here a few times as a kid. I've not been here for years, but I doubt it's changed much."

Billy looked around, alert and lively, all trace of sleep chased away. "Gran used to bring me here. In the school holidays, we'd get cheap day return tickets on the train. She always said the sea air was good for me. I loved it, and we'd spend ages in the penny arcade and paddle in the sea."

"Did you eat chips on the beach and gorge on ice creams?"

"Yeah, yeah, we did."

Billy smiled, and God, didn't that just do something weird and wonderful to me? His smile was big and bright, and the shadows that lived in those beautiful green eyes had been chased away.

I found a parking space, and we climbed out of the car. Billy stretched, and his T-shirt rode up, revealing the pale skin of his belly. It also revealed way too many sharp ribs for my liking. Anger spiked in me. Chips, ice cream, and God knows what else, food he couldn't or wouldn't eat and all out of fright. Frankie wasn't here today, he wasn't here to make Billy scared. This was our day, mine and Billy's, and all the rules that bound him would be ripped away.

"The chippies will be opening, so let's start with an early lunch al fresco on the beach."

"No. I don't eat that stuff anymore. I've already told you that."

His shoulders were hunched, and his hands stuffed into the pockets of his jeans as we made our way down through the winding streets of the Old Town towards the shingly beach.

"Do you jump in the car and come down here anymore?" I already knew the answer.

"No, of course not. Frankie would never come down here."

"Well, you're here now, aren't you? You're doing something you never normally do." I had him, and Billy knew it, too. "Is an illegal bag of chips really going to do that much damage?"

"I suppose not."

Every other shop along the front was either a fast food place or a sweet and rock shop, and I dived into a chippie that was just opening its doors. To be honest, I hardly ever ate stuff like that anymore myself. Steak, skinless chicken, steamed fish, salad, veg, protein shakes. Hardly any carbs, except when I gave in to the occasional piece of cake. That was pretty much it for me; it all sounded a bit dull, and as restrictive in its own way as Billy's diet when I thought of it. He wouldn't be the only one who'd be breaking out that day.

"I'll just have a few of your chips," Billy muttered as we waited to be served.

I looked down at him. He was staring at the crispy battered fish in the warming cabinet as if it were the second coming. A few chips? He could think again.

"Cod and chips twice, please. Open."

"Dashiell, I said—"

"Just put the freaking food thing aside for today."

I hadn't meant to snap, and it wasn't really at Billy. It was the whole fucked up situation he was in. He was as thin as a rake, and he wanted to eat, I could see it in his face, but he was scared, and he was scared because of that bastard who'd laid into him as if it were his God given right and would do so again and again. And that filled me with impotent anger because unless I forcibly removed Billy from Frankie, there wasn't a thing I could do to stop it.

I paid for the food, and we made our silent way down

to the pebbly beach, crunching our way across until we decided on a place to sit.

"Here." I handed him one of the bags, unsure whether he'd take it or not. Much as I wanted to, I couldn't make him eat it, but he took it with murmured thanks.

I plunged into mine. I was starving, and the hot salt and vinegar drenched food made me groan with unashamed pleasure. I deliberately kept my eyes from Billy because I didn't want him to feel self-conscious, but I couldn't resist a quick glance. He was eating the food. Okay, not much of it had gone, but he hadn't thrown it to the gulls who were swooping around us, and to be honest, that was what I'd half been-expecting.

"Nice?" I asked, nodding towards the bag.

"Yeah. It is. Doubt if I'll be able to eat it all, though."

If I was used to keeping fat and carbs to a minimum, Billy was way ahead of me. To be honest, I was starting to feel full myself, and tired, too. Everything that had happened the day before, lack of sleep, and the drive down from London all took its toll, along with the hot sun and the heavy food. I screwed the empty bag into a ball and lay back against the pebbly ridge just behind us, shifting around to make myself comfortable as I closed my eyes and let myself drift.

Heat seeped into my bones, a soft blanket I hugged tight. It yielded in my arms, and I pulled it closer as I breathed in its sweet vanilla scent. The shriek of a gull pierced through my foggy state, tugging me out of the cosy, snug world I'd fallen into. I opened my eyes and squinted against the bright blue sky and blinked hard to clear my fuzzy brain. The soft blanket that should have slipped from me as sleep melted away didn't. It wasn't a warm dream I was still holding on to; it was a warm body. Billy not only lay in my arms, he lay over me. One long leg was swung over my thighs, and an arm was slung across my chest, hugging me close. I didn't move, feeling the regular warm puffs of breath against the crook of my neck. Billy was fast asleep, holding me as tightly as he was held.

If I moved, I'd wake him, and I was more than happy for Billy to be coiled up in my arms. I'd have preferred that we were someplace private rather than on a public beach, but the few people who were around didn't seem to be taking any notice of us. Instead of easing myself away, I tightened my hold on him. Billy sighed and muttered something unintelligible and snuggled in closer, nuzzling further into my neck.

People always say they can remember where they were and what they were doing when major events take place in the world, like when Princess Diana died. On a stony beach, where a sleeping Billy Grace snuggled into me, I knew I'd always remember that day because it was the day my life changed. One way or another, I was going to get Billy away from Frankie Haynes and the virtual prison he was living in. I was going to take him away from the fear and violence that cast a shadow over his life. As Billy slept, and as I brushed my fingers through his hair, I had no idea how I was going to achieve that and by when, but all I knew was that living in Frankie's world was killing him, and that the world was a better place with Billy in it.

14

BILLY

I slept better than I had in I didn't know how long. I was so used to waking in the middle of night, soaked in sweat and filled with panic, that I'd forgotten what it was like to sleep and not dream of never ending darkness. When I drifted awake, I was warm, my guts weren't rumbling with hunger, and I felt kind of content and safe. I didn't want to let that go, so I hugged the pillow harder, really pulled it to me, but the more I woke up, the more I knew something wasn't right because the pillow was hard and the bed was lumpy.

I rolled away, away not from a pillow, but from Dashiell. It was him I'd wrapped myself around.

"Oh shit, sorry."

"You were out for the count."

He shifted and crossed his arms behind his head and smiled as if me falling asleep in his arms was the most natural thing in the world.

A pain speared my chest because I wished that Dashiell holding me as I slept safe and sound *was* the most natural thing. I shoved the thought aside because it was wishful thinking. Much as I may have wanted it, Dashiell wasn't my knight in shining armour who'd whisk me away. I lived in the real world, not in a fairy tale. I put the pain I'd felt down to indigestion from the fatty food that sat in my stomach.

"You know, you talk in your sleep."

"What?" My pulse rate picked up immediately. What had I said?

"Hey, I was only joking."

He was next to me like a shot, his arm around my shoulders. I shrugged him off, but I couldn't shrug off the concern I saw in his eyes.

"Don't say stuff like that." I got up and began walking along the beach, picking my way over the large grey and brown stones. The sky was a cloudless blue, and the sun shone bright and golden, but I shivered. The heavy crunch of footsteps drew up beside me.

"Why are you in a strop?"

A strop? He thought I was in a *strop*? "I'm not. But letting you bring me here was a stupid idea."

"Why? Because of Frankie? He's away for a week, you said it yourself. Just hold on for a moment."

Dashiell touched my shoulder, not hard and not forcing me to stop, but asking me to. I looked down at the pebbles, but Dashiell's fingers found their way under my chin and he tipped my head up, and when he spoke, his words were as soft and warm as the sunshine on my skin.

"It's just you and me, Billy. Nobody knows where we are or what we're doing. He's away for a week. Do you remember saying that, when we were all alone in the kitchen? This is our day, just yours and mine. It's ours, just like this is ours."

The world stopped, and everything in it disappeared except for Dashiell's heavy hand cupping my neck. His thumb brushed over the skin just below my ear, the rough callous on the pad sending a million volts down my backbone. His hand moved up, and he scraped his fingers through my hair. Dashiell's touch was sure and confident, and I closed my eyes, knowing what was coming next and wanting it with each and every part of me. His lips on mine were gentle, the kiss slow and soft, and full of tenderness. That's what hit me hard in the chest, and wet heat prickled behind my eyes, because I'd forgotten what tenderness and a soft and careful touch felt like.

"Today belongs to us, sweetheart. This is our day, nobody else's."

He breathed the words against my lips, and his warm, damp breath sent a ripple through my whole body.

Dashiell took my hand as if he did it every day, and we wandered along the beach. With his fingers wound around mine, I imagined the feel of those hands trailing over my body and clamping down on me as he pressed into the white skin of my hips and pulled me towards him, pushing into me as his fingers gripped harder and harder until they left dark evidence of what we'd done. I swallowed and tried to dislodge the solid, dry lump that had got stuck in my throat. Heat radiated out from deep in my belly, and my balls tingled and my dick twitched in response. With my free hand, I dragged my palm across my sweaty forehead.

"What?"

Dashiell was saying something to me, but I was so caught up in my thoughts, I hadn't heard him.

"Ice cream?" He quirked his brow at me.

Fish and chips, now ice cream. What next? Candy floss and sticks of rock?

"Yes, please."

Dashiell laughed and dragged me up the beach and onto the promenade. A hut selling fancy Italian style ice creams stood near to the new art gallery, which hadn't been there the last time I'd visited with Gran. The dark wood exterior was covered in seagull shit, which I doubt had been part of the architects' and planners' vision. We sat on a nearby bench. The ice cream was already melting, and I licked my way up the cone, not letting any escape. The sweetness was overwhelming, and I groaned.

"God, this is good. I can't remember the last time I had ice cream." As I lapped away at it, half my brain was calculating the calorie intake. Added to the fish and chips, I wouldn't be eating for the next couple of days. Or I could have found a public toilet, locked myself in a cubicle and chucked everything up. I'd done that a few times, when I'd been desperate. The thought of doing that was depressing; it would be like I was purging the day, and I didn't want to do that because our day at the seaside was special, my secret little dream to be brought out when I needed to chase the darkness away.

"Then you should eat more of it because you could do with gaining a few pounds. Or a stone or two."

I didn't respond, but the ice cream lost its flavour and I threw the rest into the bin next to the bench.

"I'm sorry, I shouldn't have said that. It was stupid, crass, unthinking—"

"Yeah, it was," I said, glaring at him. I should have been angry, but wasn't he just pointing out the truth? Dashiell's mouth was turned down, and his face was flushed. He looked mortified at what he'd blurted out, and I just couldn't be angry with him. "But you're right. I'm hungry all the time, but it's the way it is. But not today." He'd been blundering and tactless, but it was me who wanted to make *him* feel better when it should have been the other way around. "Maybe I was a bit hasty, throwing the rest of mine away," I added as I smiled up at him.

Dashiell's face relaxed, and the little knot of tension that had pulled tight in my stomach loosened.

"You can have a lick of mine, if you want."

Dashiell gave me an exaggerated wink, and I burst out laughing.

He carried on eating his ice cream. I'd scoffed at mine, shovelling it down my throat until I'd lost the taste for it. Dashiell was taking small licks and nibbles, and he was kind of being delicate with it. The long, graceful fingers, the gentleness of his touch, and the soft kisses, all of it was at odds with his hard masculinity, with the muscles and the tatts snaking down his arms. He was a man of contradictions. Light and shade, as my gran used to say.

His ice cream was turning into a melting mess as the creamy vanilla ran over his hand. My stomach lurched, but in a good way. Or a dirty way, depending on how you looked at it, because it wasn't ice cream I imagined oozing all over his hand and between his fingers. I licked my lips, I'm sure I did, and I caught his eye. He smiled, and the skin at the outer corners of his eyes crinkled because he'd read my mind. I looked away, unable to hold his gaze as my face burned, but I couldn't help smiling, too.

"We can't come to the seaside," he said, finishing the last part of the cone and wiping his hands on a paper tissue, "and not go to the penny arcade or have a paddle. We've got plenty of time. There's no rush, not today."

He was right, there was no rush. Penny arcades and paddling, more memories to be added to those that would be brought out to lighten the dark.

Dashiell got a whole bag of change from the bored looking woman in the corner booth. I didn't know who was the more excited, him or me, as we rushed from the penny fall machine, giving it a sneaky shove to try and dislodge the teetering pile of coins that threatened but never quite managed to collapse and pay out. At the grab-a-prize machine, the bright orange teddy bear became an object of desire and obsession as we fed in coin after coin to make the grabber clamp down on it and deliver Cheese Ball, as we called the bear, from his glass walled prison. Yes, Dashiell had called the stuffed toy Cheese Ball, and we both collapsed into laughter that was a lot longer and louder than the silly name warranted, but we were both hyped up on fat, sugar, flashing neon lights, and freedom. We never rescued Cheese Ball, and with all our change gone and nothing to show for it, we waved him goodbye and emerged back into the sunshine.

"Race you to the sea."

Dashiell ran across the beach, and a second later I was on his tail, trying my best to get to the water first. I wasn't used to running, and with the downwards slope and the pebbles shifting under my feet, I was soon out of control.

"Shit. Shit, shit, *shit*," I screamed as I hurtled forward, unable to stop my legs from getting faster and faster and slammed into Dashiell's body as his arms clamped around me, holding me up and holding me tight.

I was breathing heavily, and his arms tightened and our bodies pressed close and I could feel his hardness, and no doubt he could feel mine. He wanted me as much as I wanted him, and in that moment that was all that mattered. We couldn't do a thing about it, in the heat of the afternoon and on a public beach, but I didn't care about that. What I *did* care about was that Dashiell held me in his arms, and knowing that I was truly wanted. I looked up into his eyes, and my world went dark as he kissed me. These weren't the kisses of before, they were hard, and hot, and full of need and want.

We collapsed onto the pebbles, clinging onto each other and breathing hard. If anybody watched us and sniggered or sneered, we neither knew nor cared.

"We need to be careful." He said the words slowly, and he was frowning as though deep in concentration.

"Careful? There's nothing to be careful about, because this can't happen again Dashiell, it can't." I couldn't risk Frankie sniffing anything out. The day was a special, a one-off. It couldn't happen again because it was too dangerous.

"Is that what you really think?"

"It *can't*. You know that. I'm Frankie's—" What? I was Frankie's what? I knew what I was, but I couldn't bring myself to say the word out loud because it would be a blot on the day.

"Oh sweetheart, you don't think that, I can see it in your eyes." He stroked my face, and I began to lean into his touch before I pulled back. What had started today had to end today. I could see that, so why couldn't he?

"It has to, we've got no choice."

"There's always a choice. The trouble is, I've never been much good at making the sensible one, and I'm not about to start now."

"This time, you're going to have to." I tried to inject conviction into my voice, but when he touched my cheek again, I didn't pull back. As he stroked, he rubbed out my protest until it faded and disappeared.

"We can make this work, Billy. *I* can make this work. You just have to trust me."

Trust? I'd stopped trusting years before, but something told me that was about to change, and I didn't know whether the thump in my chest was due to fear, exhilaration, or a mix of both. Whatever it was, it was forgotten as Dashiell pulled me close once more and kissed me into oblivion.

15

DASHIELL

"It's not much, so don't get your hopes up." I parked the car on the bricked over front garden outside my terraced house and cut the engine.

With Frankie away for the week, I was determined to make the most of it with Billy. I hadn't missed Lee's cool-eyed scrutiny when Billy and I had arrived back from the coast, and it'd been the same this morning. I told Lee I was taking Billy for another day out. I saw no reason to lie and pretend I was taking Billy out as 'work', not when it'd been just the two of us in the kitchen. We both had it in for Frankie, in our different ways, and to my mind that made us brothers-in-arms. Or sort of. Lee had been about to say something, some word of warning no doubt, but Billy sauntered into the kitchen, trying his best not to look excited, and that had stopped Lee in his tracks. Lee's unspoken censure pissed me off, but it was only when I'd nodded goodbye that it occurred to me that if Lee had been left in charge of the house, and by extension Billy, he wasn't doing much to enforce that.

When we'd left, I hadn't thought much about where to go because it was enough that I got Billy away from that house, but then the thought had struck hard, and it seemed so obvious. Hastings, the day before, had been a place where Billy had been happy as a child. I'd been happy high up on Hampstead Heath, free from the stresses of a home life that frequently erupted out of control, and it'd been too long since I'd been back.

We'd walked and looked at the views, and I'd stolen glances at his windswept hair that was brighter than the sun, at his flushed cheeks, and sparkling eyes that looked so alive. Fuck me, but he was beautiful. If I'd not understood it before, I understood it then why Frankie was so possessive, but Frankie's version was warped, vicious and cruel. As he'd stared out over the city, Billy had looked young and free of all his cares, and God, didn't I just want to pull him close and kiss him into tomorrow, but even more I just wanted to look at him and drink in that smile of his.

By lunchtime we were done with the Heath, and that's when the idea occurred, the idea that brought us to a newly painted front door of a late Victorian terraced house in Kilburn.

"Wow, this is great, it's just like the house I grew up in with Gran."

Billy's words, and the smile that lit up his face, pleased me more than it should. Billy had mentioned his grandmother a few times now, and I was on the point of asking him about her when I bit back the question. He always referred to her in the past tense, so I didn't want any thoughts of a much loved but dearly departed sweet old grannie coming along and killing that smile that sent a warm tingle all over my skin.

"This is so nice. I love it."

"So it meets with your approval?"

"Oh yeah."

We were in the living room, and Billy was taking it all in. The place was full of too much junk and wasn't the tidiest, but Billy's words made me look at it afresh.

The contrast to Frankie's house was stark. No featureless white walls and hard edged modern furniture for me. One wall was made over to shelving holding my collection of beaten up paperbacks. Popular crime and thriller novels, nothing remotely literary, every one of them was dog eared, tatty and loved. The books shared space with my vinyl, everything from blues to jazz to rock, the collection put together from trips to shops, market stalls and boot fairs over the years. Full of colour, framed prints and posters that had caught my eye covered the walls, with no thought as to whether they went with anything else I had. Everything was a jumbled, eclectic mess, and with the cosy, comfortable furnishings, it wasn't just a house; it was a home.

"Come on, let's get a drink, and then we'll sit in the garden."

Billy nodded, all smiles, as he followed me down the long, narrow hallway which led to the kitchen at the back of the house.

My home was my private space, and to be honest, I wasn't even all that keen on having my friends around, but Billy being there with me felt right and natural, and he was happy to be there, too, if his smiles were anything to go by.

If my home reminded him of better times, I was more than okay with that.

I opened the French windows to the patio garden, which was crammed with potted shrubs, tubs overflowing with sweet smelling plants, and vine covered trellising.

"This is lovely. Who'd have thought you were into gardening?" Billy said as he looked around and smiled.

"When my job finished, I had time on my hands I needed to fill. My friend Andy, the one I told you about, is into gardening, and we spent hours picking all this stuff out. It cost a bloody fortune, even with his discount card." I smiled as I remembered. Andy had been so excited about all the plants, you'd have thought he was buying them for his own much larger, and immaculate, garden. "I don't even know what half of it's called. I water, feed and prune, and they repay me by smelling nice."

We sat at my little patio table, neither of us saying a word as we sipped our drinks and looked out over my small but private and secluded garden. I was content having Billy there with me and knowing that once again nobody knew where we were and what we were doing, and one glance told me he felt the same. He was with me where he was safe, and no harm would come to him.

Billy, as he'd gradually opened up, had been a revelation. He was everything I thought I never wanted but knew I did, but he'd also brought out a strong protective streak I'd never suspected existed.

Trying to get him to eat, making sure he was comfortable, wanting him to relax and have some fun – wanting, I suppose, for him to be the twenty-three-year-old he was. Whether Billy knew it or not, he needed protection, not just from that bastard Frankie, but from himself, too. The rigid, strict regime he lived by, not giving himself any slack and living in a constant state of tension, had made him scared, wary and vulnerable. Days out and snatched time, for now it was all we had, but it wasn't enough.

"You're quiet."

Billy's comment dragged me out of my dark thoughts. It was too perfect a day to have them, and I pushed them aside and smiled.

"Just thinking."

"What about?"

"You."

"Oh."

Billy's cheeks flared red, and he buried his face in his mug, but not before I spotted the shy, upward curve of his lips.

The sudden and unexpected noise of the doorbell cut through the quiet of the house and garden. Who the hell was calling in the middle of the day?

"It's probably the Jehovah's Witnesses." I tried to make a joke, but Billy's eyes were huge and round as he stared at me.

"You don't think it's—?"

"No."

Frankie. Had Billy really thought he'd turned up on my doorstep, to drag him back to the house and do God knows what with him? One look at his rigid, white face told me all I needed to know.

"Wait here."

Whoever was at the door, they were insistent and kept their finger pressed to the bell. I darted into the living room and looked around the edge of the, thankfully, closed blind.

"Fucking hell, Andy." I swore under my breath.

Andy was a good friend, the best, but why he wasn't at work and was calling around in the middle of the day, I neither knew nor cared. Today was about me and Billy, nobody else, and that was how it was going to stay. I watched as he stepped back and looked up at the house and decided I wasn't at home after all. He turned and walked off, and I watched him until he was out of sight before I made my way back to the garden.

"I'm not sure if it's a good idea, me being here. Perhaps we should go back."

Billy was perched on the edge of his seat and looked like he was ready to make a bolt for it. He was seriously spooked, and I needed to put a stop to that. He didn't realise it, but he was in the safest place in the world.

"That was Andy, that's all. He doesn't live too far away and was probably on the scrounge for a coffee. Billy, there's nothing to worry about. Do you really, truly, honestly, one hundred percent want me to take you back?" I stood over him and planted my hands on my hips and prayed he said no.

"No, of course I don't, but—"

"Then we won't." I sat back down and picked up my coffee, aiming for casual and unconcerned, but I had no idea how the next few minutes, or even seconds, were going to play out. *Fuck it.* Our perfect day was on the edge of being ruined, and I wasn't going to let that happen. I wanted to put everything back as it had been and make it right again.

"Come here." I was throwing the dice; it was a gamble I could lose, but one I had to take.

"What? Why?"

It took me a second or two to answer before I licked dry lips, ready to say the truest words I'd ever uttered.

"Why? Because I want to kiss you until you can't breathe." I wanted to do a whole lot more, but that wasn't what I needed to tell him, not at that moment.

Billy didn't say anything. He still looked scared and nervous, but I swore his shoulders relaxed, just a little, as he got up and stood before me. I eased him down on to my lap; he came willingly, and my heart gave a little lurch. He was feather light, and I draped my arms around him, nice and loose, so he didn't feel trapped or restrained, making it clear he could get up any time he wanted and I'd take him back to the house, no questions asked.

"You ask me why? I'll tell you. Because you look at the world with eyes that are too old for a twenty-three year old. Because you're too thin and you're always hungry, but you'll hardly ever eat enough to satiate that hunger. Because you've made a deal with a bad man who abuses you and who's bleeding you dry. If I can make things better by bringing you here, with me, and where you're safer than you could ever know, isn't that enough to answer *why*?"

For a man who'd spent much of his life indulging the physical, I was in grave danger of becoming emotional. I'd never said anything like that before to any other man. Maybe that was because no other man had needed me to say those things, or maybe it was because I'd never *wanted* to say them. But I meant every word because I wanted not just to be Billy's friend, I wanted to be his lover.

Lover. The word sent a shiver through me.

I'd had boyfriends, too many to count. One night stands, week and month long stands and a tiny handful that had gone beyond that, making my pulse race with the promise of more. But a lover? No, not if I were honest with myself, and I'd always been that. A lover was uncharted territory, and I needed to tread with care.

Billy stared at me, silent and still, and dread crawled down my spine as I feared I'd said too much.

He lifted his hand and trailed his fingers down my cheek and along my jaw, scraping at the dark scruff that pushed through my skin, and I shivered.

"You said, you *promised* me, Dashiell, that you could make this work. But before you can do that, you have to have something to *make* work."

He leaned into me and brushed his lips across mine, his breath warm and damp on my parched lips.

"I don't want you to take me back; I want you to take me upstairs."

Over the years I'd taken countless men into my bed, but Billy wasn't like any of the others, and he never could be, just like this couldn't be just some casual affair. There was too much at stake. Despite my conviction that we could work, the risk of discovery was real. An indiscreet look, a word overheard, or a kiss observed, all of that was possible no matter how careful we were. The enormity of what we were about to embark upon, of what making our way to my bedroom meant, hit me with a force that knocked the breath from my lungs. But was I going to turn away from the risk and the danger that went with it? No. I never took the easy path, and I wasn't about to start.

I set Billy on his feet, took his hand and led him back through the house, and upstairs.

I'd always been a man who took the lead. There weren't many times in my life I'd danced to somebody else's tune, and that included when it came to sex, but as I led Billy into my bedroom, the tingle that raced across my skin, and the hard, hard beat of my heart told me that this time the tables had been turned.

"Sweetheart—"

"Sshhh."

Billy wound his arms around my neck and stopped my words with a hard kiss.

And all hell broke loose.

Who pushed whom on the bed, I neither knew nor cared; all that mattered was that we *were* on the bed. I'd kissed him deep and hard when we'd been on the beach, and sure enough he'd kissed me back, but that had been a chaste peck in comparison. He took my breath away as we rolled around on the bed, me on top, then Billy, then me again.

I was taken aback by his passion and fervour. There was a hunger about him, almost a desperation, as he kissed me with a ferocity that left me reeling. But kissing could take us only so far, and I pushed forward and ground my aching dick against him. And he was hard. God, he was hard as a rock, and if I didn't get inside him, I was going to go off like a fucking rocket then and there.

I pulled away and scrambled for the drawer of the bedside cabinet, hand going straight to the foil packet I knew was there.

"No."

Billy was on his knees on the bed, just inches from me.

No. . . the word rang in my ears. I knew what it meant, and I'd not cross it if he didn't want me to, but as I turned and saw his pupil-blown eyes, his wet and swollen lip and his flushed skin, I didn't *understand* it. And nor did my dick.

"What? But. . ?" My hand fell away from the drawer.

"I want—no, I need—for this to be. . . oh *fuck*."

Billy screwed his eyes closed and raked his fingers through his hair, and his brow furrowed as if he were in physical pain. And it hit me, right between the eyes. What he needed was *not* to be hammered into the mattress. He needed it *not* to be a hard, aggressive fuck; he needed *not* to be crushed under my weight.

He needed it *not to be like it was with Frankie.*

God, had he really thought it would be like that between us? The scramble for a condom, the unspoken, arrogant assumption that he was going to take whatever it was I wanted to give him. Of course he'd thought all that because I'd given him no reason not to. I wasn't Frankie, I would never be Frankie, and unless I made Billy understand that, I'd lose him, and somehow I didn't think I'd get him back.

"I'm sorry. Billy, I'm so sorry, I should have thought." And I should have, too, but with the head on my shoulders, not the one between my legs. "We can just do this if this is what you want. Anything, anything you want." I pulled him into my arms and kissed that silky soft hair of his. Cuddles and kisses. It hadn't been what I'd had in mind, but honestly, just having him in my arms made me feel like I'd won first prize. Whatever he wanted or needed, now that I was thinking straight, it was all about Billy. I'd realised almost too late.

"We could just do this," Billy murmured, his face snug against the side of my neck. "Or we could do this."

Billy eased me onto my back. Was I pushed, or did I

fall? I didn't know, and I didn't care; all that mattered was that Billy took what Billy needed. What he needed, for reasons I knew but wouldn't examine, not in that moment and when it was just the two of us, was to take control.

Flat on my back in the middle of my bed, I closed my eyes. Billy straddled my thighs, and it was a struggle not to groan out loud. He wasn't even sitting across my groin, and my nerve endings were sparking. One by one, Billy undid each button, and the soft cotton of my shirt fell open.

Billy sighed, and I couldn't help feeling pleased, and not a little smug. I took care of myself, and alongside a lucky set of genes, the result was a flat, hard stomach and broad chest, smooth and adorned with tattoos. I jumped and squeezed my eyes tight when he trailed his fingers across and over my very hard, very erect nipples, which were not the only things that were hard and erect. This time I did groan and didn't bother trying to stop it.

Billy laughed. It was rough and throaty, and completely at odds with his blond skinniness. At odds, and one hell of a fucking turn on. My eyes shot open. He was staring down at me, his eyes bright and mischievous.

"Not a Spurs fan, then?"

He ran his fingers across the inked image of the wheeled cannon, the emblem of Arsenal FC, Spurs' greatest football rival.

"If I were, you'd be running your hand over my cock." I grinned up at him as I referred to the cockerel that was Spurs' mascot.

A slow, lazy smile and a glance through a thick curtain of lashes, and I was melting.

"And what makes you think I won't be doing that?"

If I'd been melting just a second before, his words turned me into a giant puddle of mush. *Sweet Jesus.* Just the thought of Billy's fingers curled around and sliding up and down my fit to burst—

I made some kind of weird choking sound as every bit of breath was crushed out of my lungs, but I don't think Billy noticed as he inched down my body, trailing his tongue over my twitching, sweat slicked stomach, towards the top of my jeans.

I itched to push Billy onto his back, rip his jeans off and dive in deep, and plough him into the next day. Yep, there was no denying that's what my body wanted, and it demanded with a strong voice that was very, very hard to resist. But it wasn't what my *mind* wanted. That was something new and unfamiliar, and I forced myself to listen.

Being with Billy, giving up control and letting him take the lead was so, so far from my comfort zone, and I was being led into the unknown, but with Billy as my guide I was ready and willing to see what might be discovered. I closed my eyes again and willingly gave myself up to his touch.

My belt buckle came loose, the zip on my jeans was slid down and I shifted a bit, letting him pull them down over my arse. I knew what was coming, or I thought I did, but it didn't prepare me for the heat or the weight of Billy's hand as he pressed down on my cock, still trapped in my briefs.

"Oh fuck, oh Jesus."

My voice filled the bedroom, but it didn't stop me from hearing the hitch of Billy breath. I pushed my hips up as he squeezed down and stroked me from the base to the tip. The friction of the cotton against my nervy skin sent pulses deep into my balls, but it wasn't cotton I needed to feel, but the skin of Billy's hand, slipping and sliding and soaked with pre-cum.

It was the work of a second or two to free my cock, and my briefs were pulled, or pushed off, and cast aside.

Billy was tentative. His touch on my uncovered shaft was less sure, not as confident as it had been just a moment before. I dragged open my eyes, and Christ almighty, I almost died and went straight to heaven. Billy didn't look unsure, and his touch wasn't unsure either. What I'd mistaken for a sudden loss of confidence hadn't been that at all. His face was serious, and contemplative, as though knowing we'd finally reached the bridge that once crossed would allow no way back.

"Billy? We can stop, here and now. If this is a step too far, even now, you only have to say." What I'd have said if he *had* taken a step back will never be known because he shook his head, then leaned forward and slid his lips down my shaft, all the way to the base.

A starting pistol went off in my head, signalling the start of the race. Much as I wanted this to be long distance, I knew it would be a sprint. Every flick of Billy's tongue across the pulsing, nervy head of my dick, every suck and wet *pop* as he released me before he slid his soaking lips all the way back down, and every twist of his wrist wrung groans, cries, and even fucking *whimpers* from the back of my throat. I didn't have a chance to as much as catch my breath as he sucked my tight, heavy balls into the heat of his mouth, rolling and caressing them with his tongue, letting them slip free before he licked me from root to tip, where he teased and flicked at my swollen, wet slit before circling over the ridge of my glans. I cried out as all that undiluted pleasure that was almost pain merged with something deep in my chest, something that my barely functioning brain was in no state to name or examine, but I knew was warm and solid, and sure.

I couldn't pull back, not even if I'd wanted to, as I crashed over the finishing line and exploded into Billy mouth.

I'm not sure how long we lay there, panting on the bed. I was dazed, breathless and sweat-soaked. I couldn't move because all my bones had dissolved. Billy obviously fared better because he crawled up my body until we were nose to nose. He was smiling, and my heart, already under serious pressure, almost gave out.

"I could kiss you," he said, his lips glossy from more than spit.

"Only if you clean your teeth first."

Billy laughed, soft and light, replacing the throaty chuckle from earlier. He shook his head before he snuggled into my side and entwined himself around me.

"We'll make this work, Billy, we will, I promise. But you have to trust me."

I wasn't sure if I was talking to Billy or myself, but whoever the words were for, they were the truest I'd ever spoken. But it didn't matter because Billy was asleep, and I was tumbling fast behind him.

16

BILLY

I didn't know where I was when I woke up. Everything was different; the light on the ceiling, the colour of the curtains, the pictures on the walls.

The man in my bed.

Dashiell was propped up on his elbow, and he was looking down at me with a big, lazy smile. My face heated up, and I must have been going red as what we'd done came back to me. I wasn't embarrassed or ashamed – why should I have been? – but I kind of felt a bit shy. Yeah, who'd believe it?

"Do you always watch the men in your bed when they're asleep?" I didn't think about the words, but as soon as they were out of my mouth, I regretted them.

"You look peaceful and relaxed," he said, choosing to ignore my comment. "I like that look and want to keep it on your face for as long as possible."

Dashiell leaned down and kissed me. The sweep of his tongue across my lips filled my belly with warmth, and I closed my eyes as he coaxed my mouth open, and didn't that warmth just turn into an inferno as his tongue slid over mine? I slid my arms around his neck and pulled him in tight as I kissed him back as though my life depended on it.

It was mental, what I was doing. Being with Dashiell, I was putting everything at risk. It wasn't myself I cared about, but I was so tired of walking on a tightrope all the time, where a day without a smack was a win. Peaceful and relaxed. Dashiell didn't know how powerful those words were and what they meant to me. I couldn't remember the last time I'd felt peaceful and relaxed and as he cupped my face and stared at me with those long lashed eyes of his, I knew I'd do anything just to forget for a little while what my life was, and what depended on it.

We were dishevelled from earlier and still partially dressed, and we both stripped off and I slid under the duvet. Dashiell had never seen me properly undressed before, and I became conscious of how I must have looked to him. I was so skinny, and I had no muscle to speak of, and being half-starved all the time, I felt like I wasn't much more than a bag of bones. I pulled the cover up and wondered what the hell he saw in me.

"Billy? What's wrong?"

The bed dipped as he knelt on it, but I kept my eyes down. His fingers tipped up my chin. He wasn't rough, but there was a firmness in his touch that wouldn't take no for an answer.

"How can you want me? I'm all skin and bone. At best, I'm snappy and irritable, I'm—"

His fingers went from under my chin to my lips, stopping the words that were spewing out of my mouth.

"Enough. Do you hear? I said, do you hear?"

I nodded. Dashiell was expecting an answer, and he wasn't going to be satisfied until he got one. His face was serious but calm and thoughtful, as though he were thinking about what he needed to say.

"The question you should be asking is, how could I not want you?" He leaned back a little and took his hand from my mouth and tipped his head to the side and looked at me full in the face. He was stark naked, and I had the duvet pulled up so high, only my head was on show, like some scared virgin. I forgot it all when he smiled, and his words echoed in my head.

"You don't know how beautiful you are, Billy. Yes, you're too thin – why do you think I keep trying to feed you up?" He quirked his brow at me, and I couldn't help smiling. "But it isn't just how you look; it's who you are. Yes, you can be snappy. In fact, I'd go further than that, you can be a snotty little bitch—"

"Thanks a lot. Is this your version of talking dirty?" Okay, he was right, but I didn't need it pushed in my face.

"If it turns you on."

His lips twitched a smile, that cocky, smug smile that sent a shiver racing through me. He could smile like that and I'd forgive him anything, even being called a snotty little bitch.

"All that's surface stuff," he said as his smile fell away. "It's your coat of armour. It's how you protect yourself, but it's not the real you."

"No? Then who is?" I needed to be reminded because the real me felt like he'd disappeared long ago.

"The real you is smart and insightful. A bit sassy. For that read sarcastic—"

"Now you know how I rock my inner little bitch so well."

"It's a fine line, and yes, you do it well. And of course, you're as sexy as fuck. Despite being too thin."

"You're a sweet talker."

"And you're just sweet."

Dashiell leaned forward and kissed me. Sweet. I don't think I'd ever been called sweet before, but that's just what the word tasted like on his lips.

The kiss didn't stay sweet, and we had to pull apart for air.

"Are you sure? I won't put any pressure on you, Billy."

Pressure? Dashiell thought he was putting pressure on me? He had no idea, and God I loved him for it. I kissed him again because I couldn't find any words. It was also my answer because in that moment I didn't think I'd ever been as sure as anything.

"I don't think we need this, it's far too warm in here."

He pulled the duvet aside, and it slid to the floor. Moments ago I'd been hiding beneath it, ashamed for him to see me as I was, but now I wanted his eyes on me because he'd called me beautiful. Too thin, yeah, okay, but beautiful, and it had been way too long since anybody had called me that.

Foil packets appeared as if by magic, a condom and lube. Maybe they'd been on the bedside cabinet all along, from earlier when I'd said no.

I put my hand on his to stop him from opening up the condom.

"Not yet."

"What—?"

Dashiell was confused, and no wonder, but the truth

was that I wanted touch him again. Yeah, we'd need that condom, but not just at that moment. I always wanted sex to be over, in the life that lay in wait for me on the other side of the street door. But I wasn't in that life, if only for a while; I was with Dashiell, and I wanted to savour every moment.

I placed my hand on his warm chest, and the beat of his heart seemed to travel all the way up my arm and join with mine, and I pressed against him.

"Sit up, on the edge of the bed."

He did what I asked, without question. His eyes were full of curiosity, but he wouldn't be curious for long. I shifted and straddled him as I wrapped my legs behind him on the bed, my arse planted on his lap. He yanked me closer, nudging our cocks together.

"Skinny boys are always so flexible," he said as he clamped his hands to my hips.

"Thought you didn't like skinny boys?"

"I like—oh fuck," he gasped as I took hold of both our cocks.

My hand was slick with our mixed juice, and I slid my grip to the base and back up again, moving our foreskins over their swollen heads. I caught his mouth with mine, and we moaned into each other as I repeated the motion, keeping everything slow and smooth. The feel of our cocks, flushed with heat, hard yet at the same time silky smooth in my hand, was doing all sorts of things to my heart rate and was sending tingling pulses deep into my balls. I could have come then and there if I'd have gone much further, so I eased off, just enough to stop what we were about to do being over before it'd really started. With my free hand, I felt for the abandoned condom and held it up.

Within a couple of seconds, the foil was discarded as Dashiell suited up.

"Anybody would think you'd done this before." It was a joke, to hide my nerves that jangled below the surface. Of course he would have done this before, in this room and on this bed, but with the world locked away outside, I wanted to believe that it was just us, that there had never been and would never be anybody else. I wanted to believe in a fairy tale, even if it did only last for the rest of the afternoon.

"You're right, I have done this before, but not with anybody who mattered the way you do."

Dashiell's words punched the air from my lungs. I mattered, I really mattered to him. . . it was easy to say all sorts of stuff when your balls were full and your cock rock hard. It was easy to say anything then and believe you meant it. Afterwards, he might forget he'd ever said those words, but he *had* said them, and in that moment that was the only thing that was important.

The little packet of lube was ripped open, and the cool slick shared before I shifted so I was kneeling astride him. I batted away his hand when he attempted to open me up. It wasn't his fingers I wanted.

Dashiell positioned the head of his cock up against me, nudging me with gentle pressure and making my muscle tingle and flutter. My mouth was suddenly dry, and I licked my lips. I wanted this, I wanted Dashiell so much, but what I was doing, it was dangerous, it was crazy, it was—

He pushed me down as he pushed himself up.

I must have cried out because his arms were around me and he was pulling me hard against his chest.

"I've got you, I've got you. I won't hurt you, I'd never do that," he said over and over again.

Yeah, he'd got me all right. In that moment, he'd got my heart and soul as I shuddered and panted in his arms. He began to move cautiously, not wanting to hurt me, just as he promised he wouldn't.

Long, slow rolls of his hips, his hands clamped tight to mine as he guided me. And it felt good, no doubt about it, but I didn't want slow and gentle. I wanted him to fuck me with every piece of strength he had. I rolled forward and came up a bit, feeling the drag of his cock inside me that set off every nerve in my body. I hesitated, just for a heart-beat, before I slammed down, signalling exactly what it was I wanted him to do to me. His eyes widened just for an instant, before he grinned. He'd understood the order loud and clear and was ready to obey.

Our bodies were slick with sweat as we pounded against each other. He was like a jackhammer, and as he pummelled into me, each thrust went harder and deeper. He hit my gland, and Jesus, I really did scream out then. He was saying something, his words hot against my ear, but they were fast and slurred, and I couldn't understand them because the noise in my head was too loud and high pitched, and the thump of my heart was erratic and out of control. Everything was too much, too intense, and I tried to speak but couldn't because his mouth was on mine and Dashiell was kissing me. And I forgot it all, and nothing mattered except for the taste of his hot, wet mouth, and the pounding of his cock as he filled me up and hit my gland over and over, and made the blackness behind my squeezed shut eyes explode in a million bright, white stars. The pressure in my balls was mounting, and the friction on my cock between our pounding bodies was too much, but it was nothing compared to when Dashiell closed his palm around me, and that was it.

I exploded into his hand, and my back arched backwards as he pumped me of every last drop of cum from my heavy, aching balls. His own climax followed on the tail of mine as he swelled inside me, and his hips jerked and spasmed as he cried out my name as he crushed me tight into chest and whispered words into my ear I couldn't hear over the deafening beat of my heart.

My eyes flew open as I heard voices from somewhere downstairs, and panic gripped me. Nobody, *nobody*, could know where I was and what I'd done, but as the memories flooded back, the warmth deep in my belly flared, and all I knew was that I didn't want what had happened between us to be a first and last.

The voices turned into a blast of music. A radio, that's all it was. I relaxed deeper into the bed, but as the sleep cleared from my head, the enormity of what had happened really began to sink in. If Frankie ever found out, even the tiniest suspicion. . . a wrong word or look resulted in cuts and bruises, so God alone knew what he'd do to me if he ever found out I'd been in Dashiell's bed. I curled up into a ball under the darkness of the duvet and tried not to think of the potential consequences of my actions. If Frankie found out, it wasn't just me who'd be in danger.

I might have wanted to, but I couldn't let what Dashiell

and I had done, in his bed that held the warm musky scent of him, of me, of *us*, blind me to the danger we'd walked into. I didn't want it to be our first and last, but that's what it had to be. How the hell was I going to tell him that, after everything he'd promised me?

The door opened, and Dashiell walked in. He was dressed, but he must have showered as his hair was damp and glued to his head. He'd washed me from his skin. It was the smart thing to do, but I couldn't help the twinge of regret that he'd done that.

"There's plenty of hot water, and I've got a pretty swanky shower, and then after there's some lunch. Even you must be hungry after all that unscheduled exercise."

Dashiell smiled at me, the smile that pretty much from day one had made my stomach tighten. I nodded but couldn't bring myself to say anything.

"Billy? What's wrong?"

Dashiell's smile turned into a frown, and he sat down on the bed. When he reached out and swept my hair back, I should have pushed his hand away. I didn't. I leaned into his touch as I felt the warmth of his skin on mine again. It felt good and right, and God, was I screwed.

"What if he finds out?" I muttered.

"He won't. Just believe me."

He sounded so sure and confident, as if he'd thought it all through and had a plan. I wanted to believe him, I really, really did, but Dashiell didn't know Frankie like I did. Frankie had a way of sniffing stuff out. He'd know, he just would, and what he would do to me, to Dashiell, to—

"Hey, come on."

Before I knew it, he'd bundled me up in his arms. I

reckon he'd seen the panic that was welling up inside me and threatening to spew out.

"You don't know what he's like, and what he's capable of," I whispered into his chest, but even as I said the words, my heartbeat slowed. The warmth of his skin pressed against mine, and the spicy, smoky scent that could have been shower gel but I already knew was Dashiell himself, was an instant shot of calm. I closed my eyes, wanting to believe him. But what would happen when he let me go? All my fears would rush back in and drown me because he couldn't hold me in his arms forever, could he?

Twenty minutes or so later, I was showered, dressed and back in Dashiell's garden, where it had all started. A plate of beans and cheese on toast was put in front of me. Any other day, in any other circumstances I'd have pushed it away and demanded another black coffee instead. It wasn't any other day, and these weren't any other circumstances as all the rules had been swept aside, if only for a little while. I dived into the food; I was starving.

We didn't speak as we ate. I guess Dashiell was as preoccupied with what had happened between us as I was.

"Do you regret it?" He didn't need to spell out what he meant by *it*. And no, I didn't, not in a million years.

"What? No, of course not, but—"

"Then why *but*?"

His question was calm and measured, but I saw beyond it when I gazed into his eyes. He was hurt, and that just about killed me.

Dashiell reached across the little table and clasped my hands in his, and their warmth seeped into my skin. They were firm and strong, but I knew how gentle they could be, too. They were hands that would hold me tight and never, ever hurt me.

"Why are you with him, Billy? Why? I don't get it. Everything he does to you—"

"Dashiell, please don't—"

"Leave him. Leave him now. I don't have to take you back, you don't have to see that house or that man ever again. Stay here, stay with me."

His words came in a rush, and as I gazed into his eyes, all I wanted to do was cry. He had no idea what he was offering and how much I wanted to grab it. I tore my gaze away and looked around the pretty little garden with its sweet-smelling shrubs and brightly coloured flowers. I thought of the living room bursting with character and comfort and the big, squishy sofa that just cried out to be snuggled on. And the bedroom, upstairs, where I'd given Dashiell not just my body, but my heart.

I turned back to look at him and shook my head. "I can't."

"Why? For God's sake, Billy, that makes you stay with him? What hold does he have over you? You don't want to be with him, so why are you?"

Why? Because of obligations and commitments; because I loved somebody so much and had to care for them because they couldn't care for themselves any longer, and being with Frankie Haynes was the only way I knew how.

The garden was quiet, there wasn't even the distant hum of traffic. The only thing I could hear, other than the rapid beat of my heart, was the buzz of a bee going from one flower to the next. Just the two of us, Dashiell and I, in that perfect little garden, and after everything we'd shared, there was no reason for secrets. I only prayed he'd understand why it was I couldn't and wouldn't walk away from Frankie.

"He—he pays the fees."

"What? What do you mean? Pays what fees?"

"The care home," I whispered. "Gran? I've mentioned her a few times."

I watched as understanding dawned.

"Your gran? I thought—"

"That she was dead?"

He nodded as his face went red. "I'm sorry, you made it sound as if she. . . I'm sorry."

I pulled my hands free and scrubbed them down my face. I couldn't be angry with him because I'd deliberately kept my words vague. I'd talked about her as though everything was way back in the past. Like a memory, I suppose. Of course Dashiell had thought my gran was dead, because I'd never given him any reason to suppose otherwise, and it had stopped him from asking questions I hadn't wanted to answer.

"She's not well, she needs loads of specialist care. It all costs money. A lot of money. Frankie, he takes care of that, in exchange for – me. That's why I'm there, and why I'm staying. That's the deal, and if I pay dearly for it, that's the way it is."

"Your gran, what—?"

"No, not now," I said, shaking my head. I couldn't answer questions about her. Not there, not then. I couldn't talk about who my gran had been and who she had become.

I pushed my plate of half-eaten food away.

"I think we should go."

"Do you? Not sure if I'd agree with that."

It was tempting, so, so tempting to stay shielded in the warm little garden, just the two of us alone and cut off from the world, and when I looked into his eyes, I almost gave in. Dashiell undid something deep inside me, it was as simple and basic as that. If I stayed any longer, he'd undo me all afternoon, into the evening and long into the night, and I couldn't let that happen. I pushed myself up from the table.

"Okay." Dashiell sighed.

He didn't try to argue or persuade me, and I didn't know if I was relieved or disappointed.

On the way back to the house, I stared out of the window. I had no idea of the roads we drove down or what was happening on the streets. The warmth, the gentle rumble of the car, a full stomach, and my stretched and strung out emotions all got the better of me and I drifted into sleep.

I suppose the car pulling to a halt and the engine being switched off was what woke me up, and I stretched.

"Hmm, what's the time?" I said on a yawn as I forced my eyes open.

Dashiell didn't answer, and as I blinked the sleep from my eyes, I saw why.

Frankie's car was parked in front of the house.

He was back.

Fuck.

17

DASHIELL

Frankie had cut short his trip. I wasn't sure if that had been deliberate on Frankie's part, a way of ensuring he kept everybody on their toes, or whether he'd concluded his business sooner than expected and had decided to catch an early flight home. Call it intuition, or me a cynical bastard, but I suspected the former. Whatever; it just confirmed that Frankie was unpredictable, and that made him dangerous as far as me and Billy were concerned.

My phone buzzed, and I pulled it from the pocket of my jeans. Two words, from Lee. *He's back.* I bit down on the groan. The warning was a bit late, but perhaps Frankie had surprised Lee, too.

"Why's he back early? Why?"

"Just take a deep breath and calm down. This is all under control."

I needed to reassure Billy, who was going into meltdown. It was an unexpected turn of events, no doubt about it, but I was confident I could handle the situation. As I cut the engine and fiddled about unbuckling my seatbelt, I kept my head down as I gave him my instructions.

"We've been to Hastings. You were feeling a lot better after your bout of gastric flu. It was a hot day, and you liked the idea of going somewhere you used to enjoy going to with your gran. You insisted I take you. That's what you're going to tell him when he asks, and the same goes for me. We're just going to bring forward to today what we did yesterday, that's all. You even had a bag of chips. We've got this, sweetheart, you and me both. Now, just get out of the car and go inside. It's fine, I promise."

He'd gone as white as a sheet, but he gave me a weak smile before he made his way to the house.

I parked in the garage and sauntered into the kitchen as if I hadn't a trouble in the world, where I found Lee talking low and fast into his mobile. He looked rattled. Frankie had taken him by surprise, too.

"I thought he was away for the whole week," I said when Lee cut the call and stuffed the phone back into his pocket.

"So did I. He turned up about fifteen minutes ago."

"I got your text, just as we pulled up. But thanks. Oh, we've been to the coast, by the way. Hastings."

"Thought you went there yesterday?"

"We liked it so much, we went for a second visit."

Lee glowered at me, and I thought he was going to make some comment about what was so patent a lie, but he must have thought better of it because he walked off without a word.

Alone in the kitchen, I got the coffee machine going. My head was spinning. Billy's revelation about his gran had taken me aback, but it made a sickening sort of sense.

I'd never had reason to visit a council run care home, but I'd seen the exposés on TV from undercover journalists and read stuff in the papers, and none of it was good. But were they really that bad? Bad enough for Billy to put up with all the shit Frankie threw at him? I poured myself a mugful of coffee and made my way to the garage to give the car I'd been driving a clean for want of anything else to do. I hoped the mindless task would help me think, not just about what Billy had told me, but about how I was going to handle Frankie when I got the inevitable call to give him a report.

"He wants to see you."

I looked up to see Lee standing just inside, and I put the soapy sponge aside and wiped my hands. The call had come sooner than expected.

"He's had a long trip, so he's tired. Just be careful what you say."

Lee said the words so quietly as I passed him, I wondered if I'd misheard, but a quick glance where we met each other's eyes told me I hadn't. It was the second heads up he'd given me in the past hour, and although it didn't make him my friend, I appreciated the warning and responded with a brief nod as I made my way back to the house, and Frankie's office.

My thoughts were flying at a million miles a second. Frankie would want to know why Billy wasn't at the house to welcome him home. What I was going to tell him wasn't technically a lie. The timeline had just been smudged a bit, that was all. The problem with out and out lies was that the more you told, the easier it was to be caught out, so the trick was to keep everything nice and simple. All I'd be doing was giving him yesterday's news because, let's face it, he really didn't need to know that Billy had spent a big chunk of the day in my bed.

Frankie sat behind his desk, rubbing his eyes as light streamed in from the window behind him. He was dressed in a casual shirt and jeans, and I could have sworn his paunch had expanded in the last couple of days, and I felt a bitchy little thrill when I made a mental comparison of my body against his. The thrill turned to bile as I imagined that gone to seed body rolling on top of Billy's. I swallowed down the sour sickness that filled my mouth, but if Frankie thought I was swallowing down apprehension because he was making me nervous, then so much the better.

"Well?"

"I took him to the coast. He seemed a bit better after his illness, and he told me he wanted to go to Hastings. Something about going there as a kid? It was a bit of a drive, but he insisted, so. . ." I let my words trail, and I shrugged as if to say I hadn't had a lot of choice in the matter.

"You're back early for a day out."

"I insisted on getting back before the traffic picked up." *And I screwed up again*, was the unspoken comment. Frankie heard it and nodded.

I creased my face into a worried frown. "Was that okay? To take him that far?"

"Hastings? I can't stand all those crappy, broken-down English seaside towns. It doesn't surprise me he wanted to go to that dump because it reminds him of his dear old grannie, or some such shit." Frankie huffed out a laugh.

Fury boiled up inside me, and the bitter taste of bile coated the back of my throat. Billy's stricken face filled my head, as he'd told me about the deal he'd made to buy her the care she needed, and that bastard Haynes was *laughing*.

"And what did you do when you visited this pearl of a town on the south coast?"

"We walked along the beach and had some chips." I had no idea how I pushed the words out, but I had to keep a hold of my temper and play along because I had to buy time to think, not just about the story I was feeding Frankie, but about how I could get Billy out of the shit he'd fallen into. Hurling myself over the desk and pummelling Frankie's face into a pulp, no matter how much I itched to do it, wasn't the smart move.

"Chips? Billy was eating chips? I hope you weren't attempting to lead him into bad habits. Were you, Dash? I like Billy to look a certain way, and he likes to please me."

He smiled, and my stomach turned over.

"And that's it? You went all that way to walk on a filthy, pebbly beach and eat a bag of chips?"

"We also went into the penny arcade," I added as an afterthought. "That was pretty much it. Like you say, it's a bit crappy and there's not much to do there. And I told him I didn't want to get stuck in traffic."

I'd made everything sound dull and prosaic when it had been anything but. Everything I told him was technically the truth, so there was nothing to trip me up. I'd just left out the more interesting details, like Billy having an ice cream. Ha bloody ha.

Frankie studied me as though trying to decide whether or not I was to be believed before he exhaled through his nose, which I took as a sign that what I'd told him was satisfactory.

"I'm taking Billy away on a little holiday. Ibiza. I have

a home there, very secluded. Very private. A bit of an improvement on Hastings, don't you think?"

"Nice." I don't know how I choked the word out because it'd be anything but *nice* for Billy.

"Have you been to Ibiza, Dash?"

"Only to San Antonio when I was a bit younger." A bit younger as in the previous year, where I'd shagged my way through the clubs for a fortnight.

"Yes, well," he sniggered, leaving it unsaid that he didn't think I was the sort who'd be accustomed to a luxurious private villa.

"We're leaving tomorrow afternoon, but you'll report for work as usual. Don't think because he's not here it's a chance for you to sit around drinking coffee and doing fuck all. After all, you need to earn your pay, and that means more than eating chips on the beach. Lee will assign your duties."

He waved me off, and as I walked out the door, I knew I'd never hated anybody as much as I hated Frankie Haynes.

18

BILLY

It was my idea of hell, being holed up in the villa with Frankie. Actually, the place was really, really nice, it was just the company I could've done without.

When I'd rushed into the house from the car, the first thing Frankie had done was fuck me, and the second was question me about why I hadn't been at the house waiting for him. I had the story Dashiell had told me to tell ready and waiting. I didn't know what was worse, Frankie trying to trip me up or him attempting to get some life into his half dead dick. He needed another appointment with creepy Khan, because the pills weren't working very well.

At the villa, Frankie spent a lot of time dealing with business, but on one of the days he'd had visitors and they'd locked themselves away in his office. I didn't think it had been a social call, but whatever had been discussed, or agreed, Frankie had emerged as smug as the cat who'd got the cream, and that meant he'd been ready to *paar-tay*. Trouble was, he'd got angry when he couldn't get it up properly – again – and seemed to think it was my fault.

Even the toys didn't help much, and I had to pull out all the stops and use all the tricks of the trade, as it were, to keep him happy because a happy Frankie made my life a lot easier

When I wasn't racking my brains to find ways to keep Frankie entertained, I spent my time day dreaming about Dashiell. I relived every single moment I'd been in his bed. Every kiss and touch, the sound, smell and taste of him. And God, I missed him. Not just what we'd done, I missed *him*, the man who made me laugh, made me eat chips and who could make my legs go weak at the knees with just a hint of that cocky smile of his.

I also thought about what I'd told him, about Gran. I found it really hard, talking about her. It wasn't like I was ashamed or anything; she was ill, there was nothing to be ashamed of. What it was, I think, was that I'd carried all the stress of her illness on my own for so long, I didn't know *how* to talk to anybody about her. Even when Frankie had agreed to pick up the tab in exchange for having me in his bed, he never asked, not even to find out if he was getting his money's worth for the fees. I didn't want to talk to him about her anyway.

The first thing Frankie did when we got back was go straight to his office with Lee, with strict instructions not to be disturbed. All I wanted was to run and find Dashiell, but I had to bide my time, so I tried to act casual as I wandered into the kitchen, hoping he'd be there so I could at least see him.

He was there, just like I'd hoped he'd be, leaning against the counter with his legs crossed at the ankles.

"Hello, Billy. Nice holiday?"

"Yes, thanks."

I started up the coffee machine, which just happened to be next to Dashiell. I glanced at him, and his eyes narrowed, just a little bit, but I could see the smile in them. I wanted to throw myself on him, crawl up his body and kiss him to death, but with Tony sitting in the corner like a fat, ugly toad, there wasn't much I could do.

"Do you need me to drive you anywhere today?"

Yes, I did. I needed Dashiell to drive me away and never bring me back. It was a nice dream, but that was all it was.

"Maybe later."

"Okay. I'll be in the garage if you need me. Just give me a shout."

He pushed himself away from the table and wandered out without another word or glance in my direction.

"Tony!"

Lee's voice cut through the silence of the kitchen, seconds before he walked in.

"Billy." Lee nodded in my direction before he turned his attention to Tony.

"Move your lazy arse. We've got some deliveries to make, but first we're dropping Frankie off at Blue."

All of them were going out, and within minutes the house would be empty. In a few words, Lee had told me all I needed to know. My stomach was doing somersaults, but I just kept scrolling and scrolling through my phone as I sipped my coffee and did my best to look bored.

"How long's the delivery expected to take?" Tony lumbered up, chewing on the last mouthful of a bacon sandwich which had left grease smears over his lips.

"All afternoon, we've got a lot of drop-offs to make. Frankie's got meetings back to back until 7.00pm. I'll be bringing him home, around 8.00pm I should think," he added. What had been meant to sound like an afterthought had been a deliberate, precise piece of info about Frankie's movements for the rest of the day.

Hours and hours. I didn't know how I kept from jumping up and down, but I did what I was good at and kept everything I was feeling under lock and key. Seconds later, I was alone in the kitchen. Dashiell was waiting for me in the garage, but I had to take my time and wait until everybody had left, until I was sure Frankie didn't want to see me before he went. About ten minutes later, the longest ten minutes of my life, I watched him climb in to the back of the car as Lee and Tony got in the front. Seconds later they were through the electric gates and gone, and I was racing to the garage.

Dashiell was leaning against the bonnet of the Range Rover, legs crossed at the ankles just like they'd been in the kitchen. And waiting for me, with the biggest smile spread out on that gorgeous face of his. I was in his arms in a flash. He held me tight, but I wanted him to hold me even tighter, and I pressed against him as hard as I could. And the kisses. God, it was like we were starving and trying to eat each other. Yeah, I was starving all right, and for a change it wasn't for food.

"They've gone – and they're – gonna – be out – for – hours and the house – is empty," I breathed against his lips, kissing him between words. I'd missed him so much, I couldn't even speak a whole sentence without needing to kiss him.

I grabbed his hand and pulled him towards the garage door and in the direction of the house. What I was doing was beyond dangerous, and I was putting everything I was with Frankie for at risk. I should have been doing what I'd been determined to do, when I'd woken up in Dashiell's bed, and stepped back. But how could I? The week I'd just spent away from him had been one of the worst in my life, and I'd had a lot of bad, bad weeks over the last few years, and I knew I couldn't take another like the one that'd just gone. I dragged him upstairs and into one of the spare bedrooms, because there was no way I was going be with Dashiell in the bed I was forced to share with Frankie.

We slammed the door closed, and we were on each other, kissing, kissing, and kissing.

"Miss me much?"

There was a laugh in Dashiell's voice, and I couldn't help smiling. Missed him? That didn't even get close.

"Might have," I murmured into his chest, and his arms tightened around me. I closed my eyes and shuddered. I'd missed the kisses for sure, but what I'd really missed was just having Dashiell close and knowing that I was wanted for who I really and truly was.

"And what about you? Have *you* missed *me*, or have you gone and found somebody a whole lot less complicated?" I'd spoken as if it were a joke, but when he stared down at me and didn't say a word, my heart lurched. I hadn't been entirely joking. Who I was, and my situation, was so screwed up that any man in his right mind should have run a mile.

"I hated you being away, and with him. I hated every minute of it, Billy, every fucking minute."

I looked away. I didn't want to be reminded of Frankie, not when it was just me and Dashiell. Our time together, just the two of us, was too precious to waste.

"Thinking of you was what got me through it."

I glanced up. Dashiell was smiling down at me, but it wasn't his normal cocky smile; it was kind of dozy.

"Is that true?"

It was truer than he could know. A lump formed in my throat, and I answered with a kiss. I'd meant it to be a simple *yes*, but with the two of us alone for hours in the house, that wasn't all it was going to be.

We sunk down onto the bed, and every inch of me felt his lips. My mouth, along my jaw, and down my neck until he worked his way to the little hollow at the base of my throat. I groaned, and Dashiell answered with his deep, rumbly laugh that sent shocks through every nerve in my body.

Dashiell straddled me, his arms braced either side of my head. He was a big man, and heavy, but I welcomed his weight on me because in all that solid, comforting warmth, there was safety.

He leaned down and kissed me, and it was the softest, most tender kiss ever. It was light and gentle, and there wasn't any of the heat of just moments before. But there was something else there, something I'd forgotten existed since I'd become chained to Frankie.

Respect.

There was respect in that kiss, and consideration. We were desperate for each other after our enforced week apart, and it would have been so easy just to tear each other's clothes off and screw ourselves stupid on the bed. But he knew what my time away with Frankie had been, and he wasn't going to grab and paw at me as though it were his right and without thinking. In placing that soft kiss on my lips, Dashiell was asking for permission.

It was in that moment that I knew I loved him. He'd

never take from me but would always ask for what I had to give. I couldn't breathe, or speak, and my only answer was to reach up and touch.

"Let me undress you."

I nodded and shuddered in anticipation as Dashiell's hands travelled over my T-shirt covered body, across my belly and up to my chest, where his thumbs swept across my nipples.

"Oh fuck," I breathed.

Dashiell laughed as he ran his nail around the hard little nubs hidden under the thin, fine cotton. We hadn't even got to skin on skin, but I was already dissolving into mush.

"Get this off."

He tugged at my T-shirt, and I sat up so we could both pull it off over my head.

Dashiell went still as he stared. I didn't get what had changed until I saw where he was looking, and at what; then I knew as my insides shrivelled and my shoulders stiffened and hunched as I tried to make myself as small as possible.

"He did this to you? He did *this*?"

"It doesn't matter." Of course it mattered, but the sad fact was that the marks Frankie left on my body were no longer remarkable to me, or not very much. I was used to it, which was a sign of how messed up my life was. My torso, as usual, was covered in bruises. The scratches had almost healed, along with the worst of the teeth marks, but what was new were the cigarette burns. God, they'd really hurt. There was a whole bunch of them, near my hip bone, and it looked like I'd been branded just like an animal would be. Frankie had gone to town on me, one night after he'd too much whisky, and his dick had been shrivelled and unresponsive.

"How can you say it doesn't matter?"

I reached out for my discarded T-shirt, ready to pull it back on, but he stopped me.

"Do they hurt? They must do."

I shook my head, not trusting my voice.

"This can't carry on, Billy. It just can't. The man's an animal. How do you know it won't go beyond punches and scratches? Or cigarette burns? Or *bites*, for Christ's sake? What if next time he has a knife, or a razor, or a baseball bat?"

I didn't know, and I was ashamed to meet his eyes.

"Can't we just forget about it? Just for now, when it's just us? Please?"

"How can we forget it, Billy? Those marks, they're assault. The man's beating you up and worse, and you just take it."

He moved to the edge of the bed and slumped forward and leaned his head in his hands.

I pulled my T-shirt back on and tucked it in tight, not wanting an inch of my beaten, abused flesh on show. The promised few hours, where it was just us, slipped away out of reach. Our reunion had grown awkward and angry.

"I do take it, you're right. And you know why."

"There's got to be another way." He lifted his head, and his eyes bored into mine.

"There isn't."

"No, I don't believe that. The residential home fees, I could help. I've got some savings, my redundancy money. I could get a loan—"

"And then another, and another, getting yourself into

debt, putting your house at risk. These private places, they eat money, and you'd be broke within a few months. I won't let you do that, Dashiell. You'd end up hating me, and I couldn't take that, not on top of everything else."

"I'd never, ever hate you Billy. Don't ever say that again."

His words were harsh and rough, and his cheeks flushed red. He was angry, not at me, but at the whole screwed-up, fucked-up situation that blocked us at every turn. I looked down. I was ashamed of what I'd said, but I had to try and get through to him that there was no easy answer or quick fix.

I couldn't explain, not with words, but I could show him and pray he'd finally understand.

19

DASHIELL

Billy gave me the post code to enter into the sat nav, and we set off for a location every bit as exclusive as the one we were leaving.

The journey was silent because he was absorbed and turned in on himself and preoccupied with thoughts I couldn't even begin to guess at. He wasn't purposely ignoring me; he'd simply forgotten I was there.

"Take the second on the left."

They were the first words Billy had said since we'd left the house, and I glanced across at him. His face was pale and pinched, and a small V wrinkled the space above his nose. I did as he instructed and turned off into a small no-through road, where I was completely taken aback by what was at the end.

"There's a car park on the left as you drive through the gates."

The Larches. If I hadn't known where we were going, and why, I could have believed we'd pulled up at a luxury hotel or upmarket spa, but the fine Georgian mansion house that reared up in front of me was neither of those places.

"Billy Grace for Mrs. Eileen Grace, please."

The young woman behind the reception desk tapped into her computer and then asked us to sign in. A few seconds later, we were hanging name tags around our necks bearing the word VISITOR.

"You'll find her in The Oakes, it's—"

"Thanks, I know where to go."

I followed Billy down a long corridor painted in muted, neutral tones, and the walls were hung with soft water colours. The Pines, The Firs. . . each room we passed was named after a type of tree until we reached The Oakes and walked through the wide open double doors.

"Gran? It's Billy. Oh, you're looking lovely today, Gran, but you always look lovely, don't you?"

I swallowed down the lump that lodged in my throat as Billy leaned down and hugged a tiny bird-like woman, hunched in an easy chair, before he pressed a gentle kiss to her cheek. It was a warm day, but she was swathed in a heavy shawl and her feet were encased in big, pink, fluffy slippers, the grinning kitten motif as vacant and gormless as the grin on the old lady's face.

"This is a friend of mine, Gran, this is Dashiell. You mustn't call him Dash, though, 'cause he doesn't like it. Do you want to say hello to him? Dashiell's driven me all the way here today. That was good of him, wasn't it?"

I coughed to clear my throat, and I wasn't convinced my voice wasn't shaking when I spoke.

"Hello, Mrs. Grace. Or can I call you Eileen?"

Eileen's face didn't move, and she stared through me with dull, vacant eyes. Drool had pooled in the corner of her mouth and began to weave its way down the crease of her chin.

"Dashiell can call you Eileen, can't he, Gran? You'll let him, won't you?"

Billy glanced up at me, his eyes bleak and full of pain, and you know what? All I wanted to do was hold him and never let him go. Whether that was for him, or me, or a bit of both, I hadn't a clue because at that moment my heart was breaking as I watched him pour his love and devotion into the lap of a husk of a woman who probably didn't even know he was there.

"Your hair's a bit messy, Gran. You won't like that, will you? You were always so proud of your hair. Soft, thick and bright blonde. No bleach job for you. Everything else may have gone to pot, but your hair was tip top. That's what you used to say, wasn't it, Gran? Do you remember? I do."

Billy pulled a brush from a bag on the floor beside Eileen's chair and stroked through the lush head of hair that still retained a few strands of cornfield gold amid the white, the same beautiful golden hair her grandson had inherited.

The old lady sat mute and still as Billy brushed and brushed, murmuring endearments and encouragement as the tears fell silently down his face. What I said about my heart breaking? Those tears that were soaking Billy's face and I could do nothing about? They ripped it into a million, bloody shreds. I looked away. What I was witnessing was love. Pure, unquestioning, unconditional love, and I felt like an interloper, a witness to an intimacy I had no rights in. I should have left and given Billy the privacy to pour all that love into the lap of the silent, still woman, but I didn't, because Billy had brought me for a purpose; he'd brought me to bring me face to face with what bound him to Frankie and why he wouldn't and couldn't leave.

"Hello, Billy."

I turned towards the voice. A care assistant, around about Billy's age and dressed in the home's uniform of blue and cream, smiled at Billy before his gaze flickered over to me and back again. I didn't miss the interest that lurked behind his professional smile, but it wasn't directed at me. Briefly, his eyes darted back to me, and I met his look full on and without flinching. A flush coloured his cheeks as he once again turned his attention back to Billy, still brushing his gran's hair. I said nothing because it was neither the time nor the place for the flash of possession that burned through me, so instead I gave him a nod and the tiniest of smiles.

"Hello, Chas." Billy put the hair brush back into Eileen's bag and looked up at the care assistant. "How's she been? Has that chest infection cleared up?"

"Yes, all sorted now. Isn't that right, Eileen?"

Chas took one of Eileen's limp, lifeless hands and gave it a gentle squeeze and was rewarded with a warm smile from Billy. I wasn't sure if I wanted to give Chas a kick up the arse and tell him to piss off or give him my heartfelt thanks for being the cause of Billy's one and only smile since we'd left the house.

"I'll bring you and your guest some tea. There's a fresh supply of custard creams in, as well."

Chas grinned, and Billy responded in kind. They were sharing a private joke, something I wasn't a part of. I was the outsider, and again that surge of jealousy rose up in me. In that place, and in those circumstances, it was pathetic, wrong and despicable. Chas left, and Billy turned to me.

"We'd always sit at the kitchen table when I got back from school each day. She'd have a pot of tea and a plate of custard creams ready. I'd tell her what I'd done in class, who was my best friend that day and who wasn't. She used to listen like it was the most important thing in the world, rather than the stupid ramblings of a kid."

Billy shrugged, and his mouth turned downwards in a sad, resigned smile.

I leaned across and took up both his hands in my own and held them tight.

"Not *like* it was the most important thing in the world, but *was*."

Somebody had loved Billy enough to listen to his childhood victories and woes. They'd made time, with the daily ritual of tea and biscuits, all cosy around the kitchen table. It was a rare thing, or at least that was my experience. My grandparents had all died years before I'd been born, and my parents had been too busy screaming at each other to take any notice of me and my brother. Billy had childhood memories he could treasure forever, and as he turned back to his gran, pulled her shawl in closer and made sure the blanket placed across her knees was tucked in, I envied him.

Chas returned with the tea and biscuits. As well as the mugs, there was one of those plastic cups with a small funnel, the type of thing young kids used.

"Thanks, Chas, that's great."

Billy smiled up at Chas, who seemed to take it as his cue to hang around and gawp at Billy, but he must have felt the force of my disapproval because he glanced at me before he said his goodbyes, adding that he hoped to see Billy again soon.

"I know, and stop it," Billy murmured into his tea.

"What's that?" My attempts at feigning ignorance weren't working.

"Chas. Do you think I don't know he fancies me? But he's okay, and he's nice to Gran, and that's all that matters. So, don't get funny with him."

I continued to sip my tea. Billy, twelve years my junior, was scolding me, and I deserved every word of it. I opened my mouth to apologise, but I stopped before I could start. Billy stared ahead of him, far away and wrapped up in memories of a life that, though he was still so young, was long gone.

I thought of my own family. My parents had divorced, and my brother had joined the merchant navy, soon after I started sharing a house with Andy and the other guys I'd remained close to. The family I'd been born into had fallen apart and had been replaced by a family of friends that was a sight more important to me. Where my parents and brother were, and what they'd become, I didn't have a clue, but seeing the love Billy had for his gran made me sorry for that for the first time in years.

"Come on, Gran, your tea'll get cold."

Billy's voice jolted me out of my thoughts, and I watched as he placed the funnel of the plastic cup to Eileen's slack mouth, giving words of encouragement and the promise of a biscuit as a reward for taking a few sips. I didn't expect a reaction. Eileen was a husk, whatever life had been in that tiny body had long since departed, but as Billy encouraged and cajoled, I could have sworn to God that Eileen's lips twitched the tiniest of smiles. It was probably a trick of the light, but for the second time that day I had a lump in my throat and my vision glazed over; not because of the imagined smile of a sick old lady, but because of the love I saw in Billy's face as he wiped at her tea-wet lips and chin and told her what a good girl she was.

Billy broke up a biscuit into a saucer and wet it with tea, making pureed sludge. Taking a little on the end of a spoon, he gently prodded at her lips, encouraging her to open up as if she were a baby in need of being talked into eating. Billy's whole focus was on his gran, for him they were the only two people in the room, and again I felt like an interloper with no right to be there. I was about to get up to give them some private time together, but also, I've got to be honest, to escape the discomfort I was starting to feel at being a witness to what felt like a ritual when Billy's words stopped me.

"She doesn't want a biscuit today. You don't want a custard cream, Gran? No?"

If Billy hoped for some reaction, the tiniest of signs that something of Eileen Grace still existed, he'd have been waiting a long time. Eileen stared ahead of her, lost in whatever world she now lived in as drool once more made its way down her chin. Billy dabbed it away before he placed a soft kiss on her cheek and promised to be back again soon.

"I need to tell them we're going. Don't forget to sign out."

Billy all but fled from the room. With his head bowed and his shoulders hunched, he was gone in seconds, leaving me with the still and silent Eileen.

I sat there for a minute or two, knowing Billy needed a moment alone, before I got up to leave. For all that Eileen didn't know I was there, it seemed wrong to just walk away. It was disrespectful, and I wouldn't treat somebody loved by Billy like that. I placed a small kiss on top of her head and promised to return again soon with her grandson.

Billy was outside and perched on the edge of a bench, with his head slumped forward in his hands. When he pulled himself up straight, it looked like it took every ounce of strength he had. He plunged his hand into his pocket and pulled out a flattened, battered packet of cigarettes. My eyes opened wide; he'd never given any indication he smoked. He lit one up and drew in a deep lungful of smoke and released it on a trembling sigh. It'd been years since I'd been a smoker, but the scent of tobacco, so close, still had the power to make my nose twitch.

"I gave up when I got together with Frankie," Billy said, staring in front of him. "He didn't like it, so I had to stop. It's for the best, but when I've been here, to see Gran, I really, really need a cig. Just the one, it's all I need."

He smoked the cigarette as if it were his last, burning the paper all the way down to the filter, which he dropped to the ground and crushed under his heel. The tension that had held him stiff fell away, and at last he turned and looked at me.

"Do you understand, now, why I do what I do? Why I have to? Gran being here, in this place where she's cared for every minute of the day, this is why I have to be with him."

Billy's eyes were beseeching. Every humiliation, every put down, every slap he took from Frankie, he took it willingly, and he'd do so until Eileen took her last breath.

"Billy—"

"I want to go, I need to get away from here."

He got up and headed for the carpark without waiting for an answer, and I had no option but to follow him. Whatever he wanted, or needed, I'd give it. I just wished that what he wanted at that moment was to be enfolded in my arms and held close.

20

BILLY

Dashiell put the two big mugs of coffee on the table, along with the muffin, and for once I didn't argue about the food.

Some fresh flowers sat in a small glass vase in the middle of the table, which was pretty apt seeing as we were in the café of a garden centre. The flowers were small and had a strong, sweet smell, and it reminded me of the expensive perfume I'd bought and had dabbed on Gran's wrists, and behind her ears, the last time I visited.

"Eileen's my gran. She brought me up." I was shaking as I picked up the mug, and I had to put it down again. Dashiell put his hands over mine and began to massage, and I sighed at the comfort of his touch.

"Dementia." I didn't really know why I said that, because it wouldn't exactly be news to him, not now he'd seen her.

"How long has she been—?"

"Like that? Like a fucking vegetable?" I pulled my hands away as anger erupted from me, but it wasn't Dashiell I was angry with; it was the world, or God, or whatever, because what had happened to Gran was so wrong and unfair.

"No, how long has she been unwell?"

Dashiell's calm and steady voice brought me back down.

"I'm sorry," I mumbled. I picked at the muffin, breaking pieces off but not eating. "Four, five years. It's hard to say for sure because it – the dementia – it kind of crept up on her. It's like that, it eats away little by little. . . she's been in the home for two years. The same amount of time I've been living with Frankie."

"I see."

"Do you? What do you see?" Sometimes I wondered, when he was carrying my endless shopping bags, driving me around, trying to make me eat. And when he was kissing me and taking care of me, that's when I wondered most of all.

"I see somebody who's kind and loving, and who'd do anything for the one they cherished, no matter how much it hurts them. Do you want to tell me about her?"

I nodded. Yeah, I wanted to tell Dashiell about Gran, about the woman she'd been, not the shell he'd seen in the home.

"Her daughter was called Kirsty, and she was my mum and under age when I was born. I've got no idea who my dad was. She went when I was about five, just upped and left, but she'd send me birthday and Christmas cards, and I got the last ones when I was eleven. The postmarks were never the same, because they were posted from all over the country."

The memory, as clear as day, hit me. Gran at the kitchen table, her cigarette burning in the ashtray next to her. And crying as she held what turned out to be the last birthday card I ever got from my mum. It'd been years since I'd thought of that, but suddenly it was like I was an eleven-year-old kid again and wondering why it was my gran was crying.

"Did you ever hear from her again?"

"No, but I didn't care because I didn't need her. I had Gran, I didn't need anybody else to love me. All she was to me was a cheap card a couple of times a year. It was only when I got older that I started to think about her properly and tried to understand why she did what she did."

"And did you?"

"Yeah, I think so. It didn't make what she did right, but I understood it to some extent." I'd never really put my thoughts into words about what I felt about my mum's actions because me and Gran never talked about it, and finding the right words after so many years was difficult. "For me, it just didn't matter that she wasn't around, but for Gran it was painful. Kirsty was her only child, who'd chosen to walk out not just on her own mum, but on her kid as well." I put a piece of the muffin in my mouth, but it was dry and tasteless, and I had to swallow some of my drink to make it go down.

"It was only a lot later that I finally really got why she'd done what she had. Kirsty hadn't been much more than a child when she had me. A kid with a kid, she must have thought her life had closed in on her and that she was trapped. And I understood it, that feeling of being helpless and knowing there was no way out. Once we got Gran's diagnosis, that's how I felt, and I just wanted to run away, too."

"But you didn't."

"No." I swigged down the rest of my coffee as I thought about how everything had started to unravel. "We got the diagnosis about four years ago, but I'd noticed stuff before then. Little things you could have put down to old age, I suppose, not that Gran was old. Like, when she went to the shops to get some cigs and was brought back an hour later by a neighbour who'd found her wandering because she couldn't remember the way back. Well, it's obvious then, isn't it?"

"How old were you when this happened?"

"Nineteen. I was shit scared and had no idea what to do. I'd been working for a company as an accounts clerk. Remember? They were paying for my studies? I got called in to see the HR woman because the college had reported that I'd started missing a lot of classes and my marks were going down the toilet. I also kept phoning in to work pretending to be sick because I was getting scared of leaving Gran on her own. I hadn't told anybody at work about what was happening, and I ended up breaking down and telling her everything. I'd hoped I'd get some sort of support, but instead they ended up putting me on an official warning."

I pulled off some more of the muffin, but I couldn't stomach it and crumbled it between my fingers, adding to the mess I'd already made. Dashiell pulled the plate away, and I looked up and met his eyes. They were kind, but more than that, they were understanding; something in those deep blue eyes told me he understood.

"Andy," he said, answering my unasked question. "Or more precisely, his mum. Even after I split with Andy, Helen and I remained friends. She remained in the family home, and I used to visit her whenever I could, but it was difficult, seeing the vibrant and loving woman who'd welcomed me with open arms just fade—"

"To nothing."

We stared at each other across the crumb-strewn table, a moment of shared and absolute understanding.

Dashiell leaned across and cupped his hands to my cheeks, and I pressed into his warm palms. Here was somebody who understood, and for the first time in over four years I didn't feel as though I was carrying the anger, and guilt and upset, and the sheer hopelessness alone. I closed my eyes, wanting only to feel the understanding in Dashiell's warm touch.

The table jolted, and my eyes flew open as a waiter came and cleared our things. Dashiell's hands dropped away from my face, and I looked up at the table clearer, an old bloke with barely concealed disapproval in his eyes. My nerves were shot, the visit to Gran had upset me just as it always did, and for the first time I was being given the comfort of somebody who *understood* and knew all about seeing somebody you loved fade away in front of you. And all I could see was censure and the tinge of disgust in the old bastard's eyes. I looked around, almost expecting to see a *no dogs, no Irish, no queers* sign. He wiped the table with quick, jerky movements and scuttled off.

I met Dashiell's eye.

"Do you want to go?" he asked.

"No. I want another coffee."

He grinned and made his way to the counter, singling out the old guy.

Dashiell's voice carried as he told him to bring over the drinks for him and his boyfriend. A few heads turned, and there were some raised eyebrows, but also a cheeky grin from a very pretty young mum with her toddler.

Boyfriend.

The word hit me hard in the chest. Another time, place and situation, it would be that easy, but my life was mapped out for as long as it needed to be. Boyfriends were for a world where people lived normal lives, and my life was as far from normal as it was possible to get.

"He'll bring them over in a tick," Dashiell said as he sat down.

"You know he'll spit in them?"

"How do you think they make all the froth?"

I couldn't help laughing; for a split second Dashiell had made me forget, and I loved him for it.

With fresh coffees in front of us, I picked up the story.

"Gran had all the tests that confirmed what I already knew. Social Services were rubbish, and were hardly any help. And then I got the sack from work."

"What? Even though they knew what was going on?"

"Yeah." No job, no money, and Gran, who didn't know what day it was or what she'd said or done just seconds before, but who recalled every detail about her childhood in Dublin and would talk, and talk, and talk about it.

"We were getting some state benefit, not much, though, and there was Gran's pension, so we were just about surviving, but it was tough. One day, I bumped into somebody I knew, just by chance. He was kind of an old boyfriend, and we went for a coffee. I should have got back to the house, but I just needed some time away from Gran. I told him what was going on and about losing my job. There was a way, he said, I could make some easy money, and he offered to introduce me."

"Billy—"

I stared hard into Dashiell's eyes. I knew what he as thinking, but he was wrong.

"Dancing. In a club." I didn't need to add that I might as well have been stark bollock naked, the little pair of shorts being *short*, as I writhed around. "That's all it was, Dashiell, that's all," I whispered. Or that's all it'd been at first.

"I made serious money. More in one night than I did in a whole month in my old job. And I danced there six nights a week. It meant I could pay somebody to sit with Gran in the evening and sort out her meds, get her to bed and all that, and make sure the rent got paid."

"Where was the club? Maybe I saw you dance."

Dashiell gave me a smile, and I knew he was just joking, but my blood went cold. I hated the thought that he might have seen me, that he might have been one of the men who'd stuffed money down my shorts as they tried to touch me. I wasn't ashamed of what I'd been doing, because all I'd been doing was dancing.

"It was in the West End," I mumbled. It wasn't far from that nice little café we'd been to in Soho, but I didn't want to tell him where. "The club turned out to belong to Frankie."

I caught Dashiell's eye, but I couldn't read his expression; he had his poker face well and truly in place.

"He came in one night, not long after I started. When I'd finished and was getting ready to go home, somebody came over and told me there was a guy who'd seen me dance and wanted to buy me a drink. It was Tony who came over. I said thanks, but no, 'cause there was always somebody who wanted to do that, and once I'd finished for the night, all I wanted to do was get away. Tony was very insistent. It was just one quick drink, he said, and told me Mr. Haynes would be very disappointed if I said no."

"Did you know who Haynes was?"

"No. I had no idea who owned the club and didn't care. All I was interested in was making as much money as I could without cosying up to any of the punters, but one of the other dancers overheard and told me who Frankie Haynes was. Saying no wasn't such a good idea. I didn't want to risk losing the job, so I said I'd stay, but just for one. Famous last words."

I didn't know what Dashiell read in my face, but it was enough for him to scoot his chair around the little table so he was sitting up close to me. He pulled me into him, and I rested my head on his shoulder as he brushed his fingers through my hair. I didn't care about the looks I knew we were getting or the whispered comments in that prim little garden centre café, because all I cared about was being in Dashiell's arms.

"So I stayed for a drink, just the one as I promised myself. Frankie had perfect manners, and he didn't try to touch or proposition me, which was what I thought was going to happen. He was slimmer then, and his hair hadn't thinned so much, and I guess I was flattered that the boss was taking an interest. We just chatted, that's all, and when I left, I didn't think too much about it. He was there the next night, and the next, and each time he sent Tony, or somebody else, to ask me to stay for a drink. And I did."

"Didn't you think it was a bit odd?" Dashiell asked as he carried on running his fingers through my hair.

"Of course I did. I know it's difficult to believe, but Frankie was easy company. He asked me about my life, what I liked doing when I wasn't working, that sort of thing. He was never intrusive, though, and I think that just encouraged me to tell him about Gran. It was a relief, having somebody to talk to about it all. But I knew I was in a tricky situation because I wasn't interested in him at all, not in that way, and I didn't know how I was going to handle it if he *did* want anything more from me than to have a drink at the end of the night. He'd never once tried to touch me, though, not in all the weeks I'd been staying behind, so I thought that if he did ask, he'd be okay about it, and that would be that. But everything deteriorated at home, and that changed everything."

I sat up, pulling myself away from Dashiell. I looked at him and saw the question in his eyes.

"Gran took a turn for the worse. She'd been kind of steady, but suddenly she just went downhill. Having somebody sit with her wasn't enough. She needed to be in care because she had no control over herself anymore." I stopped and took a deep breath. Talking about Gran like that, it was as though I were stripping her of all her dignity.

"I looked at some private homes, because the thought of her going into council care made me feel sick. They're horrible, Dashiell, they're really fucking horrible. They're understaffed, they're dirty, they're—"

"Come on, hey, she's not in one of those places." Dashiell rubbed my hands between his own.

"No, she isn't, but she will be if I don't keep playing along." He knew what I was talking about, he had to. "These private places, they're so, so expensive. Even though I was making really good money, there was no way I could ever afford them. I had no choice. I couldn't look after her anymore. She needed specialist attention. Everything was arranged for her to go to the council home. I felt like a traitor and that I was betraying her. After all the love she'd given me, all I was doing was packing her off to a hellhole that stank of piss." I rubbed my eyes as Dashiell rubbed my back. Big, slow circles, his hand was warm, and bit by bit it calmed me down.

"I was having one of my regular drinks with Frankie. He said my eyes were too pretty to be sad. It all came out, everything that was happening. He just listened and didn't say very much, and I thought he was being a friend. How stupid was I? He was working out how he could use what I told him for his own benefit, and he knew just what to do to get what he wanted. He said he was sorry to hear of my troubles, and he arranged for somebody to drive me home. He'd offered before, and I'd always said no, but I gave in that time because the night bus didn't hold much appeal."

"So he made you an offer you felt duty bound to take."

"Why do I think you know where this story's going?"

Dashiell didn't answer, and I took a moment to gather my thoughts.

"That's exactly what he did. He wanted me, which I kind of already knew, and I suppose I was flattered that the boss had singled me out. I'd begun to notice that the other boys and the rest of the staff were treating me differently, with a bit more respect, I suppose. Anyway, when I'd spewed out the whole story about Gran, he had the perfect hook. Those homes were terrible, no place for a loved one, he said. She deserved the best. Around the clock care, where she'd be looked after every moment on the day. I told him I couldn't afford any of that. *I can*, that's what he said. *I can*. He was offering me what I wanted, but for a price, and the price was me. In exchange for being his companion, as he put it, he'd pay for Gran's care. I'd have a good life. Just as Gran would be looked after and provided for and given everything she needed, then so would I. All I had to do was—was be his companion."

I rubbed my hands up and down my face as I remembered. A proposition over a late-night drink, and I could give her everything she needed and deserved. All I had to do was say yes.

"He told me to think about it for a couple of days. But there was nothing to think about. I had no real choice, Frankie knew that. I didn't know what kind of man he was, not really, but it didn't take me long to find out. But that didn't matter, and despite what he's done to me and still does, I can't let it matter. As long as my gran's safe and looked after, it's all that counts. A week later, Gran was moved into The Larches and I moved in with Frankie, and that's where I'll be for as long as I have to. So now you know. Everything I do and everything I take from that man is because of that lovely lady who doesn't even know I exist anymore."

21

DASHIELL

"I don't want you ever going away on holiday again. Or not unless you take me with you."

Billy mumbled the words into my chest, and the movement of his lips against my hot, damp skin sent a shiver through me. At any other time it would have gone straight to my dick, but the aforementioned dick was lying on my thigh, all tired and overworked, as we lay in my bed.

I ran my fingers through his hair, and he snuggled in closer. He loved having his hair petted, and I loved obliging. It was one of the many small things I'd learned about Billy. Like being able to turn him to mush by just kissing him from the bottom of his ear down to where his neck met his collarbone. Only on his right hand side, not his left. Or that little gasping noise he made when I—

Billy pulled himself up from the pillow of my chest and looked down at me. His face was soft and relaxed, all the tension wrung from him. It was how he should look all the time, and I'd made it my secret mission to put that look on his face as often as I could. With his bed-messed hair, the sleepy look in his eyes and the faint flush that still lingered on his pale skin, he looked totally fucking adorable. My chest tightened. I wanted him to wake up looking like that every day. The truth was, I wanted him waking up looking like that every day with *me*.

It'd been just over three weeks since he'd taken me to see Eileen, to show me why he couldn't just walk away from Frankie. I hated that he thought he was trapped, because there had to be a way out, a way where he could be free of Frankie without compromising Eileen's care.

It wasn't all I hated. The thought of Frankie's hands on Billy, of what went on in that bedroom and in that bed, made me sick. Literally. Oh yes, there were more than a few times, after I'd got home, when I'd sat and brooded, when my impotent rage had spewed into the toilet bowl, encouraged by too much scotch or beer, or whatever I happened to have in the house at the time. When Billy and I were together, I'd try to blot Frankie from my mind. The time we had was precious, and I refused to let that bastard cast a shadow. But as Billy slept in my bed, free for just a little while of all the crap in his life, my stomach would grow cold and shrivel knowing that soon it would be time to wake him and deliver him back to an existence that ground him down, day after day, after day,

After he'd taken me to see Eileen, I'd gone onto The Larches website, and my eyes had watered when I'd seen their fees. Billy had been right, I'd have been broke within months, and it was much the same story at some other places I'd looked up. I'd even trawled through estate agents' sites to see what I'd get if I rented my house out or sold it. A lot, was the answer. But even if I moved some-where cheap, I'd only be able to fund the comprehensive care she needed for a limited time before the funds dried up and we were back at square one.

But I refused to believe there was no way out.

My thoughts kept returning to Lee. He'd made it plain as day that if I did anything to compromise the investigation, it'd be Billy who'd suffer. Was that threat real, or just to keep me compliant? I had no idea. I may have been able to sum up just about everybody I met, but Lee was the exception. It was almost impossible to really know what was going on behind those cool grey eyes of his. The investigation into Frankie's activities may well have been drawing to a close, but until he was thrown into the back of a police car, he was free to inflict whatever damage he liked on Billy, with every attack seeming to be more savage than the last. I was going to get Billy out of that house, and that meant I had to confront Lee.

"Tell me about the wedding," Billy said.

"Hmm?" Billy's question dragged me out of my tangled, jumbled thoughts. "Oh, yes. It was fun."

"Is that it? *It was fun.*"

"Ouch!" I yelped when Billy gave me a hard flick on the nose.

Billy liked to chat after a post-coital nap. That was another thing I'd discovered about him. Whereas I was content to stare up at the ceiling and wonder when I'd be ready for round two, Billy always liked to snuggle up and drift off to sleep for a few minutes.

"The wedding was wonderful, and Sam and Wes really went to town. I've got photos on my phone I can show you later."

Two old friends, Sam and Wes, had been at Blue the

night I'd met Billy, and they'd finally tied the knot in Ibiza, where I'd been for ten days.

Ten days without Billy had been bad enough, but when I'd turned up for work on Monday morning, Tony had told me Frankie, along with Lee, had gone to Bucharest and wasn't going to be back until Friday. I'd have been more than happy with Frankie being out the way; the only problem was, he'd taken Billy with him, too. I had to put on an air of not being bothered, although my guts had clenched down on themselves. So, I'd been stuck with Tony and I'd kept out of his way as much as he kept out of mine. By Friday, I'd been climbing the walls. I'd hung around in the hope there'd be word from Frankie to pick them up from the airport, anything, just to see Billy, but there'd been nothing and I'd gone home, slumped in front of the TV, and worked my way through some duty-free and wished it was Monday morning. It wasn't until Wednesday that we'd been able to find time. Billy had said he needed driving, and I'd driven him all the way to my bed.

"When you told Frankie you were going to Ibiza, I thought he might offer you the villa. Well, not really the villa, but the annex." Billy lay back down again, against my chest, and I shivered as he trailed his fingertips across my nipples.

"The annex? You mean there's a granny flat?"

Billy's laugh shuddered through my body. "The annex is a two bedroom house hidden away at the bottom of the garden. I prefer it to the main villa."

"Why would he do that?" It seemed an odd thing for Frankie to do.

"He does stuff like that sometimes. I think he likes to be seen as – what's the word? Magnanimous?"

I nodded. "Yep. Well, he didn't. In fact, he was really pissed off when I reminded him I was going away, so an offer of this annex wasn't on the cards."

Pissed off was putting it mildly. If I could not have gone, I wouldn't because the idea of leaving Billy alone with Frankie turned my stomach, but I was heavily involved in the wedding, which included being one of the best men. There was no way on Earth I could have let them down. They'd spent a fortune on the wedding, which included hiring some ultra-smart apartments in an exclusive complex so their closest friends could share their honeymoon, and that included me. The days had dragged, and I'd plastered a fake smile over my face for my friends' sake, all the time wishing I was back in London, with Billy.

"So how do you know them again? I've forgotten."

"We shared a house. Along with Andy, they were the other two. Three posh-boy students, and a bit of rough who worked on a building site."

"It seems a strange mix. How did you end up living together?"

"Friend of a friend kind of thing. I needed somewhere to live, and they needed to rent the spare room. I wasn't keen on sharing with students because I thought they'd all be snotty bastards, but they weren't. It was an eye opener living with them. None of them hid who they were, and that in turn encouraged me to be more open about myself. Building sites aren't the most liberal or accepting of environments, so I spent a lot of my time keeping who I was under wraps."

"And you started seeing Andy."

I looked down at Billy. If I detected an awkward note in his voice, I needed to put that right.

"Yes, but it was all a long time ago. We were in an on-off relationship for a couple of years. I think he saw me as a walk on the wild side, and I was happy to play along with that because in return he encouraged me, without pushing, to be honest about myself *to myself*, as well as to others. But we were always better as friends rather than boyfriends, and that's how we've stayed over the years."

Billy snuggled in closer, which I saw as an acceptance of what I'd said. He lay so still against me for a few minutes, I thought he'd fallen asleep. It was late afternoon, and we'd spent a large part of the day in bed. A visit to see Eileen, where this time I'd sat in the waiting room, had left him sad and exhausted. He hadn't said anything when we drove away and had only come to life when I turned into the small square where my house was. Minutes later, we were in my bed, and that's where we'd stayed, and would stay for the rest of the day and all through the night if I had my way. Billy stirred against me and ran his fingers up and down my chest in a way that sent a shiver deep into my belly, and groin, and perked up my dick.

"You don't talk much about your past, do you? I mean, why didn't you tell me before that you'd been in the Army Reserve?"

It was a good question, but the truth was I wasn't much of one for looking back. What was in the past should stay in the past, as far as I was concerned. What mattered was the present, and the future, and besides, I'd joined up when I was in my early twenties, so it'd been years since my stint playing at being an action man.

"If I hadn't have taken a closer look at that photo on the bookshelf, I'd have never have known."

The one of me in full uniform at my passing out parade, with Andy and his mum Helen, and Sam and Wes. The family I'd made rather than the one I'd been born into.

"Did you go undercover on secret missions?"

Undercover. The word flipped in my stomach. I had a few photos from that time scattered around on the walls, I was just thankful Lee wasn't in any of them.

"No. I went abroad on and off, where I was involved in humanitarian type stuff, but mostly I ran around yelling and shouting on Salisbury Plain while pretending to be the hero in an action film. I joined up for the adventure, and to get a few more qualifications under my belt."

Billy had shifted onto his side and looked at me with what I could only describe as an impish grin spread all over his face.

"Have you still got the uniform? Maybe you could wear it in bed."

"Got a thing for soldier boys, have you?"

Billy's grin grew wider, and I shook my head in mock disbelief. Thing was, the uniform *had* been a bit of a man magnet, but I decided to keep that little nugget to myself.

"I bet wearing it snagged you loads of boyfriends."

So, he'd read my mind. Ah, well.

"Maybe one or two, but the best boyfriend is the one I've got right now."

The grin on Billy's face faded.

"I'm not your boyfriend, Dashiell. It might be what I want, but how I can be? You know what my situation is."

His words cut me to the core, but I clamped my mouth shut.

Fury, scalding hot fury, coursed through my veins, but it was impotent. I'd never been a man to sit back and do nothing, but wasn't that exactly what I was doing? Snatched hours, a morning here or an afternoon there, before I had to deliver Billy back into Frankie's hands to take whatever punishment he thought Billy deserved. I'd seen too many bruises, and I didn't want to see any more. What was happening to Billy had to stop, and the only route to that was Lee. And if he refused to help? I'd issue my own threat, and mean every word of it.

I took a deep breath before I spoke because, God alone knew, he needed some hope. We both did.

"There's a way out, for you and Eileen. Don't stop believing in that, Billy."

He shrugged, and my heart broke because he didn't believe me, so that meant I had to believe for the both of us.

A phone pinged, somewhere amid the discarded and jumbled clothes on the floor. Neither of us moved, ignoring the intrusion of the outside world, but the second and third pings, just moments later, were signals that our time together was coming to an end. Billy pulled himself away, and it was all I could do not to grab him back.

"It's Frankie," he said as he sat on the edge of the bed and stared at his phone. His face was tight, holding the tension once more that had melted away as soon as we were alone. "I have to be back at the house."

"Billy, you have to get—"

"No." He shook his head as he tapped in a quick reply. "Don't say it, Dashiell. Please."

He pulled on his clothes, his movements slow and laboured.

I got out of bed, picked up my clothes and dressed in silence as my thoughts turned over and over and over.

22

BILLY

"Dr. Cope will meet you in the relatives' room, that's—"

"Thank you, I know where to find it."

I'd had a few visits to the relatives' room over the past two years. The last one had been when Gran had slipped, broken her ankle, and smacked her head open. It was where they gave you bad news. Your loved one had had an accident, was ill. Or dying.

I waited there and looked out over the manicured gardens and watched the hunched residents in their wheel-chairs being pushed around by the carers. The Larches was a beautiful place, and I had to give Frankie his due that he paid the fees without a murmur.

God, but I wished Dashiell had been with me. I missed him, even more than I usually did. I hadn't seen much of him for the best part of a week because Frankie'd had him doing all sorts of running around and we'd not found any time to be together.

The door opened, and Dr. Jane Cope came in, and I joined her on the sofa.

I liked Jane. She wasn't above cracking a joke, and she had the dirtiest laugh I'd ever heard. Well, she wasn't laughing as she switched the sign to *occupied* before she closed the door behind her, and she didn't tell me a joke either. My heart rate picked up as panic started to roll through me. This wasn't good; this was fucking *bad*.

"Billy, thanks for coming. The first thing is, don't panic."

Don't panic? *Don't panic*? If there were any words guaranteed to make me panic, she'd just said them.

"What is it you don't want me panicking about, Jane?"

I'd got the call from the home earlier that day. Dr. Cope, I was told, wanted to discuss Gran's *care plan* with me. Dashiell hadn't been around to drive me, so I'd walked into the kitchen and ordered Tony to take me, then and there. He took one look at my face and didn't argue.

Heart. It was all I heard. Gran had had problems with her heart for years, ever since I was a kid. She'd survived a minor heart attack and a couple of operations, so she'd get through, right? But there was an infection, too, and she wasn't responding well to the meds.

"Your gran's got advanced heart disease, Billy. The bout of pneumonia she had not so long ago has weakened her heart further, so we need to be very careful about what medication we give her."

"Is she dying?" That's what I was there for. Was my gran dying? "Jane, don't give me any bullshit."

"No, she's not, but she's very weak, and given her condition, we do need to reassess—"

"Reassess what? If she's not dying, what's to reassess?"

"Billy, please. I don't underestimate how difficult this is for you—"

"Difficult? That's the understatement of the year, Jane. You call me up to discuss Gran's *care plan*, you tell me her heart's got weaker and she's not responding to her meds, and you tell me you understand how fucking *difficult* it is for me?"

I glared at her. Jane didn't deserve the full force of my anger, and fear, but I had to rave and rant at somebody because if I didn't, I would've gone into meltdown, and I couldn't afford to do that. Jane didn't react; she was just as calm as she always was, but then I guess having relatives go off the deep end at her was water off a duck's back.

"Eileen's health has been deteriorating for some time now, Billy. As you know. She's not in any immediate danger, but if her health deteriorates further, we need a clear and agreed understanding about how we deal with that and move forward."

How we deal with that. . . move forward. . . It was just code for *do we let her live or die?*

Big, fat tears began to roll down my face as I sat hunched on the sofa. A box of tissues was pushed my way, and I grabbed one.

"I'm sorry Billy, I really am, but we do have to update her care plan so that we're sure—"

"Re-suss or not. That's what it comes down to, isn't it? Should she live, or should she die."

"It's probably the hardest decision anybody has to make when it comes to a loved one. But I have to be frank with you. If she were to have another heart attack, which isn't beyond the realms of possibility given her history, if she survived it, her quality of life would decrease dramatically. So yes, as distressing as it is, we do need to re-evaluate our course of action."

I sat there, staring at the floor, at the cream carpet, as I clutched the soaking tissue. Gran's quality of life? *What* quality of life? She didn't know whether I was with her or not as I brushed her hair and droned on about how lovely she looked. All the fancy gifts I brought her, she didn't have a clue. I think I did it to make myself feel better. If I never visited her again, she wouldn't have even known. The gran who'd cuddled and kissed me and made everything better, whether it'd been a bruised knee or a bruised heart, was long gone.

I sucked in a long, shuddering breath and wiped the heel of my hand across my eyes as I looked up at Jane.

"Okay. I—" I coughed as I tried to clear my throat of the big, dry lump that had become stuck there. "There are papers to sign, right?"

Jane nodded.

"All right, I want to see her first, though, before I. . ."

"Of course. I'll walk you down to her."

I followed Jane out, expecting us to go to Gran's room, but instead we went to what was effectively the hospital wing. Gran was in bed, with tubes attached to the backs of her hands and stands with plastic bags hanging from them.

"You didn't tell me she was—"

"We're looking after her hydration levels, Billy, and we're administering her medication intravenously. I'll leave you with her."

A second later, Jane was gone, and it was just me and Gran.

I didn't know how long I sat there for. She lay there with her eyes closed, and the only way I knew she was alive was because of the very small rise and fall of her chest. I talked and talked, stuff from when I was a kid. I talked about our day trips to Hastings in the summer holidays. We even got to stay there once, for a week, but only once because she couldn't afford to do it more than the one time.

Eventually, my words dried up and I just sat and stared at her and held her hand. My phone rang, and it was too loud and shrill in that silent room.

Frankie. My stomach clenched. I never rejected a call from him, never, but I couldn't bring myself to speak to him, and for once he'd have to wait.

"I'll be back to see you again soon, Gran, I promise. I'll bring you a new scarf, because you like your scarves, don't you? A nice bright red one, it'll set off that lovely hair of yours beautifully. And some chocolate mints, they were always your favourite." A scarf she'd never wear, and sweets she'd never eat. "Be good, and don't you give any of those nice nurses any trouble, okay? I know what you're like." I kissed her on the forehead, hoping for the tiniest of smiles or a flutter of her eyelids, anything to show me she knew I was there. But it didn't come, because it never did. I turned away as I wiped away the fresh tears that were making their way down my cheeks so she wouldn't see, which was stupid because she had her eyes closed, but even if they'd have been open, she wouldn't have known.

I left that silent room, found Jane and put my name to the papers she put in front of me. I felt like I was signing Gran's death warrant. As soon as I could, I got out, lit up a cigarette and took a long, trembling drag.

In the carpark, I found Tony dozing in the driver's seat. I climbed in the back and slammed the door closed.

"Take me back."

Tony jerked awake, looked at me through the rear-view mirror, and started up the engine without a word.

As soon as we got back to the house, I was summoned.

"Billy, in here. Now." Frankie's voice boomed from his office. My heart sank, and it must have shown on my face because I saw Tony smirk, as if he knew I was in for trouble.

Frankie was frowning at something on his laptop as he nursed a scotch. It was early in the day to be drinking, even for him. My nerves were shot, and I was stretched thin enough to snap, but that's just what I couldn't do. I sat down across the desk from him and waited for him to speak.

"Why are you so late?"

Frankie might not have been around when I'd left earlier, but I'd sent him a text to tell him where I'd gone, and why. I squeezed my hands into fists in my lap as Frankie looked me full in the face.

"I'm sorry. I had to see the doctor, there was paper-work, and it all took time. Gran, she's not good."

I looked down, unable to hold Frankie's cold, hard stare, but it wasn't just that. I didn't want him to see the tears pooling in my eyes that I *wouldn't* let fall in front of him.

"She's old, Billy. Old people get ill."

I glanced up. Frankie's face had relented a bit, the hard edge not quite so hard. I nodded, not knowing what to say.

A glass of scotch appeared before me.

"You look like you need a drink."

I wasn't keen on scotch, and on an empty stomach it'd hit my system in seconds, but it was never a good idea to refuse Frankie anything, so I picked it up and took the smallest sip possible.

"She's well looked after in that place, isn't she? She should be, the amount it costs each month." Frankie barked out a laugh. I'd heard it before, the reminder of our deal. I took another sip and kept my eyes lowered.

"Yes, she's cared for. Everything she needs. All those gifts you buy her – or I buy her because it's my money, isn't it, Billy? Look at me when I'm talking to you."

My eyes snapped up. Frankie's eyes were like lasers as they burned into mine. This was more than a reminder of who paid the bills. There was more going on. The softening I thought I'd seen had vanished. There was something different to the way he normally looked at me, and in his tone. Then he smiled, and it froze me down to the bone.

"It's very expensive to keep poor ol' Gran in that place. I don't begrudge it. Or not much. So much better than those local authority places, stinking of shit and piss. She wouldn't fare too well in one of them, would she? Not if she had to be moved for any reason."

I didn't have a clue what was going on, but my mind was racing. Dashiell, it had to be about Dashiell. Had Frankie found out about us? We'd been so careful, we hadn't left any clues, and Dashiell had told me he could make it work, and scared though I was, I'd believed him as I'd put everything on the line and risked it all.

"You know how much I appreciate what you're doing for me and Gran. She'd tell you that herself if she could."

"I'm sure she would, Billy, I'm sure she would. Just as I'm sure you wouldn't do anything to put her continued care and comfort at risk. Would you?"

"No, no, 'course I wouldn't. You know I wouldn't." What did he know? What did he suspect? Did Frankie really have suspicions, or was he playing some sick game? He liked to remind me how bad things could be for Gran, as if I didn't know, because he was an evil bastard. Was this all it was, my regular reminder? If it wasn't, I was in serious danger. But not just me, but Gran and Dashiell, too. Putting myself first had not just put me in harm's way, but also the two most important people in the world to me.

"No, Frankie. I'd never, ever do anything that would affect Gran's care and comfort." I looked him straight in the eye when I said it. I felt sick, and I didn't know how I kept down the little bit of scotch I'd swallowed.

I'd been selfish. I'd put what I'd wanted first, and that had to stop.

"Good boy, Billy, good boy. Just as long as we're clear." His smile grew wider, and it had as much warmth as a shark bearing down on its prey. He waved his hand at me. He'd made his point, and I was dismissed.

As I walked out that room, I knew I'd got off lightly, but it had been a warning. And now I had no choice. If hearts really could break, that was what mine was doing.

Dashiell. We were over before we'd really begun, and somehow I had to find the words to tell him.

23

DASHIELL

I hadn't seen Billy for two or three days, because Frankie had me running around like a blue arsed fly. Airport runs, delivering packages of Christ knew what to addresses all over London, all stuff that kept me away from the house. When I did get to see Billy, I found him in the kitchen as though he'd been waiting for me.

He was leaning against the counter, a mug of coffee clamped between his hands, and it took only one look at his face for my heart to crash through my chest and hit the floor.

"What's wrong?" My first thought was Frankie and his overly handy fists, but Billy must have read my mind because he shook his head. Which only left his gran. "It is something to do with Eileen?"

"Yeah, or kind of. I—"

Whatever he was about to say was cut short by Frankie's voice, and another I didn't recognise, followed by the slam of a door. We were alone in the kitchen, but with others in the house we had to be careful.

"Billy, what's going on?" Something was, because the air around us crackled with tension, and something deep inside my chest twisted and turned.

"I need to speak to you, but not now. Alone. I need to speak to you alone."

He was nervous and ill at ease and kept glancing over my shoulder towards the open door as if expecting somebody – read Frankie – to burst through and catch us whispering together.

"What is it? I'll help, you know I will, whatever it is." I ached to hold him and tell him that whatever it was, we'd be able to work it out even though I knew he wouldn't believe me. I stepped towards him, but he moved away as he shook his head.

"No, no, don't. Just don't."

"Billy, for God's sake—"

"Frankie's out later. I'll come and find you."

"Billy—"

But it was too late, he was gone. I stood alone in the kitchen and stared after him, with the knowledge creeping through my bones that whatever it was he had to tell, I didn't want to hear.

The encounter earlier in the day had shaken me, and not knowing what was wrong was screwing me up. I was snappy and bad-tempered, and my nerves were frayed as I waited for word from Billy. Tony attempted to give me an order, and I told him to go fuck himself. It would have been comical, the way he reared back with his mean little mouth formed into a perfect O, but I was in no mood to laugh. Even Lee raised an eyebrow, but his cool eyes kept their own counsel, and he turned back to whatever it was he was doing.

Lee. I had to speak to him, but I had to make sure we were alone because I couldn't risk any interruption from either Frankie or Tony, not with what I had to say.

Eventually, Frankie left for wherever it was he was going, with Lee in tow, and Tony departed soon after, his face screwed up in its habitual bad temper when Lee had issued *his* orders about supervising the drop-offs, whatever they were.

Billy appeared in the doorway of the kitchen, and like me he must have been waiting and watching for everybody to leave. I rushed across and did what I'd wanted to earlier and pulled him into my arms. He didn't resist, but his body was stiff and unresponsive. His arms didn't snake around my waist, and he didn't nuzzle into my chest with a contented sigh. He did nothing, and that's when my heart broke, because I knew. I knew what he had to say, and why he couldn't meet my eye.

He stepped back and out of my arms. It felt as though he had given me one last chance to hold and to touch.

"Why, sweetheart, why?"

"I'm sorry." He dragged out a chair from the table and all but collapsed into it and let his head fall forward into his hands.

I sat opposite him. I wanted to hug him, shake him, be angry, and plead. I wanted to do all those things at once, but instead I sat there, mute and still and waited for Billy to bring down the axe.

At last, after what seemed like ages, he looked up.

"It's too dangerous. There's too much at risk—"

"Billy, please just—"

"No! Listen to me. Please. Frankie suspects. We can't make it work. Being careful and discreet, keeping our distance when we're around the house. We were fooling ourselves. None of it's worked because he knows, I'm sure of it."

Billy's voice had risen, and panic coloured every word. He was a frightened animal, and his instinct was to run. I grabbed his hands and yanked them so hard, I pulled him from his seat and dragged him forward across the table so he was no more than inches from my face. He huffed out a sharp breath, and surprise lit up his face and shocked him into silence, just as I'd intended.

"Billy, just stop. Stop and think. What makes you believe he suspects anything? Tell me what makes you think that. What did he say to you?"

His breathing was shallow and rapid, but the panic that had made his pupils swallow the green of his eyes was subsiding.

"When I got back from seeing Gran, he called me in. He—he talked about the home, how well she was looked after, and how bad it'd be for her if she had to be moved. It was a warning, and it frightened me. It made me realise the danger I was putting her in."

"It's a bluff, Billy. Frankie's an evil bastard, and he gets a kick out of pressing your buttons. If he really thought something was going on, he'd be doing a lot more than making veiled threats to move your gran."

Would Frankie react so coolly if he knew Billy was spending afternoons in another man's bed? In my bed? No, I was sure of it. If he so much as had the smallest suspicion about Billy, Frankie wouldn't be able to serve up revenge cold. He'd be explosive because he wouldn't be able to contain himself, not when it came to Billy.

"He doesn't know. He's playing with you." I believed that, I honestly did.

Billy stared back at me with eyes that were so sad and tired, and devoid of any hope. I couldn't let him carry on thinking there was no way out. I had to tell him. I had to tell him about Lee, and the investigation, and that I was going to confront Lee and put pressure on him to get Billy out and Eileen's care paid for in return for my co-operation. What I knew was a powder keg, and I'd light the fuse if I didn't get what I wanted.

"Listen to me. Don't say anything, just listen and—"

Both our heads snapped around at the sound of car doors slamming hard, and I saw the confusion, and fear, in Billy's face.

We stood and listened as the front door opened and slow, deliberate footsteps made their way into the hallway, loud in that house that was all hard lines and surfaces, and no comfort. The footsteps stopped as though whoever was there was deciding where they would go next. I placed a finger to my lips as I looked down into Billy's wide, scared eyes and made my slow, quiet way out of the kitchen. With my back flattened against the wall, I edged along the corridor just far enough for me to see who'd come in.

Frankie stood in the middle of the hallway, his head tilted upward a little as if he were sniffing the air for the scent of blood, watchful and waiting for his prey. Behind him, Lee stood in the open doorway, his mouth pushed into a thin line as a deep and worried frown furrowed his brow. Frankie spun around, and I jerked, ready to flee, but instead of coming my way, the hard click of his heels went towards his office and was followed by the slam of the office door. I turned to go, to get back to Billy, but not before Lee's long, shaky breath filled the hallway as he scrubbed his fingers through his hair before he walked back out, no doubt to drive the car around to the garage.

"It's Frankie," I said when I got back to the kitchen. "He's gone to his office, but—" I went to take Billy's hands, but he pulled them away and stepped back as he shook his head.

"No, Dashiell, no. I can't do this anymore. He's back, and we didn't even notice until it was almost too late. I love you, Dashiell, I love you so much, and God knows that's the honest truth, but it's over because it has to be."

He pushed past me and fled, leaving me standing in the middle of the kitchen, with the word *love* echoing through my head.

24

BILLY

Telling Dashiell we had to end it was the hardest thing I've ever had to do, but I just knew Frankie was suspicious. Carrying on would have been like putting a gun to our heads and pulling the trigger, and I wasn't prepared to do that to the man I loved.

I didn't know when I'd fallen in love with Dashiell, I just had. I used to dream about falling in love and imagined the big, public declarations, fireworks exploding, and shooting stars racing across the sky. I'd even thought there'd be unicorns jumping over rainbows. What I'd never imagined was that I'd just *know*, kind of all quietly and without any fanfare. But that's how it was, and the warmth that filled me up just through knowing was better than any prancing, dancing unicorn any day of the week. I loved him, I loved him and wanted him with every bone in my body, but for however long I had to, I had to put aside what and who I wanted.

I'd deliberately avoided Dashiell, and it wasn't hard to

do. In the days since I'd told him we couldn't carry on, a big chunk of time had been spent abroad, with Frankie on one of his business trips. I'd spent the days on my own in the hotel suite, thinking about Dashiell and missing him so much it hurt, and the evenings swallowing down on the sickness as Frankie grunted and sweated on top of me, hugging myself into a little ball when he'd finished and rolled off to fall into a whisky soaked sleep. Being wide awake in the early hours, with my body as bruised and battered as my heart was the lowest, darkest point. It would have been so easy to slip out of bed and call Dashiell and tell him I hadn't meant what I'd said. Anything, to set me free from the nightmare of my life. But lying in bed and taking long, deep breaths to steady my nerves and bring my heart rate down, the panic would ease and I'd know I'd done the right thing, even if it was killing me inside.

Back at the house, I knew it wouldn't be long before I ran into Dashiell, and my heart was going crazy when I walked into the kitchen the day after I'd returned home. The only person in there was Lee. He'd come with me and Frankie to Istanbul. That had surprised me, because he always stayed in London when Frankie was away. I was glad he'd come along, though, because Frankie seemed to like him, or as much as Frankie liked anybody, and with Lee around it kind of felt like it kept some of the pressure off me.

"Any chance you can take me to see my gran?"

"Dashiell will be back soon, he can take you."

"No, I—no, I need to go now."

Lee didn't say anything as he looked at me. His face

was straight, just like it always was, but as he carried on staring at me I began to wonder if he was going to ask me why I wasn't prepared to wait for Dashiell.

"I can't, Billy. I'm sorry. Are you sure you don't want Dashiell to take you?" he added.

"No." It came out as a croak.

He blew out a long breath, and his brow wrinkled, like he was thinking hard about something.

"Okay, if that's what you want. I can get Tony to drive you, but he needs to be back here for 3.00pm."

Three hours, which meant I could spend about an hour and half with Gran. An hour and a half that would feel like too long, but not long enough.

"Thanks." I was about to go, but his words stopped me in my tracks.

"Is everything all right?"

"What?"

No, nothing was all right, and it felt like it never would be.

Lee's eyes flickered between me and the open kitchen door, then back to me.

"You know what I mean. You and Dashiell."

"I—" The words dried up on my tongue. How could I answer that?

"Billy, don't panic. I'm not going to—"

"Lee, I need to speak to—"

Dashiell strode into the kitchen, jingling a set of car keys in his hand. There were dark shadows under his eyes I swear I'd not seen before, and all I wanted to do was run to him and jump into his arms and kiss him into tomorrow.

"You're back." Dashiell locked his beautiful blue-eyed

gaze to mine, and I asked myself how could I have ever told him we were over?

The only sound in the kitchen was the gurgle of the coffee maker, and it felt as if all three of us were holding our breath.

"Billy wants to go and see his gran," Lee said, bursting the weird bubble we were in. "Are you free to take him?"

"Frankie's just told me to drive another business contact and his wife around all day, and I've got to go soon. Show 'em the sights, he said. It's like I'm some bloody tour guide. *Fuck it*. Can Tony do the sightseeing stuff?" Dashiell looked between me and Lee, and we both shook our heads.

"If Frankie's asked you to do it, it's not a good idea to palm it off," Lee said. "And he'll want to know why you decided to ditch his orders in favour of taking Billy out. You need to think and act more carefully, Dashiell."

I tried to swallow down the dry, hard lump that'd lodged in my throat as I looked between the pair of them. It was a warning, it had to be, but there was something else there, too, something that was understood between them and didn't need spelling out. I could feel it, it crawled along my nerves, and it hadn't been the first time I'd seen that, I realised, as I stood there like a bystander watching them stare each other out.

"You think I don't know that?" Dashiell asked without dropping his gaze.

Lee shrugged and turned away.

"I wouldn't leave Frankie's people waiting too long, if I were you. Billy, I'll go and find Tony, and he'll be out the front in fifteen minutes. But back by 3.00pm, remember?"

The kitchen door was always left open, but Lee closed it behind him, leaving Dashiell and myself alone.

"You look tired," I said. I wanted to run my thumbs across those shadows and wipe them away. Instead, I just stood there, hardly daring to move.

Dashiell shrugged. "I'm not sleeping properly because I've got a lot on my mind."

"Please, don't—"

"Don't what, Billy?" He stepped towards me. His face, like his words, was tight and tense. "Don't give up on us? Don't stop believing? Don't love you?"

"Love me?" Of course he loved me. I knew it with every ounce of blood in my veins, but it was the first time the words had passed his lips. Even though there wasn't a thing either of us could do with those words, I smiled wider than I'd ever done before because, at last, he'd said them.

"Did you think I didn't? How could you have thought that?"

Dashiell cupped the back of my head, just like he'd done on the beach in Hastings, and just like then, I groaned as I pushed into his touch. He leaned forward, and I closed my eyes as I gave myself up to his kiss.

I could have kissed him all day, all through the night, and into the next day. Yeah, I wanted to kiss him into forever, but instead I pressed my hands to his chest and pushed him away.

"I'm not giving up on us, Billy. Whatever you do or say, I won't give up."

"We don't have a choice, not with the way things are."

"There's always a choice. What choice do you think Eileen would want you to make?"

"What?"

Dashiell's words were hard, unlike the soft kisses just moments before. "Asking me that question, it's not fair, and you know it."

"No, it's not, but why should I play fair when there's so much at stake? So, I'll ask you again. Would she want you to do what you're doing? Would she want you to give up on your own life? Would she?"

I knew the answer, of course I did. My gran had loved me without question. Everything she'd done, she'd done for me, *never* putting her own needs before mine. Everything had been about me, and for me. No, she wouldn't have wanted me to do what I was doing. She wouldn't have wanted me to turn away from the man I loved, and who loved me. *Live your life to the fullest, Billy, just don't hurt anybody as you do it.* Gran's words came back to me, it was what she'd want me to do. And God, but I wanted it, too. If I took Dashiell by the hand and walked away without a backwards glance, I'd have done it with her blessing. I wavered, in that moment, with that question, I wavered.

"I—I can't, Dashiell, I can't do it. I'm sorry, I'm sorry, but I—"

My world was falling apart around me, and I collapsed into his arms and he caught me, like he'd done on that evening in Blue, and like he'd been doing ever since.

There was a light tap, and I stepped back and out from the warmth and security of Dashiell's arms as Lee peered around the door.

"Tony's out front with the car, Billy." Lee's tone was matter of fact, but I thought I heard a small apology, almost as if he didn't want to tell us our time was up.

I nodded and walked out, without looking back. As the car set off towards the home, I told myself over and over that I was doing the right thing, however much it hurt, I *was* doing the right thing. But Dashiell's questions, no matter how much I denied them, had caused a tiny doubt, deep down inside me, to start gnawing.

25

DASHIELL

"Half an hour, Dashiell, then you're heading out."

Lee's head appeared around the side door to the garage, and he was just about to disappear when I called him back.

"I want to speak to you. Come in and close the door."

I threw aside the soft cloth I'd been using to put a final sheen on the car. It was the first chance I'd had to get Lee on his own, in the few days since he'd given me and Billy time alone in the kitchen. At first I didn't think he was going to take any notice, but he gave me a curt nod and took a pointed look at his watch.

"Make it quick." He closed the door and leaned against it.

"I want you to get Billy out."

"*What?*"

In a flash he was in my space, so close I could feel his warm breath on my face. Once, he would have been exactly my type, but times had changed, and so had my type. For a split moment, I wondered why it was he'd been chosen to infiltrate Frankie's world. Was he gay? He'd never given off any vibe, but that didn't mean a thing, though it would make sense. I didn't think it was quite the right time to ask, and I shoved him away.

"You heard me, Lee. I want Billy out of this house and out of range of that bastard's fists."

"No. No way. Everything needs to stay just as it is for now. And that includes Billy."

"For fuck's sake, what's Billy got to do with your investigation? How is his being here, or not, going to make a difference?"

"Keep your voice down," Lee hissed.

He scrubbed his fingers through his hair, the same gesture he'd made as he'd stood watching Frankie sniff the air in the hallway.

"We're on the brink of bringing Frankie down. And what that means is that nothing, and I mean *nothing*, can get in the way."

He took a step towards me, and his grey eyes narrowed as they stared into mine.

"For a while longer, everything's got to carry on as normal, nothing unusual or out of place. That means Billy stays right here. Understand? If you're thinking about whisking him away to your place, forget it. Frankie would find you because I'd make sure he did, and what he's done to Billy up to now would be *nothing* to what he'd do then."

I slammed my arms forward, and Lee stumbled back-wards, his fall stopped by the garage wall, and I pressed my body hard against him as I used all my weight to pin his back to the bricks. My face was so close to his, anybody seeing us would have assumed we were lovers and on the brink of a kiss. But kissing him was the last thing in the world I wanted to do.

"If you don't get Billy away, I'll go straight to Frankie and tell him who you are, and what you're doing here. I mean it, Lee. Your precious investigation will go up in smoke. Remember what you said to me? All the time and money, and resources that have been spent. And it'd all be your fault, because *you* fucked up, because *you* got caught snooping in Frankie's office. Do they know that, your bosses? Or did you leave out that juicy little nugget when you told them your cover had been blown? Bit sloppy, that, wasn't it? I don't reckon much for your chances of promotion if they find out about that. So, what's it going to be?"

I stepped back out of his reach, and just like I had when I'd caught him red handed, I watched him thinking hard and weighing up his options before he came to a decision he really didn't want to make.

"All right, all right. I can get him to a safe house. *Shit.*"

He pushed his fingers through his hair again. It was a nervous gesture, and I wondered whether he knew he was doing it. I tamped down the grin that wanted to break out over my face, because he knew I meant every word I'd said. But I hadn't quite crossed the finishing line.

"When?"

"A couple of days, no more than that. I need to speak to my commander."

"What about Billy's gran?"

"What about her? Oh, come on," he said, looking at me with wide, incredulous eyes. "Do you think The Met is going to pay for her to stay in that care home?"

"Why not?" I shrugged. "It's a small price to pay, in the

grand scheme of things. Billy won't leave Frankie for the safe house without assurances about Eileen, and if Billy refuses to go. . ." I let my words trail off; I didn't need to spell it out that one couldn't happen without the other.

"You're a fucking madman, Slater."

Lee was right about that. I had no idea whether The Met would cough up for Eileen's care or not, but without assurances, Billy would refuse to leave, and I tried to keep my words steady as I voiced my fear.

"He won't go unless they do."

"He won't have a choice." He looked at his watch. "You need to get moving unless you want Frankie on your case. I'll get in touch with my commander, and in the meantime you don't say a word, all right? If you want Billy out of harm's way, keep your mouth *closed*."

Lee stomped off, slamming the door behind him.

Would I go to Frankie? As I let out a long and shaky breath, I hoped to God I wouldn't have to put that to the test.

"Stay in the car. I'll call when I need you."

If I'd been wearing a cap, no doubt Frankie would have expected me to doff it. Maybe I should have acknowledged his order, even if were only with a nod, but I kept my mouth shut because to be honest, I didn't trust myself to speak.

Frankie got out the car, and Billy followed on his heels. Billy kept his gaze cast down, like he'd been doing for the whole of the journey. I knew that, because I'd been trying and failing to catch his eye in the rear-view mirror during the drive across London.

I parked the car alongside a number of others and settled down, resigned to a long afternoon. Late nights and weekend work wasn't unheard of, but it wasn't the norm, and I wondered why Frankie had told me I'd be working on a Saturday, and all to take him and Billy to some afternoon BBQ, or party. Whatever the reason, I was happy to work as any time spent near Billy was good by me, even if he barely acknowledged me.

About an hour in, I got fed up with messing with the radio. I was also getting uncomfortable, and I needed to stretch my legs and take a leak. Frankie had told me to stay in the car, and he liked his orders taken literally, but I wasn't going to take any notice of that.

I made my way into the house through the back and found a ground floor bathroom, and when I came out I decided to take a look around. As I made my way down a corridor, a door burst open and a tall, thin guy rushed out, gabbling away in what I thought was Turkish, into a mobile phone. What was more important, though, was that I caught a brief glimpse of Frankie inside the room, having what appeared to be a heated discussion with a handful of other men gathered around a table. I moved away quickly, as I didn't want to risk being seen. But it told me everything I needed to know: Billy was somewhere around, and on his own.

I followed the sound of voices, and music, which led me out to the garden. I spotted him immediately; it was like my eyes knew exactly where to look. My stomach tightened, and my mouth went dry, and all I wanted was to fold him up in my arms and take him home with me. I also wanted to tell him there was a way out, and that plans were afoot to take him out of the life that was slowly killing him, but Lee's words of warning echoed in my head. Much as I wanted to tell Billy what was happening, I knew I couldn't and that I'd just have to bide my time.

"Hey."

I'd come up alongside of him, and he swung around, his eyes wide with shock.

"Frankie told you to stay in the car."

"Since when did I do as I was told?" I asked with a shrug.

"He'll be angry if he catches you here."

"He won't. He's tucked away with his cronies, so that gives us time."

"Time for what?"

"For whatever we want."

"Dashiell—"

"Champagne, sir?"

The waitress appeared as if from nowhere, and I smiled and took a glass. Billy shook his head, and in a moment she was gone.

"I have to speak to you, Billy. You've been avoiding me in the house, but you won't avoid me here."

Billy rubbed at his forehead, and his eyes were screwed up as though he were fighting pain. And he was, because I was hurting him, I was causing him pain and anguish. It was the last thing I wanted to do, because life had made a good job of that already.

"No."

"Yes."

He hesitated, and sighed. "Okay. But a few minutes,

that's all. There's an outhouse at the end of the garden, behind some trees and shrubs. I'll meet you there."

His voice was resigned and weary, and it twisted my heart.

Billy got up and walked away, and I tried to look like I belonged at the BBQ or garden party of whatever the hell it was. I didn't know how long we had, but when Frankie had business meetings at the house, they could last for hours, and I was banking on this one doing the same. I waited for a minute and then sauntered in the direction Billy had taken as I wound around knots of people knocking back the same champagne I'd taken but not touched. There were a lot of people, but the garden was huge, and I was soon clear of them and heading towards the trees and shrubs, the outhouse and Billy.

After the sunlight of the garden, the sudden gloom took a moment to get used to, but when my eyes adjusted, I saw Billy leaning against an old billiard table, the baize warped and ripped in places.

"We're not finished, Billy. I don't believe that, and deep down you don't either." I walked over and stepped in close.

Billy tried to move back, but he had no place to go; he was hemmed in between me and the billiard table. I put my arms to either side of him, my hands palm down on the battered baize. He couldn't match my height or weight as I bore down on him and used my advantage. It was a cheap shot, you could even have called it aggressive, but I wasn't above using every weapon in my arsenal.

"Dashiell, please don't do this to me."

His voice was quiet, and shaking, and he looked up at me with the saddest eyes I'd ever seen. But he didn't flinch.

He was summoning all the strength and bravery he had, even though it was breaking both our hearts. I gave him the only answer I could. I kissed him.

It was as though flood gates had been opened, the water pouring in and knocking us off our feet. Need, want, and hunger. I wanted to pull Billy so close into me, he'd melt into my body. Our hands were all over each other, there was no finesse, and no taking time to savour. We were men who'd emerged from a desert craving only clear, cold water to bring us back to life.

We pulled apart, but it was hardly apart, the fraction so small I could feel the hot dampness of Billy's breath against my lips as surely as he could feel mine.

"Don't ever tell me to stop, Billy. Don't ever tell me to walk away and stop loving you." My words were hard and ragged as I glared into his wide, green eyes.

"But how can we make it work? How? Everything's against us. He holds all the cards, Dashiell, he holds all the damn cards, he—"

"No. No, he doesn't. Listen to me, Billy, just listen to me." I clamped my hands to his cheeks, forcing him not to look away, not to spiral down and down in his belief that there was no way out. "Listen to me. I can take care of all of us. Eileen can be looked after, and you can be free of Frankie. But you have to have belief."

"What? What do you mean? I don't understand."

Maybe I'd said too much, but even though Lee's warning was seared on my brain, as I gazed down into Billy's eyes, I *had* to give him something to cling to, some sign of hope.

"You don't need to know, you just need to believe. Do you have that? Do you have belief in me?"

If he'd said no or shook his head, I didn't know what I would have done. My heart was in my mouth as I watched him stare at me, not saying a word and hardly even breathing, but at last, eventually, *finally*, he answered with a tiny, hesitant nod.

"Don't let me down, Dashiell. Just don't let me down."

"I'd never do that, sweetheart. Never."

My hands slipped from his face, and I pulled him into my chest, happy for the moment to hold him in my arms, breathe him in and feel the steady, strong thump of his heart. Billy's arms snaked around my neck, and as much as I'd pulled him in, he pushed into me, his cock hard against my thigh. My hands cupped him under the arse, and whether I lifted him or he jumped up, who knew or cared. All that mattered was that he was perched on the edge of the old billiard table, and I was unbuckling and unzipping him just as he was doing to me. I scrambled my wallet from my jeans and pulled out the two foil packets, and seconds after, our jeans and underwear lay discarded on the dusty floor.

"The door."

I followed the direction of Billy's gaze. It was ajar, and a shaft of sunlight was streaming through.

"Shit," I muttered as I rushed across. There was no lock or latch as far as I could see, but an old, ripped sofa provided a perfect barrier.

I'd abandoned the foil packets on the table and grabbed them up, but Billy stilled my hand.

"No. Let me do this."

A moment later, the packet was discarded and Billy smoothed the condom down over my dick. His hands were warm but shaking as nerves coursed through him. Outside, at the other end of the garden were dozens and dozens of people, any one of whom could wander to the outhouse and decide to take a look. At any moment, Frankie could emerge and be on the lookout for Billy – which meant we had to be quick. Electricity sparked every nerve ending in my body. A stolen moment, this was always going to be quick.

Lube followed condom, and the stroke of Billy's hands all the way down my dick was exquisite agony. If I wasn't inside him in the next few seconds, I was going to explode.

"Fuck, sweetheart, I'm not going to last if I have to wait."

"Then don't wait."

Billy locked his legs around my waist and jerked me forward, making his own need and urgency known. I didn't need to be told twice, as I pulled his legs further up my body and positioned my cock against him. Billy leaned back, his weight on his forearms, his arched spine lifting his arse a fraction higher. He was breathing hard, and those beautiful lips I'd kissed so hard were loose and damp.

I pushed inside him, and I swear my heart almost exploded in my chest.

He was hot, and tight, as his muscles pulsed around my dick. I clamped my hands to his sharp hips and surged forward, slamming into him as hard and fast and as deep as I could. Billy gasped, and a cry was dragged up from deep in his chest, and I slowed even though my body was screaming no, but I wouldn't hurt him, not ever, not in any way.

"No. Don't stop, don't you fucking stop," Billy panted.

He was staring at me with a hunger I'd never before seen in him, and even though every drop of blood had drained from my brain, I saw the fire in his eyes and his sharp, white teeth mashing down on his swollen lower lip. He was flushed and sweating, he looked wild, and feral, and full of need, and I didn't think I'd ever wanted him as much as I did at that moment.

Somewhere, a phone rang. I didn't know if it was Billy's, or mine, or from outside. I didn't care because all I cared about was wrapped around me and urging me to push harder, harder, *harder*.

I came with a force that made my knees buckle, and I had to steady myself against the edge of the old billiard table. I sagged forward, and sweat dripped from me as I kissed my way across Billy's warm stomach, damp with sweat and his own release.

We were breathing hard, but we held our breaths as voices sounded outside the outhouse and the door rattled in its frame. But we didn't recognise the voices as they drifted away and we were left on our own once more.

We dressed, as quickly as our trembling limbs would allow.

"Let me go first," I said, pushing my damp hair from my forehead.

"What's going to happen, Dashiell? What happens next, to us?"

"Leave it to me," I said as I placed a small kiss on his lips. "Just trust me, okay? *Okay*?"

"I've got no choice, have I?"

"No, not when it comes to me and you."

Moments later, I was heading back to the car and wondering what the hell *was* going to happen next.

26

BILLY

After Dashiell left me with a kiss, I waited a few minutes before I made my way back. My skin was hot and sticky, and I was sure everybody would know what I'd done, but nobody took any notice of me and I fled inside the house to find a bathroom. Apart from a slight flush, the face that stared back at me from the mirror looked the same as always.

Back in the garden, I took a flute of champagne and tucked myself back in the same corner where Dashiell had found me. I'd have normally have stuck to mineral water, but I needed a drink. I'd tried so, so hard to say no to Dashiell. There was too much at risk for all of us. I kept telling myself that, over and over, but when he told me he loved me, every little piece of my resistance crumbled to dust and blew away in the wind. My life had changed and would never be the same again. But I was scared because Frankie had the power to destroy everything, but Dashiell had asked for my belief and trust, and in the end I'd given it freely.

"Enjoying the party?"

The voice jerked me out of my tangled thoughts, my head shot up and I stared into Frankie's eyes. It was a sign of how shaken I was that I hadn't noticed him come and stand over me. I always knew if Frankie was close by, it was like I had some kind of radar always switched on, because it was all about self-preservation, knowing where he was and being aware of his moods. I gulped, and he smiled.

Memories hit you out of nowhere, and I remembered a stray cat me and Gran adopted. It would bring home mice and small birds and play around with them before it went in for the kill. As Frankie smiled down at me, I felt like I was one of those mice or birds and that he'd kill me with just as much thought.

"Yes, it's good," I croaked. My mouth was dust-dry, and I took a swallow of champagne.

"A drink?" Frankie nodded towards my glass. "Not like you, Billy, to have a drink. Why's that then, eh? Are you feeling the need to be fortified with alcohol for some reason?"

The cold grin never left Frankie's face, and he sat down next to me, hemming me in. In the corner, and partially hidden, we were effectively alone and nobody would hear a word he said to me.

"It was given to me. I thought it would be impolite not to take it. Don't really want it, though." With a shaking hand, I put the glass on the ground next to me.

"You were always a polite boy, Billy. Such good manners. It's a sign of being well brought up, did you know that?"

"I—er—"

"How's Gran?"

"What?" The sudden question threw me. "She's, erm—"

"To be honest, Billy, I don't really give a flying fuck how the old bitch is. But you care, don't you? You care very much."

I froze. I couldn't move or speak, and I could hardly breathe. All I could do was stare at Frankie and the cold grin that never left his face.

"I think it's time to go home."

In one quick move, he yanked me up from the chair, his fingers digging into my arm as he pulled me through the garden and out to the waiting car.

Frankie wrenched open the door and threw me inside.

"Frankie, what—?"

"Shut the fuck up." Frankie snarled, baring his teeth like an angry, vicious dog.

I pushed myself into the corner, as far as I could go, as I tried to make myself as small as possible. Panic rose up like a tidal wave. Tony was behind the wheel. What the fuck was going on?

"Where's Dashiell?" The words were out of my mouth before I could stop them.

Frankie didn't bother to answer, and I knew I was just moments from freaking out.

"What's wrong, Billy? You seem nervous. Why's that? What do you have to be nervous about?"

"No, I'm not—"

"You're such a bad liar, Billy. You're so easy to see through. Back to the house," Frankie said to Tony, who started up the car without a word.

"Frankie, I don't—"

"Oh, Billy, Billy, Billy. Don't make it any worse for yourself."

I never saw it coming, the punch to the head. He put enough force behind it to throw me down between the seats. Kicks and punches rained down on me, and something wet streamed from my nose. Blood, salty and metallic, filled my mouth. I was hauled up and slung back into the seat.

"Do you think I didn't work out what was going on?"

Frankie grabbed me by my shirt and pulled me towards him. His face was red and blotchy with rage, and spit bubbled at the corners of his mouth.

"Was I getting his sloppy seconds, Billy? Was I?"

Frankie bunched up my shirt in his fist and twisted it tight. The material cut into my throat, and in my panic I tore at his hands as I fought for breath.

"You were so eager, you didn't notice Tony follow you to the bottom of the garden."

Frankie pushed me away so hard, my head smashed against the window and pain exploded behind my eyes. I curled up into a ball and hugged my legs into my chest. For a moment, Frankie forgot all about me as he pulled his phone from his pocket and tapped something into it with sharp stabs of his fingers. I glanced up at the rear-view mirror, reflecting Tony's nasty, smug grin.

"Once a whore, always a whore, Billy," Frankie said as he shoved his phone back into his pocket. "I'll take care of you later, along with that bastard who takes my money and fucks what's mine on the side. Were you laughing, Billy, as he shoved it inside you? I tell you, you won't be laughing anymore. Neither of you will."

"Frankie, please."

What was I going to say? Plead with him, tell him he was mistaken? It was too late for that.

"I don't want to hear another fucking word from you." He slapped me hard across the face, so hard my teeth shook.

As soon as we pulled up at the house, Frankie kicked me out of the car. I tried to push myself up to standing, but I was bruised and bleeding, and every part of me hurt so much. Frankie yanked me up by the collar and dragged me, stumbling, into the house, and up the stairs to the bedroom.

"Get in there, and don't even think of trying to get out." He rifled through my jeans for my phone before he slung me through the door and I collapsed on the bed.

Lee appeared in the doorway, at Frankie's shoulder.

"Make sure he stays in the house, and keep that bastard Dashiell here, too. No contact between them, and use force if you have to. I'll be back to deal with them later."

A second later, Frankie was gone and I heard the front door bang closed.

The adrenaline that had flooded through me started to wear off, and I began to shake. Dashiell. Frankie had said he was in the house. I pushed myself up and winced at the pain. No matter how much it hurt, I had to find Dashiell. We had to run, we had to get away, we had to—

"Right, let's get you sorted out."

Lee picked me up like I was nothing more than a feather and carried me to the bathroom.

"Dashiell—"

"Don't worry, he's here. We'll get you fixed up for now, then I'll get you both out."

I couldn't think straight, but what Lee was saying and

doing didn't make sense. He was Frankie's man, but he was talking about getting us, me and Dashiell, out, but where, and why?

"Be back in a tick," he said as he rushed off. Seconds or minutes later, I didn't know, Lee returned with Dashiell just behind him.

"What the fuck has he done to you? Is he here, is he still here? Because I'm going to kill him, I'm going to *fucking kill him.*"

"He's not here. Just hold on to your temper and start thinking. The first thing is to get Billy sorted, he's the priority at the moment."

Dashiell glared at Lee, but Lee didn't back away as they glared at each other. I was in pain and more frightened than I'd ever been, but I sensed it again, that unspoken communication between them.

Lee tipped the contents of the first aid kit he was holding into the sink and began rummaging through them.

"Where were you? Frankie dragged me to the car, but there was only Tony."

"A couple of minutes after I got back, Tony showed up. Said there'd been a change of plan and I had to return to the house. Frankie's orders."

"Frankie called to tell me you were coming back," Lee said as he plucked a couple of packets from the tipped up first aid bag. "He told me to keep you here. I guessed he'd rumbled the pair of you. When Frankie smells blood, he goes in for the kill. You should know that by now."

"I told you he was suspicious, I told you," I said through my split and bloody lips. "You said you'd make this work." I hadn't meant my words to be an accusation, but Dashiell *hadn't* made it work, despite all his promises and making me believe.

"I'm so sorry, sweetheart, I'm so sorry. But he'll never touch you again. I swear."

Dashiell laid a small, trembling kiss on my head.

"Save it for later."

Lee pushed Dashiell aside and leaned down in front of me, holding a wad of cotton wool which smelled of antiseptic.

"I'm going to clean your cuts and then put a stitch in your lip and across the cut over your left eye."

"Why? Why are you doing this? Why are you helping us?"

Lee smiled, just the ghost of one. "There's no time to explain. Dashiell can tell you later."

He dabbed the cotton wool to my mouth, as much to stop me from asking any further questions, I reckoned. The antiseptic made my eyes water and I winced, but the gel he smeared on numbed the area. I'd had stitches before, more than once, and closed my eyes and waited for it to be over.

"I'll do it."

Dashiell's voice was low and rough. I snapped my eyes open and looked up at the Lee and Dashiell facing each other.

"Do you remember how? And you need to be quick." Lee was staring at Dashiell and frowning hard.

"Yes. I got a gold star in first aid. Remember? Now give it to me."

With a curt nod, Lee handed over the needle and thread. "You need to hurry. I've got a call to make. When I'm back, you go, whether you're finished or not."

A second later, Lee was gone, leaving the two of us alone.

"Dashiell, what's happening? I don't understand?" Everything was running away from me, and I couldn't catch up.

"Later. For now, let me help you. I won't hurt you, I promise."

Dashiell's words were quiet and solemn. I met his gaze, and despite everything, and all the danger we were in, we both understood he was talking about more than my split lip. I nodded. It wasn't my swollen, cut mouth that stopped me from speaking; it was the lump that blocked up my throat.

With total concentration, Dashiell pulled together my torn flesh. His hands were sure and confident, and I calmed under his touch. My breathing slowed, and knowing I was in safe hands, I closed my eyes.

When he'd finished, he helped me stand. I was sore and stiff, like I'd been a million times since setting foot in that house. Despite Frankie's attack, I'd got off lightly. My stomach turned over. He'd laid into me, but he could have done so much more damage. Instead, he'd held back, because my cuts and bruises were just a foretaste of what was to come.

I began to shake, and my legs went from under me, but Dashiell caught me in his arms.

"I'm scared, I'm so fucking scared. What—"

Lee burst into the bathroom, his face set in a deep frown as he stuffed his phone back into this pocket.

"Good, you're finished. There's a car out the front, with a couple of plain clothes officers inside. Billy, go down and wait in the car. Dashiell, you stay here a minute, I need to speak to you."

"Go? Go where? Officers? What are you on about?"

None of it was making sense. Lee was talking, but I couldn't understand a word he was saying.

"Dashiell?"

"Just do as he says."

"But—"

"Billy, you're in safe hands. Dashiell will be with you in a minute, and he'll explain everything. But for now you need to go and wait in the car."

Lee wasn't asking, he was telling.

"Sweetheart, please. I'll be with you before you know it, and then we're out of here. Okay?"

Whatever questions I had weren't going to be answered as we huddled together in the bathroom. I had no idea where we were going, but as long as it got us away from Frankie and whatever revenge he was planning, I'm not sure I really cared.

27

_____

DASHIELL

"So what's going on?"

Whatever it was Lee had to tell me, he'd been keen for Billy not to hear. To be honest, even though the shit was well and truly hitting the fan with Frankie, my thoughts went to Eileen. Was Lee expecting me to break some bad news to Billy as the car took us to fuck knew where?

"What isn't?" Lee exhaled a long breath as he rubbed his eyes.

I hadn't noticed before then how exhausted he looked, but then to be fair, I hadn't been looking, but working undercover against Frankie had clearly taken its toll.

"I told you we were just about on the brink of bringing Frankie in. Well, we've reached it a bit quicker than expected. Frankie's being arrested today, along with Tony and several others. We're picking them up at the same time as a number of coordinated raids take place across London and elsewhere in the UK."

God alone knew what Frankie was involved in, but whatever it was it would have been vicious and sordid.

Drug dealing, I assumed, because that would almost be a given. But the rest? I could only surmise. Or I could ask Lee. What the hell, he would tell me, or he wouldn't.

"What's he involved in?"

"I'm not at liberty to tell you."

"Like you weren't at liberty to tell me you were a copper when I found you snooping around in his office?"

Lee's phone rang, and he was saved by the bell from answering my question. He turned away to speak for a few seconds before cutting the call.

"The car downstairs will take you to the safe house. The pair of you are to remain there until further notice."

"If Frankie's being arrested today—"

"No, you can't take Billy back to your place," Lee said, reading my thoughts. It was exactly what I was going to suggest.

"The pair of you aren't walking off into the sunset just yet." He peered at me and licked his lips before he carried on. "I didn't want to say anything in front of Billy, but he was right. Frankie did know about the two of you."

How the hell could he have known? I'd been so careful. *We'd* been so careful. Or I thought we had. What had given us away?

"How?"

"I told him, or at least a version. He had me keep an eye on you. I didn't like doing it, but I had to in order to maintain my own cover and to keep me in Frankie's confidence. I had to feed him something."

Lee had fed Billy to the dogs, just as he'd threatened, because *it maintained his cover,* because it *kept Frankie's confidence*. Anger, blind fury, boiling hot and explosive built up in me as I launched myself forward, but Lee had anticipated my reaction, and I found myself shoved backwards and pinned to the door.

"Listen," he said, banging me hard against the door. "I had to make sure I maintained my value to Frankie, and if that meant using you and Billy as bait, I was prepared to do it. I fed him enough, that's all."

"Enough for him to lay into Billy like a fucking mad man. You saw the mess Frankie made of him. We had to sew up his face, for Christ's sake. What was he, collateral damage? Was that all he was? When did you tell him, Lee, *when*?"

"A few days back."

A few days back. When Frankie had been standing in the hallway and sniffing the air like he'd been sniffing for blood, when Lee had stood in the doorway with his face screwed up in worry. That was *when*. Frankie hadn't exploded; he waited and was ready to serve his vengeance cold. So much for me being able to read people.

"I know you're angry, and I'd be reacting just like you, but you need to listen to me."

"You set Billy up for a beating because of what you told Frankie. That makes you as much as a bastard as him, because you may as well have beaten him up yourself."

So close, I saw Lee's reaction to my words. Shock and anger at what I'd said, but there was something else there, too, something that looked like shame and sorrow. My anger was still hard and sharp, but what I saw blunted the edge. Lee must have sensed that, because he let me go and took a step back.

The room was thick with anger and our ragged breaths. I still itched to hit him, but I needed to know the rest of what he had to tell me even more.

"What is it you don't want Billy to hear?"

"At nine o'clock this evening, Tony's due to turn up here with a couple of others. Instruction's been given for you and Billy to be taken to a warehouse on the Kent coast. You're to be murdered and your bodies weighed down and disposed of at sea. Or that's what Frankie thinks is going to happen, at least for now. He'll be in custody along with Tony and the others well before then. But we're not taking any chances, which is why the car will take you to the safe house, where you'll stay for as long as we think necessary."

Lee's words chilled me all the way to my marrow. Billy had said that if Frankie found out about us, he'd go for us and we wouldn't even see it coming. It had almost happened. Our lives were to have been stamped out as though we'd never existed, our deaths secret and unrecorded.

"Fucking hell." I rubbed my shaking hand across my brow.

"But none of it's going to happen. Instead, today's the day you both gain your freedom. He's waiting for you in the car, Dashiell. Now go."

"I'm not going without seeing Gran."

I climbed into the back of the unmarked car and sat next to Billy. His beautiful, battered and bruised face was set hard, and his chin jutted out, and you know, I felt a surge of pride wash through me. Billy, who'd taken so much shit in his life, wasn't taking any more.

"Is a detour really going to make that much difference?" I asked Lee, who'd come out with me.

Lee leaned into the car and spoke to the driver before he turned to me and Billy. "A quick visit only. Is that understood?"

He was looking at me intently, the unspoken communication between us that it was too risky for Billy and myself to be anywhere Frankie or his henchmen could get at us. If Billy argued, Lee would spell out Frankie's plans for the pair of us in syllables of one word. Fortunately, he didn't have to because Billy nodded in agreement.

A minute later, we turned out onto the road and the house disappeared from view, and I let out a long and relieved breath, knowing I'd never see the place again.

The two plainclothes policemen in the front didn't say a word to us as we drove away. Billy pressed into me, and I pulled him close. It wasn't long before he was asleep and I, too, closed my eyes and drifted as fatigue weighed me down.

I woke with a start as the car pulled into The Larches, and I gave Billy a gentle shake to wake him.

The two policemen got out with us.

"We've orders to stay with you until we reach the safe house. We'll wait outside the patient's door," the one who'd driven added. "But you need to keep the visit short."

I nodded; there was no point in arguing.

Once inside, we made our way to a room deep inside the building until we reached a door with a sign hanging outside, with Eileen's name on it. A woman I assumed to be a doctor appeared and pulled Billy aside. If she was shocked by the state of Billy's face, or the fact that he'd turned up accompanied by three large men, she didn't show it.

Whatever it was she told Billy, it made his head drop and his shoulders sag, and I rushed over. If there was bad news, I wouldn't let him take it alone.

Billy looked up at me. His face was pallid and pinched, and deep furrows crossed his forehead. But it was his eyes that broke my heart. Sad and devoid of hope, it was as though he'd looked at the world and seen the lights go out one by one. I knew, without being told, that Billy had come to say his farewells to the woman who'd loved and cared for him. This would be the last time he saw Eileen. I stepped back to allow them their privacy, but Billy took my hand and led me inside.

Eileen seemed even smaller, if that were possible, and if it hadn't have been for the green line on a monitor recording small peaks and troughs of a heartbeat, I would have sworn she'd already died.

"Jane – the doctor – she'd been trying to call me. But Frankie took my phone, so I didn't know. *I didn't know*."

His voice was as small and thin as Eileen herself. All I could do was squeeze Billy's hand, then stand aside, letting him know I was there for him as he said his goodbyes.

"Hello, Gran. Sorry I've not brought you any presents. It was a last-minute thing, to come today. But next time, okay?"

I stood by the wall, completely still. It ripped my heart out as Billy placed a soft kiss on her sunken cheek and stroked her hair with a trembling hand. My nails dug into my palms, and I pressed my back into the wall, anything to stop myself from rushing over and dragging Billy into my arms. I hated that he was suffering, and there wasn't a thing I could do to take that away from him.

"I'm going away for a little while, Gran. Just a few days, probably, but it means I won't be able to come as often as I'd like. But I'm going away with my friend Dashiell. Do you remember him? I brought him with me before. You liked him, I could tell. And so do I, Gran, I like him a lot."

I looked down, and I had to blink to clear my vision.

"Here, let me brush your hair. You used to let me do this when I was little. Do you remember? It was long, all the way down to your waist when you weren't wearing it all piled up on top of your head. You always looked so glamorous, and I was so proud of you. But I liked it best when it was loose, because you looked like a princess."

I let myself out as quietly as I could. I'm not ashamed to say that my face was wet with tears. I knew time was running out, that one of the coppers would call us away, and I wanted Billy to spend the last few minutes alone with his gran.

"Excuse me, are you with Eileen's grandson?"

The same doctor I'd seen speak to Billy came over.

"I'm Dr. Cope, the senior doctor here. Is Billy still with Eileen?"

"Yes." I cleared my throat and ducked away as I dragged my hand across my face. Why, I didn't know, because she'd probably seen the tears of hundreds of grown men. "How long has she got?"

"I'm afraid that's not something I can discuss with you, Mr. . . ?"

"Slater, Dashiell Slater. I'm Billy's partner." The words

slipped from my tongue, as smooth and natural as day following night.

"I'm sorry, I still can't discuss Eileen's condition with you." She glanced over at the door and sucked in her lower lip as she considered what it was she *could* tell me. She looked back at me and drew me aside.

"Have you seen Eileen?"

I nodded.

"Then you'll have seen that she's unwell. Very unwell. It's good that Billy's come to see her today."

"Can you take my number? In case you need to get in touch with Billy quickly?"

"We've already got his contact details, and—"

"He's lost his phone and hasn't got a replacement yet. Please, can you just take it?"

She was about to refuse, I just knew it, when the door opened and Billy walked out. I forgot all about Dr. Cope and strode over to Billy and hugged him tight. He was so small and light, and I feared the ferocity of my embrace would snap him in two, but he hugged me back before he pulled himself away and turned to the doctor.

"How long, Jane?"

She might not have been able to tell me, but she couldn't deny Billy.

"Let's go to my office—"

"No, I don't have time. We have to go away for a while."

Her eyes flitted between the two of us, and she nodded.

"It's difficult to say with any certainty. She's stable for the moment, but very, very weak. We're talking days rather than weeks or more."

Billy flinched, as though he'd been struck. The doctor's words would have hurt him more than any punch Frankie had delivered, and in that moment I hated her for it.

Her eyes flickered over to me, then back to Billy. "I'd advise that we have up to date contact details on file."

"I'll give the doctor my number, while you're without a phone."

Billy nodded, and I scribbled my number down on a small pad she pulled from her pocket.

"Thanks, Jane. For everything."

Billy leaned in and gave her a long, hard hug, which she returned in kind. There was real and genuine affection there, and I felt petty and mean spirited for what I'd felt towards her just a moment before.

I heard a cough behind me, and I turned around. The copper who had driven gave an apologetic shrug of his shoulders. It was time to go.

The car sped away to God alone knew where, and I hugged Billy to my chest as his silent tears shook his body. The steady motion of the car, and the soft rumble of the engine lulled him into sleep, and I kissed the top of his head.

"I love you, Billy. I love you more than you could ever know," I whispered as I closed my eyes and wondered what tomorrow would bring, and all the tomorrows after that until I, too, let sleep claim me.

EPILOGUE
ONE YEAR LATER

BILLY

When I was a kid, I dreamed of living by the sea in Hastings. In that dream, I had a big shaggy dog I'd take for walks on the beach, and I'd throw a ball for him to chase after as seagulls swooped and screamed in a sky that was always blue. Well, I'm not a kid anymore, but the dream has become a reality. Okay, the sky more often than not is grey, not blue, and the noise of those bloody seagulls can do my head in. There's no dog either. But there is a man, a man who asked me to marry him, and I took, like, all of a nanosecond to say yes to.

"Billy? Billy, where are you?"

"In here." I looked up from the computer, where I was working through a spreadsheet detailing goods received and paid for, and all the other stuff that was part and parcel of owning a thriving bed and breakfast business.

Dashiell walked through the door of the tiny office, and just like it always did, my heart skipped a beat. Wearing nothing more than a pair of cut-off jeans and a battered pair of trainers, it meant all those glorious tatts were on show. Sweaty and covered in ground-in dirt from going ten rounds in the garden with a stubborn shrub that needed removing, my dick began a happy dance, and all I wanted to do was jump in then and there. We'd already spent way too much time in the shower together, earlier that morning, and besides, we needed to be ready for our very important guest who was coming to stay for a couple of days.

"I've just had a call from Lee, and he reckons he should be here for 6.00pm. He says he's got some news."

"News?" I met Dashiell's eyes, and my stomach bit down on itself. News about Frankie?

I'd deliberately avoided anything to do with the trial that had taken up weeks at the Old Bailey in London. When Frankie's case had first gone to court, his face had flashed up on the TV and I'd almost had a meltdown, but the jury had done its job, and the judge had sent him down for years, and that was all I needed to know. But the word *news*. . . it sent a shiver down my spine. It couldn't be an appeal against the sentence, it just couldn't, the evidence against him had been overwhelming, and—

"Hey, stop fretting."

Dashiell's hand, rubbing big, slow circles on my back, instantly stilled my panic. His touch was like magic, it had the power to calm and heal, as I'd learned in those dark days after we'd fled to the safe house and when I'd been given the news of Gran's death.

"He didn't mention anything to do with Frankie. If

there was anything unexpected, he wouldn't just spring it on us."

"Yeah, yeah I know." I did know it, too.

After Dashiell had revealed who and what Lee was, and how he'd first known him, I hadn't known what to think. Part of me had been furious with Lee. If he was a policeman, couldn't he have done something to stop Frankie from beating the shit out of me? Why had he stood by and let Frankie do what he had? But then I remembered the times I'd seen the anger flicker in his eyes when he saw Frankie's handiwork on me, and how he'd always spoken to me with some degree of respect when all I got from everybody else were ill-concealed sneers. Ultimately, it had been Lee's evidence that had put Frankie away, and for that alone I'd be eternally grateful. Tony had joined Frankie in prison, along with the rest of the zombies. Oh, yeah, I was really, *really* pleased when I heard about Tony.

"Come for a walk with me?" Dashiell asked as he kissed the top of my head. He knew just what to say to me, as walks along the beach and listening to the hiss of the waves as they ebbed and flowed over the rocky shore never failed to calm me down. Just as always, Dashiell was there to catch me as I fell, and God, didn't I just love him for it.

"We can be all romantic and hold each other's hands. I might even let you give me a blow job behind one of the fisherman's huts on the beach."

He gave me a dirty leer, and I burst out laughing because The Beach Hut Blow Job was a standing joke. It was exactly what I'd done after we'd had our offer accepted on our beautiful Regency house that had become the foundation of our livelihood. I'd only done it the once, though, because all those pebbles were a bitch on the knees.

As we made our way to the beach, a young boy, holding a stick of candy floss that was bigger than his head, was pulling an older lady by the hand towards the penny arcade. Laughing together, they didn't seem to have a care in the world. She shooed him off, but not before she ruffled his hair, and the boy raced ahead and disappeared into the arcade, leaving her to make her slow way. As I watched the strangers, no doubt on a day out by the seaside, the pain of Gran's loss hit me square in the stomach. It had been almost a year since she'd died, but a day didn't go by when I didn't think of her, not as she'd been in the home, but as the loving, vibrant woman who'd made my childhood the best in the world.

"I really wish Gran could've seen what we've achieved because she'd have been so proud." I coughed to clear the catch in my throat, but I didn't fool Dashiell and he squeezed my hand.

"She'd have been proud of you, period. Of *you*, of the man you are. Anything else would have just been window dressing."

He was right, Gran would have been proud. Every achievement, no matter how small, had been celebrated with enthusiastic hugs and kisses and sometimes, too, by her disastrous efforts at home baking. And when things didn't quite go to plan? Well, I still got the hugs and kisses and some wreck of a cake. The point was, she'd loved and supported me unconditionally, and had she still been alive, that wouldn't have changed.

It had been a rough few days, though, as the anniversary of Gran's death had come and gone, and I'm not ashamed to say I cried big, wet, ugly tears. Dashiell had held me close until I couldn't cry anymore, and that evening, rather than spending it wrapped in a blanket of sadness, we'd gone out and drank champagne. To celebrate the life of a lady who loved, and was loved, Dashiell had said as we raised our glasses in a toast to Eileen Mary Grace, my gran. Somehow, I think she'd have approved.

"Hungry?" Dashiell asked.

"Hmm, I'd love a bag of chips."

"Add in a piece of cod?"

"Haddock. With a battered sausage on the side, maybe."

"You're on."

When I'd been with Frankie, I hadn't been just slim; I'd been painfully thin and all sharp angles. That might look great in some cool fashion shoot, but the reality's way different. Gnawing hunger, fear of putting on so much as a few ounces of weight because the consequences that could come from that, chucking up illegal, excess calories down the toilet. . . it had taken some time to learn how to eat properly without panicking. Sounds so stupid, doesn't it? Thing was, I'd been so beaten down by Frankie not just physically, but mentally, too, I'd felt as though I needed permission to eat what I wanted and when.

We dived into our favourite chippy and emerged clutching steaming hot bags of food and made our way down onto the beach. I got through every mouthful in no time, and although Dashiell didn't say anything, I knew he was pleased.

Sheltered from the breeze by the bank of pebbles we'd settled back against, I snuggled into Dashiell's side, under the warm afternoon sun.

"Happy?" Dashiell ran his fingers through my hair.

"Do you have to ask?"

"Just checking."

I was happy, no doubt about it. I had everything. A man I loved so hard I ached, a lovely home in my favourite place in the world, a business that gave the two of us plenty of time to spend together and was going from strength to strength. I shouldn't have had a care in the world.

"*But?*"

I couldn't hide anything from Dashiell, and I seriously wondered whether he had the power to read minds, or maybe it was just mine he could read.

"Sometimes I can't believe we're here, and I don't think I could stand it if something happened to make it all collapse around our ears." It wasn't a worry that kept me awake at night, but it was there like an itch I couldn't quite scratch.

"We got through everything that happened, *you* got through it and made it out the other side. You're safe, sweetheart. Nothing's going to fall down around you, the rug's not going to be pulled from under your feet, the sky's not about to collapse, and the sun will rise again in the morning. Even if you can't see it in Hastings."

I huffed out a small laugh. Dashiell always had the knack of putting everything into perspective and dissolving away my fears.

Dashiell shifted around and took my face between his hands. His big blue eyes were so, so serious as they stared into mine.

"Frankie, nor any of his henchmen, are a threat to us. Everything that happened, it's gone. Finished. Finito. It's all in the past, Billy, and that's where it's going to stay. It's the future you need to concentrate on. Your future, with me. Life's not just *going* to be good, it *is* good. Remember what I said before, about believing? About trust?"

I nodded, because I was too choked up to speak. Of course I believed him because he'd never let me down, and I knew he never would.

"That's settled, then. Come on," he said, standing and pulling me to my feet as a smile lit up his face. "I'll race you home."

DASHIELL

"Have another." I topped up Lee's glass. The three of us had eaten our combined body weight in food. Lee and I were sprawled out across a couple of sofas, drinking up the last of the wine we'd had at dinner, and Billy had gone to make coffee.

"You've done well with this place."

I couldn't help feeling a little bit smug. Okay, a lot smug.

When Billy and I had re-emerged back into the world, we'd needed to find a new life for ourselves, and that meant moving away and starting afresh. I loved my house, but I had no qualms about selling up, and as soon as it had gone on the market, I got an offer at the full asking price. Billy needed a new life, and I'd been determined to give it to him. From somewhere, the idea of the seaside B&B had come up. I blame those endless get-a-new-life programmes on the telly. Whatever, it had filled us both with excitement and a sense of purpose, and we knew exactly where we wanted our new life to be.

"We got lucky with the house because the previous owners needed to move fast, so we got it at a knockdown price. There was an opportunity to be had, and we grabbed it with both hands."

We'd also taken a crash course in studying the luxury end of the B&B market, cherry picked ideas from established, successful businesses and applied them to Longshore, as we'd named the house, and marketed aggressively on the gay websites. By good luck and a lot of very, very hard work, it'd paid off. I had every reason to be smug.

"Sometimes you have to take a leap of faith."

Something in Lee's tone made my ears prick up, and I knew it wasn't just me and Billy he was talking about, it was himself, too. I opened my mouth to say something, but he beat me to it, and the moment passed.

"You've got yourself something of a reputation, and in under a year, too. Best New B&B in Southern England, according to The Gaylist."

Ah, so I had been right when I'd wondered if Lee was gay.

Lee shrugged, and his lips curled up in a sheepish grin.

"It was one of the reasons I was chosen to go undercover. The powers that be thought Frankie might be less guarded with me, I suppose."

"So, you were what? Some kind of bait? A honey trap?"

Lee laughed and shook his head. "I think that was the original idea, but those cretins at the top of the food chain got their intel wrong. I was as far from Frankie's type as it was possible to get. He had no interest in me whatsoever, he preferred younger and thinner, somebody he could dominate, I guess. Ah, shit. Sorry."

"No need to be." And there wasn't. The fact that Frankie's taste didn't run to tall and muscled wasn't Lee's fault.

"Billy seems well, and very happy," Lee said after a minute or so of silence, when he no doubt chewed on his mortification. He nodded in the general direction of the kitchen.

"He is. We both are. Considering what he went through, he's come through pretty unscathed, I'd say."

"I'm glad, because he deserves it."

I smiled and could have given Lee a big, fat kiss but there was only one man, now, who'd ever get kisses from me. What Lee said was true, Billy did deserve to be happy after all the crap he'd gone through. Billy had drawn on a reservoir of strength in the days, weeks and months after we'd fled. He'd been frightened and grieving for his gran, but he'd held it together as we'd spent weeks in the safe house not knowing where we'd go after and what our future would be. I'd been proud of him, and I always would be.

"I know I've not really said it before, but I'm sorry the two of you were given such a hard time of it. I told them over and over that neither of you had any involvement in Frankie's crimes, but, you know."

Lee didn't have to elaborate because we both knew what he meant. The questioning, the endless fucking questioning in the police station. They were just doing their job, but the interrogation we'd both received at the hands of the Serious Crime squad had left the both of us battered and bruised.

"You said you had news when we spoke on the phone. Anything I should know about?"

Billy wasn't a kid, and he'd have been pissed off if he knew I was attempting to shield him, but I wanted any information he received about Frankie Haynes filtered through me first, and our conversation on the beach earlier only reinforced that.

"Just about me, but I'll tell you when Billy's back."

I felt rather than heard Lee's hesitation. If there was anything he needed to say, I wanted him to say it then and there when Billy wasn't around to hear.

"Spit it out, Lee."

"Just so you're fully in the picture, okay? He lodged an appeal against the verdict." Lee shrugged. "But it got thrown out, of course – too much evidence against him. It's all part of the dance. It was a given he'd apply, just like it was a given he'd fail. I don't think even his legal team was fighting for him that hard in the end, not when it all came out in court."

There wasn't much I could say to that. What Lee had uncovered had been sickening, and how he'd forced himself to go deep into Frankie's world, playing the part of a willing accomplice and not go nuts, I had no idea. It must have left some kind of scar on his soul, but Lee wasn't saying, so I wasn't asking.

Billy may have refused to follow the trial, but I hadn't. I'd devoured all the coverage and had even gone to the court to sit in the back of the public gallery on one occasion, making the excuse that I'd travelled to London to see my friend Andy. It had been horrific. Drugs, naturally, but so much more. People smuggling, which were the drop-offs Tony used to scuttle away to supervise; prostitution; pornography and protection. They were the cherries on the criminal cake and ensured that Frankie was put away for years, but he had his filthy fingers in so many pies.

"Did you ever tell Billy what Frankie intended to do to the pair of you?"

I couldn't prevent the shudder that rippled through me. If anything had frightened me, it had been the thought of what could so easily have happened. It hadn't, and that's what I had to remember.

"No. I couldn't see the point, because if there was anything that would have thrown him over the edge, then that would have been it." The men who were coming to murder us. I wasn't going to lay that on Billy; he'd gone through enough. It was knowledge I'd bare alone.

"As you say, what's the point?"

Lee stared down at the remains of the red wine in the bottom of his glass before he slugged it back. When he spoke, his voice was quiet.

"I'm surprised he never spat in my face when he found out I'd told Frankie about the pair of you. It was one of the hardest things I had to do in the whole of those two years. Frankie never trusted anybody a hundred percent, and I had the feeling he was starting to become suspicious of me, which meant the whole operation went into overdrive. I had to throw him something to keep me on the inside, and you and Billy were perfect. I'd have got the two of you out, despite what I said, but events, for too many reasons to go into, started to go faster than expected. I'm surprised Billy doesn't hate me. If I'd have been in his place, I don't think I could have been so forgiving."

Lee scrubbed his hands through his hair, that same worried and nervous gesture that took me back to that house I never wanted to see again.

Billy had hated him, for a while, but there was nothing to be gained by telling Lee that. The guy was full of remorse, the slope of his shoulders and the frown furrowing his brow told me that better than any words could. What he'd been forced to do had left its mark on him. He might have been a copper, but I knew he was a good man at heart, but what was more important, so did Billy.

"I just had to sort something out for a couple of the guests. I'll be back with the coffee in a tick."

Lee and I both jumped when Billy popped his head around the door of the living room before he rushed off again.

The guests loved Billy, and he could smooth any ruffled feathers with a smile; I was convinced he was the reason why we were the success we were.

The door was nudged open, and Billy placed the tray he was carrying on the coffee table.

"All sorted. They wanted recommendations on where to eat. Now." Billy turned his full attention to Lee. "Tell us your news."

———

"That was a shock."

Billy climbed into bed, and into my arms; he nuzzled in close and tucked his head under my chin.

Snuggling up together last thing at night, warm and skin to skin, it had become my special moment of each day. Just that first minute or so, before we kissed, or made love, or just fell into an exhausted but contented sleep after a long day. To be honest, every *second* spent with Billy was special, but for some reason this always felt like that little bit extra. I cuddled him tight, and he sighed into my embrace.

"Hmm, not sure that it was, really." When Lee had told us, it hadn't surprised me one little bit.

"That he was leaving the force? But he's got a pretty senior rank and all that. It's a lot to throw away."

It had been a long time coming, Lee said when he told us he'd put in his resignation. What he'd uncovered while investigating Frankie had sickened him to the core, and he'd decided he needed to see the light in life, and not the dark. He didn't have any immediate plans; he just wanted out.

"He'll be fine." I shifted so I was hovering over Billy. "He's strong and resourceful."

Billy's lips lifted in a slow smile, and he narrowed his eyes as he gazed up at me, and didn't my heart just do every flashy, fancy acrobatic in the book.

"Yeah, and I know someone else who's strong and resourceful – *very* resourceful."

"Oh yeah? Who's that?" I tried to sound tough, but all I could do was smile.

"I think you know."

Billy trailed his fingers down my cheek and traced the line of my jaw, and every single butterfly that had ever existed and ever would fluttered their wings deep down in my belly.

"I love you so much, Dashiell. If you hadn't have come into my life—"

I pressed my fingers to his lips. Everything about the past had been said, and nothing more was needed.

"But I did, and I'll always be in your life. That's all that matters, sweetheart, you and me going forward and never looking back. Remember what I said earlier, about belief and trust?"

Billy nodded, and I released his lips.

"So, you love me. Hmm, I think actions speak louder than words, don't you? Show me how much."

Beyond number and without end, that's how much Billy loved me, and I loved him in return. As we kissed, and touched, and melted into each other, I knew in my heart that the best was yet to come. As I held the man I loved more than life, I made a silent vow that I'd do anything and everything in my power to make that true. Together we'd stepped onto a new path, and we would never, ever look back because there was only one way we could go, and that was forward.

Thank you for reading Captive Hearts — it was a pleasure to share Dashiell and Billy's story with you.

If you enjoyed Captive Hearts, please take a moment to write a review on Amazon, BookBub, and Goodreads.

<u>Ready to read more in the Deviant Hearts world?</u>

Radical Hearts
Perilous Hearts

A FEW WORDS FROM ALI

To find out more about me, my books, and to sign up to my newsletter (irreverent, chatty, packed with news and heads up on sales I'm running), check out my website at: www.ryecart.com

As a thank you for subscribing, I'll send you a juicy sweet with heat story.

I also have a readers group on Facebook, which is mainly where I hang out on social media. Come and join me!
Ryecart's Rebel Readers

Printed in Great Britain
by Amazon

62174563R00161